PRESERVE, PROTECT, AND DEFEND

BY

CHUCK MORGAN

A POLITICAL THRILLER

This book is a work of fiction. Names, characters, places and incidents are the product of the author's imagination or, if real, are used fictitiously. Any resemblance to events, locales or persons, living or dead, is coincidental.

Printed in the United States of America

First printing 2025

ISBN 978-1-968179-06-9 (Paperback)

LIBRARY OF CONGRESS CONTROL NUMBER

2025910524

DEDICATION

To those who stand against tyranny,
To the guardians of truth and democracy,
To the brave souls who fight not for power, but for justice—
This book is for you.

And to my family and friends, whose unwavering support keeps me grounded,
and to the readers who embark on this journey with me—thank you.

Chapter One

Election Night

Oliver Stevenson stood at the window of his hotel suite and looked out at the Washington Monument. He thought that someday, they would build a monument to him. It didn't seem to concern him that with a 34 percent approval rating, the lowest in the history of modern presidential elections, he would be lucky if anyone even remembered he had been a senator, let alone had run for president.

His personal life had been filled with controversy and there was even talk about a censure vote stemming from the many laws he had broken during his term in office. His election campaign would go down in history as the most divisive ever run by a candidate from either party. But Oliver Stevenson, the senior senator from Nebraska, didn't care about any of that. He didn't care about the polls that had shown him steadily losing ground to his opponent. He knew in his mind that this election would show the world that Oliver Stevenson was beloved by his followers and that he would pull off a victory of epic proportions. It would also show those who opposed him he was in full control of the Republican Party. Oliver Stevenson was on top of the world.

He turned from the window and looked around the room. Everything was perfect. He had the perfect wife, even though it had taken three test wives before he had reached this state of perfection. He had perfect children, two of whom were his closest advisors. He stood straight as a board at six foot seven and was rail thin. His gray hair was mostly gone, and he had a bit of a beer belly. The bags under his eyes were an indicator of a man who rarely slept and who ran most of the time on sheer adrenaline. He had the perfect job, having been a United States senator for close to thirty years, but being elected president would be the icing on the cake.

The rest of the room was filled with party leaders, aides and advisors, and the sycophants who, like the leeches they were, had latched on to him when he announced his candidacy two years before, if given half the chance, could suck the life out of a lesser man. How much he hated those people. They were part of the Washington he hated, the part that believed two years ago that he would do incredible things. They were also the part that kept his faithful followers fired up and longing for every utterance he made. He chuckled to himself. His faithful followers. What a laugh. What a bunch of losers.

Sure, he would get them fired up at campaign rallies, by maligning some group or chastising some individual. That's why they loved him. They thought he spoke for them, the poor, misguided souls who felt they were being run out of their own country by illegal immigrants and nonbelievers. He spoke about and promised them he would give them back their dignity and their religion and that life would be wonderful again. He had convinced them he was one of them and that even though he was a billionaire, he could feel their pain and identify with the shitty way their lives had turned out. He had convinced them that the

Democrats, the aristocrats, the abortionists, the anti-gun people and the religious persecutors were out to get them, and he was the one person who could protect them. He was their savior, and they worshipped him.

Picking up his third glass of bourbon off the table behind the couch, he walked over and stood in front of the big-screen TV that covered one entire wall of the room. The talking heads on his favorite cable news channel were filling the airtime, waiting for the first election results to come in by extolling his virtues and accomplishments, as if that stuff mattered. He would call into their talk shows and blast the president and the Democrats, and they ate it up. It was all bullshit. Pure entertainment. But it got him elected five times to the Senate, and it would get him elected president. And once this election was over, he would become the most powerful man in the world, and those who opposed him would suffer his wrath.

"Any results yet?" he asked his oldest son, Robert.

"With a half percent of the votes counted so far, they have you leading by double digits."

"This is going to be a great night for me." He downed his drink in one gulp and walked away from his son to speak with Mark Sinclair, the head of his Secret Service detail; he smiled, and they stepped through a side door. Mark was as tall as the senator at well over six feet, but where the senator had gained over sixty pounds since taking office, Mark still had a runner's physique.

The senator shook hands with Jack Cummings, one of his most trusted business partners, and his middle son, Philip, who was having a private conversation in the corner of the spare bedroom.

"Give me the status," he said to his son.

"The Chinese are royally pissed," said Philip. "Those rare earth minerals we discovered in Montana proved to be a much bigger find than we first imagined. With the legislation you helped put in place at the Department of Energy, we will undercut the Chinese and control the entire market. Once we run the Chinese companies into the ground, we will set our own price. Stevenson Mineral Resources will be the most valuable company in the world's history. Unfortunately, Dad, you won't be a part of all that wealth, because you will rule the United States."

They all laughed and clinked glasses. The senator would have to turn over control of his many companies to his various family members when he became president. He was supposed to have no part in any of the day-to-day operations, but that was not the case at all. Rules, especially those that worked against him, were made to be broken.

The senator set his glass on the credenza, looked in the mirror, straightened his red-white-and-blue-striped tie and ran a comb through his hair. Not bad for a sixty-year-old man. Luckily, his jacket covered his bulging belly. He put on his campaign ball cap to cover his thinning hair. Mark Sinclair opened the back door to the suite and led him into the hallway, where the rest of his Secret Service detail was waiting. The private elevator was waiting with the doors open, and they all stepped inside. Mark pushed the button for the lobby.

The senator stood behind the curtain and looked at the mass of his faithful followers who had gathered in the hotel ballroom for what they had been led to believe was a victory party. He felt the love all around, and he stepped out onto the stage to the thrill of those gathered. He hadn't been expected until much later in the evening. The crowd roared, and the music turned up full blast. He waved to the faithful and stepped to the podium. He let the cheers continue for ten minutes. He leaned into the microphone.

"Tonight, we have won a great victory, and I owe it all to you." Cheers and applause from the crowd. "We are leading our opponent by huge numbers and there is no way he will ever catch us; besides, he was never qualified to lead this country anyway. I was the only candidate in this race that can give you back the America you deserve."

It didn't seem to matter to the faithful that he hadn't been declared the winner yet and it would be a while before he could deliver everything he had promised, but they knew he wouldn't let them down. He was their salvation. The speech rambled for forty minutes and was as incoherent as his later campaign speeches had been, but it served a purpose. It got the base fired up.

James Grover, the senator's chief of staff, looked around the hotel suite. He spotted Olivia Stevenson, the senator's oldest daughter, and headed her way. Olivia was tall, like her father. The daughter of his first wife, Meridith, Olivia was a younger version of her mother, who had been a model and actress in a series of low-budget films before marrying an up-and-coming politician. Olivia had sharp features, a hawk nose and bottle-blond hair. She was her father's closest advisor, and she was the one who could talk him down from the edge when he went off the deep end.

"Where did the senator go?" he asked.

She pointed towards the TV on the wall. James Grover's chin dropped, and his mouth hung open.

"What the fuck is he doing in the ballroom?"

She looked at him. "He just declared victory on national television."

"There isn't even two percent of the vote counted. What the hell is he thinking?" asked James.

James, who was fair-skinned and had thinning gray-blond hair, turned red in the face and looked like he was going to have a heart attack.

"We need to get him off the stage before he says something stupid," he said.

"He already has," said Olivia. "You know how he gets when he sets his mind to something."

"Why didn't you stop him? He listens to you," said James.

Olivia smiled. "Tonight, he's not listening to anyone. He's in his own world, and no one is going to change that."

James turned and came face-to-face with vice presidential candidate Sandford Reese. Sandy was a former navy fighter pilot. He stood five foot eleven and was thin and fit. He had a ruddy complexion and red hair. He looked at the TV.

"He just told the faithful," said Sandford, "that there have been reports of widespread voter fraud and that he has a team of lawyers waiting to make sure this election, unlike the last presidential election, goes smoothly, and that he will do everything in his power to ensure our victory is not contested."

James Grover looked at Reese. "Where the hell did that come from?"

Sandy shook his head. "Who knows where he gets this stuff from."

Olivia Stevenson looked at them both. "While you two were talking, you missed the part where he told them that to ensure his re-election in four years, he would add additional members to the Supreme Court during his term in office."

James Grover stepped away to the bar, shaking his head, and poured himself a full glass of scotch. He downed it in one gulp.

All the guests in the room were glued to the TV as the senator continued to ramble on and on. James Grover pulled out his phone and called the two aides he had stationed in the ballroom.

"Whatever you have to do, get him off the fucking stage."

He put his phone back into his pocket and poured himself another drink. This was going to be a long night.

The senator was finally convinced to leave the stage, and he was led back to his suite, where he crashed on the bed, the alcohol taking full effect. He was sound asleep in seconds.

At four A.M. the following morning, CNN declared a winner in the presidential election. With 97 percent of the vote counted, former Montana governor Thomas Baker had 350 electoral votes to the senator's 188. It was a landslide victory, but it didn't go the way the senator had predicted. The faithful had not delivered.

The private party broke up right after the election was called. No one woke the senator to tell him the bad news. That would have to wait.

Chapter Two

The senator woke up in a great mood. He remembered little about the night, but he knew he had fired up the faithful with his inspiring speech. It would probably go down in history as one of the greatest election night speeches ever. He was on a roll, and life was good.

He didn't concern himself that the other side of the king-sized bed was empty. He hadn't slept in the same bed with his wife, Amanda, in years. She was arm candy, nothing more. She was young and beautiful, a former men's magazine centerfold, and she turned heads wherever she went, which didn't hurt his business image, or his political image. Standing beside her, he looked virile and powerful.

He grabbed a long shower to get rid of the cobwebs from the night before. He walked back into the room and stood in front of the mirror. He had gained a little weight since announcing his run for president, but he liked the way he looked. And he knew the women in his life shared that sentiment. He called down to room service and ordered his usual breakfast: scrambled eggs, bacon, French toast and coffee. He got dressed in his navy-blue suit and stepped into the adjoining living room. Empty. He wondered where everyone had gone. Must have been a hell of a victory party after he passed out on the bed. He looked out over Washington and admired the view. Nothing could ruin the way he felt today.

He turned on his favorite cable news channel and

stepped over to the bar to pour himself a small glass of bourbon, a little hair of the dog. He almost dropped the decanter on the bar as his mind registered the words being said by his most loyal news anchor.

"In an incredible upset, Thomas Baker is now the president-elect. We are still waiting for a comment from the White House, and all the country is waiting to see if Senator Stevenson will concede the election and wish the president-elect well."

Multiple news sites had reporters spread out all over the city getting comments from leading Republican lawmakers and faithful followers. The stunned reaction was the same, no matter who they asked. One man on the street interview, a member of the faithful, still wearing his ELECT STEVENSON T-shirt, ball cap and jacket and carrying a huge American flag, said that the whole election was a fraud and that he had heard that almost twenty million illegal aliens had voted for Baker. He promised that the senator's followers would not allow this vote to stand. That was the growing sentiment amongst everyone they spoke with.

The senator threw his full glass at the television, shattering it in a shower of glass shards and sparks. Three members of his security detail came running into the room. They looked at the mess.

"Senator, are you okay, sir?" asked George, the youngest agent in his detail.

Oliver Stevenson stood in the center of the living room, shaking. His face was bright red. The agent in charge of the detail looked at him and was ready to call for an ambulance. He checked the senator's eyes and sat him on one of the bar stools. He told one of the other agents to go down the hall and get the senator's doctor. The senator waved him away. "Forget the fucking doctor. Get my car ready. We're heading home. Now!"

The senator stood up, grabbed his coat and pulled the door to the suite open, scaring the room service waiter, who stepped back, leaving the cart blocking the door. The senator grabbed the side rail of the cart and shoved it, knocking it onto its side and scattering his breakfast all over the floor. He scowled at the server, who had pushed himself against the door to the room on the opposite side of the hallway. The server looked scared to death.

The Secret Service agents scrambled to catch up with the senator, who was standing in front of the closed elevator doors. The agents were all talking into their collar mics as they waited until the doors opened and headed for the lobby.

Understanding what was going on, the agent in charge had requested that the senator's limousine be brought around to the back entrance of the hotel, away from the prying eyes of the press. He didn't think it would be wise to have the senator seen by the public in the state he was in. They exited the elevator into the back service corridor and passed through the staff entrance. The senator climbed into the back seat and he told the driver to go. Protocol dictated that they wait for the police escort and follow cars, but the senator was in no mood to wait. He leaned forward and got face-to-face with the lead agent.

"If this fucking car isn't moving in the next ten

seconds, I will have your ass!"

The driver looked unsure what to do, but the lead agent turned towards him. "You heard the man. Move it!"

The driver put the car in gear and pulled out of the underground garage. Two Washington, DC, police cars were just pulling into the garage when they saw the limo and turned around. They took up positions in front of and behind the limo and headed to the senator's mansion in Alexandria, Virginia, with lights flashing and sirens wailing.

The limo moved through the gate and passed hundreds of the faithful standing along the fence, many with signs reading WE ARE WITH YOU, MR. PRESIDENT or STOP THE FRAUD. The senator didn't acknowledge them as they drove by.

They approached the front entrance of the mansion, and the senator grabbed the door handle and pushed open the door. He pushed past the agents and walked into the house.

The senator, pulling off his coat as he went, speed-walked towards his office. He threw his coat on the couch and stepped through the door leading to his chief of staff's office. His home had served as his main campaign headquarters, containing offices for all his senior and junior staff. Not finding anyone, except for a couple of aides, he walked through the house, flung open the doors and yelled at the top of his voice.

"Where the fuck are all my people?" Everyone in the hallway and surrounding offices stopped what they were doing. "You'd all better get on the goddamn phones. I want everyone here in the next twenty minutes."

He stepped back into his office and slammed the door, shaking the walls. He walked over to his desk and, with the sweep of his arm, sent everything on top of the desk flying.

James Grover came running into the office and looked at the mess on the floor. He looked at the senator, who sat behind his desk, shaking.

Stevenson picked up the newspaper that had been sitting on his desk and held up the front page so Grover could see it. He balled it up and threw it at his chief of staff, who caught it in his hand.

"How the fuck did this happen? How the fuck did I lose? There is no way that Montana ranch hand beat me. The polls said it wasn't even close."

By now, several other members of his executive staff had arrived and were looking at the carnage that used to be the office. They were all afraid to say anything. They had no idea how the senator would react, but they knew it wouldn't be good. So, they stood there silently while he ranted.

"I shut my eyes for ten minutes and my entire election goes to hell. There was obviously fraud. My people are loyal to me. A lot more loyal than the people standing in this room. You'd better figure out why I didn't win, and you'd better do it in a damn big hurry, or you are all going to be without jobs next week."

The senator walked to the door of the office and

threw it open. He turned back and faced his staff. He waved his hand. "And get this shit cleaned up before I get back."

Grover looked at Sandy Reese, who had entered the room near the end of the tirade. "That was interesting," said Reese. "Suddenly the polls matter to him. He wouldn't look at the final polls last week that showed us losing by at least fifteen points."

Grover nodded. "Welcome to my world. He believes what he sees on his media sites, and a lot of those showed a significant loss, which he ignored."

Several junior staff members came in and were cleaning up the mess the senator had made. Sandy asked the members of the senior staff to step into the back hall that led to the chief of staff's office. They walked out and closed the door.

"What are we going to do about this? The senator looks unhinged. He certainly can't go on television and concede the election looking like he does now."

Grover looked around at the faces in the hall. "This goes no further than this group. If I find his tirade on the news tonight, someone's ass is going to get kicked. Do I make myself clear?"

Everyone nodded. "Good. Go back to work. By now your staff knows we lost the election. I don't want to hear a lot of talk in the hallways. We still have a job to do, and I expect everyone to get on with it."

Everyone moved down the hall except Sandy. He stepped into Grover's office. "I don't think he is going to concede. I have a feeling he is going to push this voter fraud allegation as far as he can run with it," said Sandy.

"Let's give him a day or two to calm down and see what happens. In the meantime, we need to lay off staff and close campaign offices. I'll get folks started on that right away."

Sandy nodded. "Let's do it quietly for now. Oliver is under enough strain."

He opened the door and walked out. James Grover disbelieved his own words. He sensed a storm was on the horizon, and he wondered how far this unpredictable presidential candidate would go. That thought scared him, and even though he knew why they had lost the election, he needed to appease the senator. He pulled out his personal cell phone and dialed a number.

Quinton McCabe, the senator's attorney, one of many, answered. "Wondered when you'd be calling," he said with a thick Southern drawl. "Bet he's not happy."

"That's a bet I wouldn't take," said Grover. "Better get your team together. My gut says the senator will want to fight this loss all the way to the Supreme Court if need be."

"Jim," said McCabe. "He lost by double digits. It's over. We backed the wrong horse, but to keep him happy, I'll have my folks look for loopholes. Once he sees nothing can reverse the results, he'll back down and walk away."

James Grover sat back in his chair and pushed a

button on his desk phone. A young female voice answered. "Stacy, see if the chief justice has a few minutes he can spare for me this morning."

He dialed another number on his personal phone and connected with the campaign manager for the campaign committee. "Richard, call in all the analysts. I want a report by the end of the day of which states are vulnerable, and Richard, have someone deliver it to the house. Do not send it in an email."

He hung up and looked at the picture of Thomas Jefferson that hung on his wall next to the picture of Senator Stevenson. The irony was not lost on him. The man who helped write the Constitution and the man who might very well destroy it. They were going to have to turn the Constitution inside out if they had any chance at all. He wondered how far they would have to go. He wondered how far the senator would go.

Chapter Three

Across town, in the presidential suite at the Washingtonian Center hotel, the brainstorming had begun. Quinton McCabe sat with five of his most trusted partners and seven of the president's biggest and most generous supporters. The personal wealth in the room, if calculated, would be more than the gross domestic product of many nations. These were the people behind the many conservative PACs that fed money, sight unseen, into the campaign. They had a lot to lose if the election results were allowed to stand.

Quinton stood up and walked to the whiteboard in the front of the room. He held up the black marker.

"I want you all to remember that what we discuss in this room goes no further. Please turn off your cell phones and place them in the center of the table."

Twelve phones landed in the middle of the table next to his. "Now that that's done, let's get down to business. I spoke with the senator this morning and he wants us to pull out all the stops, particularly on this election fraud thing. The campaign staff is looking at all the election results from every county in the country. As they find close races, we will file in court to have the results recounted, and we are making lists of individual votes to challenge."

Robert Crosby, the senator's brother-in-law and CEO of the largest banking system in the country, stood up. "That's all well and good, Quin, but it's going to take forever, and you know as well as I do that we will not find twenty million votes to change this election. We're wasting time and money. Sit him down and tell him it's over."

"That's not true," said Raymond Portman, CEO of Portman Industries, the nation's largest military contractor. "At least twenty million illegals voted for Baker. All we need to do . . ."

"Come on, Ray," said Crosby. "You don't believe that shit. No one is that stupid. The senator dragged that number out of his alcohol-filled mind before the election count was even partially over. All the latest polls had him losing by large numbers, but there's no proof of that number. It's imaginary."

"You'd better hope there are a lot of stupid people out there, Bob. We need his faithful followers to keep repeating that message." Everyone turned and looked at Valerie Samson, CEO of one of the largest cosmetics companies in the world. "But I agree with Bob on this. We can file all the lawsuits we can think of. We will not find enough instances of voter fraud to make a difference. The senator lost by just under twenty million votes. That's too huge a deficit to overcome with lawsuits."

"So, what are you two suggesting?" asked Quinton McCabe.

"We don't know yet, Quin," said Crosby. "Christ, it hasn't even been three days since the election. You push the lawsuits. The more lawsuits we file, the more confusing this will become, and the average person will get lost in the crap. Val and I will work on alternative methods that might have a bigger impact."

“What about the Supreme Court?” asked Gerhard Richter, CEO of the Richter Hotel Company. “I’m not sure I want to invest any more of my money in this fight if the Supreme Court will not support our play.”

Several people nodded in agreement. Quinton McCabe looked around the table. He had the feeling he was losing some of these people.

“James Grover is meeting with the chief justice again tomorrow. I am sure the chief will support our endeavors. After all, he owes the senator big for getting four new conservative white justices approved during his tenure as the Senate majority leader. They all knew going into this that someday, we might call on them, and they had better be there.”

“That’s great,” said Crosby. “What are they going to do, declare the election null and void and make Stevenson president? They don’t have the constitutional authority to do that. How about we stop talking about stupid shit and figure out if any of this is possible or if we are wasting our time? We’ve got the entire legal brain trust from your firm, Quin. Surely, they must have better ideas.”

“If we can get those twenty million illegal votes thrown out, the senator wins.”

“Fuck, Ray,” said Crosby. “Do you know how stupid you sound? If twenty million illegals voted, don’t you think the Democrats would have figured out how to keep the House and the Senate? Do you think they had those people vote for Baker and not for the other candidates?”

“It’s possible,” yelled Portman, who was visibly

shaken by the verbal attack. "The senator said . . ."

Robert Crosby shook his head. "The senator was talking out of his ass."

Everyone stopped talking and looked at Crosby. "His speech at the victory party was the most incoherent speech he has given in a whole slew of incoherent speeches."

There was a knock at the door, and a secretary who worked for Quinton McCabe stuck her head in. "Sorry for the intrusion, sir, but I thought you should see this."

She used the remote and clicked on the big-screen television. The picture appeared, and everyone stopped and stared. Senator Stevenson was standing on the street in front of the White House, behind a podium with a photoshopped presidential seal. He was surrounded by several members of Congress, and the entire scene was surreal.

The secretary clicked up the volume.

"As Americans, we can no longer tolerate the trampling of our beloved Constitution by lawless Democrats bent on destroying this great nation, a country that we hold near and dear to our hearts. The radical left stole the last election, and they have now stolen this one. Soon we will present proof to the American people that over twenty million illegals voted for Baker in this election. Without those fraudulent votes, we would be listening to Baker making a concession speech and moving back to Montana to herd cows. Instead, we are witnessing the end of our democracy as the radical left uses every trick in the book, from faulty voting machines to illegal votes. Well, I for one will not stand for it. We can fight fire with fire. Today, as your duly elected president-elect, I am calling on President Diggs to order the joint chiefs to have National Guard units in every state confiscate the voting machines that were used on Election Day and to hold them until each state can appoint a panel of Republicans to check each machine. This will not be legislators reviewing the machines, but we are going to hire hundreds of regular Americans so that you know that the fraud they find is real and not contrived. We are in a fight for democracy, my fellow Americans, and sometimes a little blood must be shed in the name of democracy and decency. God bless you all, and God bless America."

The senator stepped away from the podium and walked toward the Capitol, followed by several congressional leaders. The folks around the table sat in stunned silence.

Ray Portman and several of the lawyers stood up and applauded. He looked at Roger Crosby. "See, the senator is going to present proof of all those illegal votes. What do you think about that?"

Robert Crosby laughed. "You're an idiot. He just made a call for an armed rebellion. That's the part you missed. Nothing will be presented because there is nothing to present. He's filling up the glasses, and fools like you are going to drink the Kool-Aid without ever questioning anything. The president, a Democrat, if you remember, will never involve the National Guard. It would be like declaring martial law. Not going to happen."

Robert Crosby stood up from the table, picked up his phone from the pile and left the room. He had more important things to do than sit and argue with people who were too stupid to know any better.

Chapter Four

The senator stood behind his desk looking out the window at the crowd gathered behind the fence on the other side of the lawn. The morning had dawned gray and dreary, seeming to match his mood. He turned around and faced the three people in the room.

Admiral Steven Archibald, the former chairman of the Joint Chiefs of Staff, stood facing the senator's desk. He was a tall man with white hair, a gray goatee and a ruddy complexion. He was wearing a blue suit and stood at attention.

Next to him stood James Grover. The weary look on his face and deep circles under his eyes spoke of many late nights. That and the fact that he had been wearing the same suit for the past three days.

The third person in the room was former attorney general Mildred Barnes. At five foot one, she was the shortest person in the room. She was heavyset with grayish blond hair and a perpetual scowl. No one could remember ever seeing her smile or laugh. A graduate of Harvard who had studied law at Cambridge University, she might have been the smartest person in the room.

"Admiral, have you heard how the National Guard is doing rounding up all the voting machines?"

Admiral Archibald stood up straighter and looked the senator in the eye. "No one is confiscating any voting machines, sir."

The senator walked around his desk, his face

turning red, not from the movement, but from the anger that was welling up inside. James Grover stepped in front of him as he rounded the corner of the desk, getting between him and the admiral. The senator glared at him, but he didn't move.

Stevenson, who was not as tall as the admiral, looked up into his eyes. "I gave you a direct order to have the National Guard confiscate the voting machines in every state. Have you chosen to just ignore me, or are you out to fuck with me?"

The senator's face was bright red, and he stepped forward, pushing against James Grover, who held his ground.

"First, Senator. You never gave me a direct order, as I haven't been on the Joint Chiefs in a long time, and you are not the president. You announced your intentions during a speech. That speech does not constitute a direct order. Second, the military and the National Guard are not here for your political use. Unless the current president declares martial law, which would be an incredibly reckless thing to do without a valid reason, there is nothing that can be done. This is a political decision and does not involve the military."

The senator was livid. "You, sir, have no loyalty. After everything I have done for the military over the years, this is how you treat me. You are a traitor, and I have lost all respect for you. If you won't follow my orders, maybe I need to find someone who will."

The admiral looked him in the eyes. "I can no longer support a man who would turn a petty political action into a military conquest. If you can find someone that will follow your insane order, then go right ahead, but you can do it without me."

The admiral turned and walked to the door. The president pushed James Grover aside and followed the admiral to the door. "You are a fucking coward. Once I am sworn in, I will have your ass."

The admiral turned and faced the president. "I don't give a shit, since I retired many years ago. Either way, I no longer work for you, and that suits me just fine."

The admiral opened the door and walked through it. He left the door open as he walked past those gathered in the reception area.

The senator stepped through the open door and at the top of his voice yelled, "I will have you court-martialed, you ungrateful son of a bitch. You wait and see."

He stepped back into the office and slammed the door, leaving everyone in the reception area dumbfounded. He looked at James Grover. "You call the military police. I want that fucker arrested and charged with treason for not supporting his president and following a legitimate order."

The senator sat at his desk, his hands shaking. He looked at Grover. "What the fuck are you waiting for?"

"Sorry, sir," said Grover. "The admiral is no longer in the military, and you have no authority over him."

The senator looked at the former attorney general.

"I want a full-blown investigation into all those illegal votes. Are you going to give me an argument too? Use every agent at your disposal. I want all twenty million votes accounted for."

"No, sir. No argument. It's not going to happen. The FBI is not your personal investigation unit, and I haven't been their boss in years. Elections are the purview of the states. If the states choose to investigate these unfounded rumors that you have been citing, then that's their decision. The FBI does not get involved unless requested by a specific state with specific evidence that major fraud occurred during the election."

The senator glared at her. "Who do you think you're talking to? You serve at the pleasure of the president, and I could fire you right now and no one would even bat an eye."

"You can't fire me, sir. I was an advisor on your election campaign. I am not the current attorney general, and you are not the president. The sitting president will not allow the FBI to investigate your made-up charges of election fraud."

The senator smiled. "Well then, Ms. Barnes. You're fired. I don't need any of you. I could run this country just fine without any of you. Now, get out of my office before I have you arrested."

The former attorney general laughed, turned and left the office. The senator looked at Grover. "What the hell is wrong with everyone? I gave these people purpose, and all I asked for in return is a little loyalty. Is that too much to ask?"

James Grover sat down opposite the senator. "Sir,

the secretaries of state of forty-six states have come out and said there is no evidence of any widespread voter fraud. Maybe it's time to accept that and concede the election."

"You too, Jim? I can't even count on you any longer?"

"That's not what I said, sir. I have been with you since the beginning, and I will be with you till the end, but we need to face the fact that you lost the election. It might be time to move on."

"No. Now is not the time to turn tail and run. The nation needs me. I'm the only one who can solve its problems."

James Grover looked at him. Over the past several months, the senator had hit that same theme in his rally speeches. It didn't seem to occur to him he had been a senator for almost thirty years and whatever problems the country had were there all along. The voters were fed up with his bluster and were no longer buying that he was the salvation of the nation.

James Grover stepped through the side door of the office and walked back to his own office. He had no idea how to convince the senator that he had lost the election, but he had to keep trying. He decided he needed a break, so he headed for the gym, which was in the senator's basement. Maybe some time in the sauna would help his mood.

The senator watched him leave. He couldn't believe that his most trusted advisors were being this disloyal when he needed them most. He pulled out his personal cell phone, clicked on a contact and waited.

The phone was answered with silence. “We need to talk,” said the senator.

He listened for a minute and then hung up. He buzzed his secretary and asked her to locate Mark Sinclair, the head of his security detail. If his so-called friends were unwilling to help him claim the White House, then he would need to reach out to others he knew would not let him down.

Chapter Five

The snow was falling lightly as Mark Sinclair turned off Interstate 66 at Front Royal and passed through the entry gate for Shenandoah National Park. He followed Skyline Drive until he reached the Browntown trailhead parking area and parked his three-year-old Ford Explorer at the end of the lot. He was glad to see that there were just two other vehicles in the parking lot, assuming that the cold and snow had forced most of the tourists to find alternate plans for the day.

Senator Stevenson slid off the passenger seat and zipped up his coat. He stepped to the back of the SUV and grabbed a small day pack, which he slung onto his shoulders. Mark Sinclair did the same thing, and he closed the hatch. He touched the pistol on his hip.

"Senator," he said. "Are you sure about this?"

The senator looked at him. "Mark, if the people closest to me won't help me take the White House, then I will go to the people I have the utmost respect for, my supporters."

"That's fine, sir, but these folks are nuts."

The senator laughed. "They are eccentric, Mark. Not nuts. There's a difference."

Mark had left the Secret Service following the election loss and had become the senator's chief of security. He liked the old guy, but since the election, he'd noticed that the senator's thinking had become more clouded. Maybe "eccentric" was the right word, but he had serious doubts about the person they were about to meet, including his choice of meeting location.

The senator looked at the trail sign. “Time’s a-wastin'”,” he said.

Mark nodded, and off they went. Into what was anyone’s guess.

After an hour of hiking through dense forest with the snow accumulating under their feet, they smelled wood smoke and coffee and came to a clearing in the forest, next to a small stream. The smoke came from a small campfire that had been started in a rock firepit, and the man sitting next to the fire, drinking coffee, looked up and smiled.

“Was wondering if you were going to show up,” he said. He picked up the pot of coffee and filled two cardboard cups sitting next to him. He stood and handed the cups to Mark and the senator, then pointed towards a log and sat down in his original spot. The senator sat across from him and warmed his hands on the cup before taking a sip.

Mark, ever vigilant, stood to the side and monitored the surrounding area. The clearing, a decent size, was surrounded by a dense pine forest, and anyone who wanted to harm the senator need only hide amongst the trees and wait for the perfect opportunity. In this wilderness, it would be months before their bodies were found, if ever. Mark hated the whole setup, and he touched the side of his hip, making sure his pistol was ready, if needed.

Calvin Mace, their host, was five foot ten and weighed 220 pounds. He wore his gray hair cut in what used to be called a flattop, and he had a couple of days' worth of stubble on his chin. He had brown eyes that were constantly looking around, especially to keep an eye on Mark. Mark was former government, and that meant that until proven otherwise, he couldn't be trusted. He sipped his coffee and watched the senator. He set his cup on the ground and looked up.

Calvin was the national president of the American Freedom Force, a hard-right Christian group that had been one of the major supporters of the Stevenson for President campaign. They weren't a wealthy organization, but between the internet presence and their media exposure, they carried a huge amount of weight in the far-right community. They were extremely radical, and following the election results, they'd started calling for armed revolution to make sure that Senator Stevenson took his rightful place as the God-chosen leader of the United States. The AFF was the media face of a vast militia network that was active in every state, and they believed they had the Bible and the Second Amendment on their side.

"So, Senator. How badly do you want to be president?" He picked up his cup and leaned forward, sipping the hot, bitter liquid.

Senator Stevenson sipped from his cup and looked at Calvin. "You know the answer to that as well as I do."

"Yeah, I do, but I want to hear you say it. Once we embark on this journey, there will be no turning back, and I want to make sure you are committed to what we are about to do."

"God has chosen me to be the next president of the United States, and I am prepared to do what is necessary to achieve that goal. Is that good enough for you?"

"That will work," said Calvin. "Now comes the hard part. How to achieve that goal, and how much it's going to cost. It will not be cheap, Senator. Are you prepared to pay handsomely to reach your goal?"

"What the fuck do you think?" asked the senator. "I'm sitting on my ass in the middle of a forest in the freezing cold, drinking the shittiest coffee I have ever tasted and talking to someone who was once called the scariest man in America. So, yeah, I'm willing to pay whatever the price."

Calvin smiled. "Good, then there will be no misunderstanding. We are to develop a plan to put you in the White House. You have the initial payment?"

The senator reached into his backpack, which was sitting on the ground next to him, and pulled out a fat envelope. He held up the envelope for Calvin to see.

"One million dollars," he said. "To guarantee me my dream."

Calvin laughed, and it echoed through the forest. He stared at the senator. "There are no guarantees, Senator. We're not starting a civil war on your behalf. What we are doing will be subtle and in keeping with the word, if not the intent, of the Constitution of this great nation. We have people working on a plan as we speak, but there are no guarantees except one. If at any time you cross us, yours will be the blood that is sacrificed to save this country. Do we have an understanding?"

The senator stood, dumped his coffee on the ground and handed Calvin the envelope. Calvin stood, took the envelope and extended his hand. The senator shook it. Calvin held the senator's hand with a viselike grip, and the heat from the fire showed in the senator's face as he winced but refused to pull away. Calvin let go, and the senator rubbed his hands together.

Calvin poured the rest of the coffee into his cup and sat on the log. He looked at the senator. "We'll be in touch. In the meantime, you keep the lawsuits going. I want the news media focused on that and not on us."

The senator put his gloves on and turned from the fire. They picked up their backpacks and headed back the way they came, leaving Calvin to finish his shitty coffee.

"I have a feeling you just made a deal with the devil, Senator," said Mark. "I hope you know what you're doing."

The senator didn't respond, but he was having serious doubts about getting involved with the AFF. They had been a valuable asset during the election, but this was something different, and he wondered how they would pull it off.

They reached the SUV, wiped off the six inches of snow that had accumulated on the windows and placed their packs in the back, and while the senator slid into the passenger seat, Mark stepped off into the woods to relieve himself. Far enough away that the senator couldn't hear him, he pulled out his phone and dialed a number. The phone was answered on the third ring with silence.

"It's done," said Mark, and he put his phone away, urinated against a tree and walked back to the SUV. The drive back to the mansion in Alexandria was slow until the snow turned to rain as they approached the Washington, DC, metro area. Mark parked under the porte cochere, and the senator grabbed his pack and wished Mark a good night. Mark pulled out and headed home. It had been a long day.

Chapter Six

Mike Branik circled around to where he started and slid under the pine branches that had been his home for the past twenty-four hours. The snow he'd packed around his nest to cut some of the wind was no longer helping, and he was growing impatient. He keyed the mic snugged against his ear.

"One to team. Still no movement."

"Three to one. How long are we gonna sit here? It looks like the info we got from our uncle was bogus."

The voice in his ear was Jeff Halsey, and he sounded as frustrated as Mike. Jeff had been wounded during a mission in Somalia and, once stateside and after a lengthy hospital stay, had crawled into a bottle of bourbon, and that was where Mike found him two years back. After extensive physical therapy and months of training, Jeff's five-foot-ten muscular frame was back in top fighting condition, but like most tier one operators, Jeff hated to sit around and wait. He was a man of action and was all about charging in and taking the fight to the enemy.

This mission was different. United States Senator Carlton Mansfield had been the senior Democratic senator from Missouri for two terms and now, as the Senate minority leader, wielded a huge amount of power and influence. Ten days ago, his two granddaughters, Carrie, age eleven, and Sasha, age fourteen, had been kidnapped from the private school outside of Chicago where they were living, while under the watchful eyes of their private security guards.

The girls had been spirited away during the night, and their disappearance wasn't discovered until the following morning when their room was found empty except for the body of the overnight guard, a young woman who had been garroted and almost decapitated.

When Chicago police discovered the identities of the girls, they were more than happy to hand the case off to the FBI, but so far, the FBI had come up dry. No one had seen the girls, and no ransom notes had been delivered. The case grew cold, and a frustrated Senator Mansfield called his longtime friend in the White House for help. The senator and President Roman Diggs had been roommates in college before entering politics. Both men had proven to be highly electable and had risen through the ranks of Democratic politics to reach their current positions. Senator Mansfield knew if anyone could help him, it would be the president. The president was happy to help.

Mike had been knee-deep in the Little Snake River in Colorado, stalking a wily German brown trout, as snowflakes fell around him. He had just cast his fly where he wanted when the phone in his wader pocket chimed. He reached into his pocket, pulled out his phone, looked at the number and almost didn't answer it, but this was one number you didn't ignore.

"Yes, sir," said Mike.

"Did you catch it, or did you miss?" the president said with a laugh.

"Missed it, sir. Just not my day."

Mike knew the president of the United States didn't call for idle chitchat, so he waited.

"You heard about Senator Mansfield's granddaughters being kidnapped. It's been ten days and nothing, no leads and no ransom demand. The FBI is stuck. I need your help. I know you just got back from a mission, but this one is important."

Mike and his team had spent the last month in Mexico tracking down a mobile fentanyl lab that was bringing massive amounts of the drug across the border. Border Patrol had no idea how the drugs were entering the country, and the DEA was stuck in a battle of wits with the Mexican authorities. Mike's team found the lab and, in a shoot-out south of Mexico City, killed several cartel enforcers, captured the top three cartel leaders and spirited them back to the United States. The battle, which led to the destruction of the lab and a couple of hundred million dollars in drugs, had been costly, and two members of Mike's team didn't make it back alive. He knew his team was still reeling from the losses, but he also knew the president didn't call unless there was no place else to turn. Mike Branik was America's last resort.

"What do you need, sir?" asked Mike.

"I need you to find those young ladies, Mike. It's that simple."

Mike laughed. Nothing in his world was ever simple. "Rules of engagement, sir?"

"Find those kids at any cost and handle the kidnappers as you see fit. Christmas is in three weeks, and I want those kids back home with their family."

"Yes, sir. We'll take care of it."

"I knew you would, Mike, semper fi." The president disconnected the call, and Mike waded towards shore, climbed from the river and headed for his ATV. He put his rod and fly vest in the back. It was too cold to take off his waders, so he climbed into the ATV and headed for the barn.

Mike and his team spent the next two days calling everyone they knew, from upstanding citizens to lowlife scum, looking for any thread they could pull. While they were working the phones, Ronnie Fleetwood was working the internet.

Veronica Fleetwood was the team computer expert. During her time in the marines, she'd learned to fight, and her time at the NSA gave her the computer skills she needed to fight the war on terrorism on any front, with bullets or keystrokes. She was short, five foot four and stocky, with short black hair and intense eyes. She gave every mission her best, and despite the losses the team had taken in Mexico, she dove right into this new assignment. It would take her mind off of their two lost comrades.

Gabe Fortenz had served with Mike all over the world, and when Mike went private, Gabe was right behind him and never looked back. He had been Mike's second-in-command until that night in Mexico when an IED went off and Gabe died in the dark, alone. Mike and the team found him the following morning, or what was left of him. It was a hard loss for Mike, but they all knew that what they did was dangerous, and the end could come at any moment. Mike had spent a week after the mission with Gabe's mom and sister, helping around the farm and making sure that Gabe received all the military honors he was entitled to, including his funeral and burial in Arlington National Cemetery.

Cassidy Miller spent ten years in the marines before joining Mike in the private sector. She was a beautiful Black woman with straight hair and a nice figure. She loved jazz music from the fifties and sixties, and she could hold her own in beer pong. She and Ronnie grew close, and before long, they let the rest of the team know they were a couple. No one on the team was surprised, and if they did their jobs, no one cared.

They ceased being a couple when the round from a cartel sniper caught Cassidy on the right side of her neck as they were evacuating their hostages. Ronnie had kept the compression bandage on her neck until they were clear of the fight, but by the time they reached safety, it was too late. Once they got Cassidy's body onto the chopper, Ronnie and Jeff went back to the scene of the firefight, tracked down the sniper and put an end to his life.

Mike never asked them if anyone else died besides the sniper. He didn't care. Justice was served. Cassidy was buried in Fort Logan National Cemetery in Colorado with full military honors.

Having grown up in East Los Angeles, in what she called a hostile environment, Ronnie hated people who hurt kids, and she told Mike that she would turn over every pile of shit she could find to get a lead on the kids.

When Ronnie was seven, her older sister was kidnapped on the way home from school. She had missed her bus because of cheerleading practice and didn't want to wait for her dad to get off work. It was six blocks from the school to their house, and at thirteen years old, she felt she was ready to walk home alone. Somewhere in those six blocks, she disappeared. Two weeks later, her mutilated body was discovered in an abandoned building. Ronnie, who cherished her older sister, was crushed.

Mike never doubted his team would succeed where others who had to deal with more restrictions could not. Mike's team lived in the shadows, and in his world, there were no rules. You either succeeded or failed, and none of his team ever accepted failure. The government had many agencies that considered themselves the tip of the spear in the battle to protect the interests of the United States. Mike and his team were the microscopic point of those spear tips, and they knew going into any mission that no matter what happened, they were going to get dirty.

It took four days of working their information network before they finally got a tip that was worthwhile. The tip had come from a reliable source they called Uncle Milt, who was embedded with all kinds of lowlife militia and neo-Nazi hate groups. Mike sensed the first time he met Uncle Milt in person that he might be a federal agent, but Mike never asked. He didn't care as long as the information was good, and so far, over several missions, Uncle Milt was right on.

He told Mike that he had heard that the girls had

been taken by a small radical fundamentalist religious group and were being held in a house in the hills in Kentucky. Ronnie had tracked them down online and their pages were full of hate and vitriol, with a lot of it directed at Senator Mansfield.

When Mansfield squashed a bill to put the Ten Commandments in every school in the United States and force teachers to teach the Bible in every grade, they had had enough and had threatened retribution. The ten followers they had on the internet agreed with them.

A quick helicopter flight to Denver and a MATS flight to Lexington followed by a long drive on the back roads of Kentucky led them to a large house in a clearing in the dense forest near a tiny town called McDowell. And here they'd been sitting since the day before, waiting for some sign that the girls were in the house.

Mike was settling into his tree fort and had opened a cold MRE when his mic went off.

"Four to team. Got movement in the barn." Arnie Stern sounded excited, or maybe it was just a break in the boredom.

Arnie Stern stood over six feet tall and had muscles on top of muscles. He had spent five years after leaving the marines as a door kicker for the U.S. Marshals Service. Mike had recruited him four years back, and Arnie had proved his mettle in several hairy situations.

"Go, four," said Mike.

"A kid just ran into the barn and was tackled by a

young man. He slapped her around and dragged her back into the house."

"Can you confirm ID?"

"Yeah, hair color and clothes are a match for what we were told was missing from the girl's room. She also had a stuffed pink poodle in her hand, just like the one in her picture."

"One to two and five," said Mike. "You all set for a rear-door breach?"

"Two, ready, just say the word." Ronnie moved from her position at the back of the house and hugged the side of the barn, out of view of the rear windows.

"Five, good to go," said Bill Rogers. Bill was the youngest member of Mike's team. He had spent several years with the FBI Hostage Rescue Team but wasn't as happy as he'd hoped to be. He came to Mike's attention during an op where Mike's team was called in to back up the HRT during a high-profile rescue. Bill had proven himself to be a sharp, strategic thinker, and Mike offered him a job with less red tape. Bill had jumped at the chance.

While Ronnie watched, Arnie circled around the barn, found a couple of loose boards on the back wall, broke them off and crawled into the barn. There was a door on the side that led into the house. He could hear a lot of screaming going on. Someone was getting chewed out for not keeping an eye on the kid.

Arnie moved next to the door just as it flew open and a red-faced young man carrying a shotgun stepped through the door and kicked at the dirt. Before he could turn to pull the door completely closed, Arnie stepped from the shadows, placed his left hand over the guy's mouth and drove his knife into the side of his throat, slashing across in one swift move. He pulled the guy away from the door and left him gurgling in a small stall.

He keyed his mic. "Four in the barn, one bad guy neutralized. In position."

Jeff had moved up closer to the front door, and Mike was in the trees off to his left. He keyed his mic. "All teams. On three, shock and awe." Jeff crawled under the front window and attached a small explosive charge next to the doorknob. He pulled a flash-bang off his vest and pulled the pin. His opposite hand held the button for the charge. Around back, Ronnie and Bill had done the same thing. Mike crawled under the window and stood behind Jeff, who was a few feet down the wall from the door. They turned their faces away from the charge. Mike keyed his mic.

"One. Two. Three."

Jeff blew the front door charge at the same time Ronnie blew the back door off its hinges, then three flash-bangs were lobbed into the house as they covered their ears and looked away.

They rushed into the house. A disoriented woman with blood streaming from her ears was waving a pistol around in the kitchen at the back of the house. Ronnie dropped her with a shot to the forehead. She turned as a big guy wearing a filthy T-shirt and bib overalls charged into the kitchen, swinging an old rusty hatchet. Arnie stepped through the door just as Ronnie ducked and shot him twice in the chest. He crashed into the refrigerator and slid onto the floor.

Mike raced up the stairs on his left to the second floor, following a heavyset bald guy with a large bowie knife. Bill was close on his heels, while Jeff rushed into the living room. The guy who was sitting on the floor shaking his head to clear the cobwebs from the blast jumped up and grabbed the little girl. He raised the pistol to the side of her head, and Jeff shot him through his right eye and then shot him a second time when he hit the floor. He grabbed the little girl, who was crying and holding her ears, and ran out the front door.

Ronnie stepped into the living room and heard six shots from upstairs. She'd turned to head up the stairs when Mike and Bill came down the stairs, Mike carrying the older granddaughter snugged close to his chest. He looked at Arnie and Ronnie.

"We clear?" he asked.

They nodded and ran out the front door. Jeff had carried the little girl to where they had hidden the SUV, had placed her in the back and was now parked in front of the house. They pulled off their ballistic vests, stripped their weapons except for their pistols and placed everything in the black duffel bags in the rear. They slid in, and Jeff pulled away from the house and headed down the dirt road that led to the highway. While he did that, Ronnie, using a digital fingerprint analyzer, confirmed the girls' identities with the fingerprints the family had provided.

Jeff drove to the coordinates Mike had received on his phone, and as they pulled to a stop, a Blackhawk helicopter, painted black and with no marking, touched down in the field next to the SUV. They carried the girls to the chopper, got them situated and threw in their gear. Mike ran back to the SUV, took the plastic container of gas from the rear hatch and poured it all over the inside of the SUV. He looked around, threw in a match and raced back to the chopper. By the time the chopper lifted off, the SUV was fully engulfed in flames.

It was dark by the time they landed at Andrews Air Force Base in Washington, DC. Before they off-loaded, the chopper was pushed into an empty hangar and the doors were closed.

The chopper was met by a grateful Senator Mansfield, his wife, son and daughter-in-law. The girls, wearing the clothes they had been kidnapped in, now filthy and torn, ran off the chopper and hugged their family. Mike and his team stayed back to let them have their moment. The senator, wiping tears from his eyes, walked over to Mike, who was standing outside the chopper, and shook his hand.

"I don't want to know how you did it, but I will be forever in your debt." He wiped the tears from his eyes and headed back to the limousine that was parked in the next bay. The large hangar doors were opened, and the limo pulled away and disappeared into the night. Mike and his crew grabbed their gear bags and headed across the tarmac to a waiting MATS flight that would take them back to Denver.

Chapter Seven

Robert E. Lee Richardson looked around his dining room table at the four men seated there. Calvin Mace had called the meeting, and the patriots he wanted to attend were all there. Robert E. Lee, conservative media mogul, was the leader of Patriot Media Enterprises, a network of television, radio and internet providers who believed that the past two elections were stolen, which was obvious since the person sitting in the White House was Black and liberal. Patriot Media Enterprises had openly led discussions with conservative Christian groups across the nation to see if there was an appetite for a civil war that would see a significant number of states secede from the union. Since Oliver Stevenson had lost the presidential election by a landslide to that cattle rancher from Montana, the talk of secession had grown louder with each passing day.

Robert E. Lee ran his hands through what was left of his gray hair. He was tall, well over six foot five and heavyset with a gray goatee and a large belly that hung over his pants. He held an unlit cigar in his mouth since his wife refused to allow him to smoke in the house, no matter how important he thought he was.

Jimmy Bronson was the youngest member at the table at thirty years old, but he had seen a lot in those thirty years, having been on several missions as a member of Seal Team 4. He was medium height with an excellent build and wore his head shaved with a scraggly beard. He had a scar that ran from his right temple to the underside of his right ear. A souvenir from a Taliban fighter who'd refused to give up but eventually did. Jimmy ran the Conservative Christian Action Team (CCAT), the direct-action division of Patriot Media Enterprises. His group handled the dirty work, and through his military connections he had put together a long list of supporters willing to lay down their lives to wrest America from the hands of the godless liberals and radical lefties.

Across from Jimmy sat Warren Turlock, Esquire. Warren had been a respected Southern lawyer for more than fifty years, but more important, he was a professor emeritus at the Duke University School of Law, where he taught constitutional law for a good part of his life. He was one of the nation's leading authorities on the Constitution and was often seen on Patriot Media Enterprise's talk shows as an expert commentator. Turlock had long gray hair and bushy eyebrows and walked with a cane following an automobile accident several years ago that killed his wife and son. He wore his signature red, white and blue bow tie, with a white shirt and tan suit.

The last member of the group was former superior court judge Harold D. Wahls. Wahls was also an esquire but only used the "Esq." after his name when he was around close friends. He had lost his license to practice law in North Carolina and Georgia after being found guilty of election fraud during the last presidential election, a charge he was still appealing. He had been a noteworthy constitutional scholar and was considered by many in his field to be the preeminent authority on the Constitution in the country. He was short, fat and balding, with a ponytail that hung to the middle of his back. Today he wore jeans and a flannel shirt along with a down vest to fight off the cold and to cover the pistol he carried in a shoulder holster under his left arm.

Dorothy Richardson placed a large plate of Christmas cookies in the middle of the table, along with a big pitcher of sweet tea, and silently left the room, closing the double sliding door.

Robert E. Lee looked around the table. "It's official, gentlemen. The senator gave Calvin the approval to move forward. He wants us to move heaven and earth to move past the election nonsense and secure his place in history as the next President of the United States. He also presented Cal with the down payment for his war chest to see that the defeat of the Montana cattle rancher is uncontested. Now it's on us to make that happen. With January sixth fast approaching, we need to make sure we have looked at every loophole to prevent the election from being certified. Where do we stand?"

Judge Wahls poured himself a glass of tea and picked up a cookie. "Can't be done," he said. "The certification issue was taken all the way to the Supreme Court following the last election, and even with the supermajority of conservative justices on the bench, they could not stop the certification. The argument of Congress not certifying the election is dead. It is a formality of the electoral process and will proceed with or without our intervention."

"What about the false electors, as the lame-stream media calls them?" asked Calvin.

The judge looked down his nose. "Been tried, as you well know. Most of the electors our candidate chose as alternates are in jail, awaiting sentencing or being released after serving their sentences. The stripping of my license to practice law because of the alternate electors is still waiting to be heard at the Supreme Court. No, gentlemen. Alternate electors are not the answer."

"Then what the hell is left?" asked Robert E. Lee. "Warren. Surely there must be another way. Calvin is going to focus his militia groups on trying to stop the certification on January sixth. He is working on getting a million of our brethren to surround the Capitol and prevent the certification from ever taking place. The chances of him taking over the Capitol and preventing the certification, even with a million patriots on hand to help, will fail. The president will activate the National Guard, and they will barricade the building. All this will do is turn people against us, and it could get many people killed. We need to talk about a more direct action. Something handled by a small secretive group. Something that can't be denied or lied about by the media. The riot on January sixth and the storming of the Capitol will give the news and law enforcement something to focus on. Our actual attack must be more subtle and draw little focus."

"That's a big ask," said Jimmy. "We're talking about putting together a covert op, but before we can do that, we need to know what the objective is. I can get a bunch of guys if you're looking for shock and awe. Subtle is going to mean a select group that will need to stay hidden at all costs."

Warren sipped from his glass and took a bite of the cranberry raisin cookie. He wiped his mouth with the linen napkin and set the rest of the cookie on his plate.

"We all know what the answer is. We've discussed this ad infinitum. We have a small window of opportunity between January sixth when the election results are certified and January twentieth when the new president and vice president are sworn in. The only way to prevent the swearing in is if the president-elect and the vice president–elect are unable to attend the swearing in at noon on that day."

"What happens if the president- and vice president–elect don't show up for the swearing in but turn up later after a new president has been selected?" asked Jimmy.

Wahls pulled a small book from his pocket. He opened the Constitution to Section 3 of the Twentieth Amendment and read.

"If, at the time fixed for the beginning of the term of the president, the president-elect shall have died, the vice president–elect shall become president. If a president shall not have been chosen before the time fixed for the beginning of his term, or if the president-elect shall have failed to qualify, then the vice president–elect shall act as president until a president shall have qualified; and the Congress may by law provide for the case wherein neither a president-elect nor a vice president–elect shall have qualified, declaring who shall then act as president, or the manner in which one who is to act shall be selected, and such person shall act accordingly until a president or vice president shall have qualified.

"Good question," said Wahls. "Based on my reading of the Constitution, I believe that situation would end up before the Supreme Court and they would most likely rule that since they were duly elected by the people, they would be immediately sworn in, but we have no idea how the removal of the placeholder president would work. That situation would create a constitutional crisis the likes of which this country has never seen, and it would probably tear the country apart."

"But that doesn't help Senator Stevenson," said Warren. "That section, coupled with the Presidential Succession Act of 1947, says that in the absence of both, the Speaker of the House becomes president."

"Or," interrupted Wahls, "the House of Representatives can choose a qualified candidate to become president."

"That has never been validated," said Turlock. "It would take the Supreme Court to rule on that issue. Furthermore . . ."

"Enough bickering, you old goats. The answer seems simple enough," said Calvin. "The president- and vice president–elect not only must miss the swearing in, but they have to disappear permanently, and since Republicans will be in charge of both the House and the Senate, they will make the rules, and the justices that we appointed will back them up. Case closed."

Robert E. Lee smiled and looked around the table. "Then you all know what that means and what we are proposing to do. Once we start down that path, there is no turning back, and if we are exposed, we will be destroyed, personally, professionally and in every way conceivable. It is also not inconceivable that we would be tried for treason and executed."

He looked at each man at the table. Each man nodded in agreement.

"Then it's settled," he said. "Jimmy, it's time for you to go to work. We are three weeks from January sixth, and we need to have a plan in place. Our first objective is to overwhelm the Capitol and prevent certification. Our second objective is that the president-elect and the vice president–elect must not live to see the inauguration. In the meantime, I will speak to the senator and the incoming Speaker and get them on board with legislation to be voted on following what would have been the inauguration to make Oliver Stevenson the President of the United States."

They all nodded in agreement. Robert E. Lee stood and walked to the credenza along the wall and filled five glasses with his best bourbon. He passed them out.

"Gentlemen, a toast to Oliver Stevenson, President of the United States."

They finished their drinks, set their empty glasses on the table and gathered up their coats, hats and gloves. They shook hands and left the Richardson house. They were ready for the start of a new era in American politics.

Chapter Eight

The Blackhawk helicopter flew in just above the treetops and settled down on the landing pad, snow billowing up from the rotor wash. The morning had dawned with a Colorado bluebird sky, and the temp had climbed to just above freezing. It was a beautiful morning by any standard.

Mike Branik stepped to the open barn door, reached under his Carhartt ranch jacket and felt his pistol. He unsnapped the thumb break and placed the pitchfork he had been holding against the stall next to him. He stood ready to meet whatever this challenge might be. He relaxed when he saw the tall, thin Black man climb down from the chopper and remove his helmet. The man's hair was grayer than the last time he had seen him, but his former team leader still stood ramrod straight. He placed his helmet on the seat, turned and strode towards the barn.

"Mr. President, this is a surprise," said Mike as he extended his hand shook Roman Diggs's hand, and then embraced. Mike stepped back and pointed to the chopper.

"They let you fly?" asked Mike.

Roman laughed. "What's the fun of being the commander in chief if you can't play with the toys?"

Roman pointed to the thumb break unsnapped on the holster on Mike's hip. "You expecting trouble?"

Mike laughed. "You never know who's dropping in for a visit. Can't be too careful. What the hell are you doing here?"

"Can we talk inside and maybe get a strong cup of coffee and some of Mary's strawberry rhubarb pie?"

"No problem, Roman. Go grab your copilot and I'll see what Mary has lying around in the kitchen."

Roman turned and walked back to the chopper, and Mike snapped the thumb break on his holster and walked to the back door of the house. He took off his gloves and Stetson and placed them on the counter. Mary turned from the counter.

"Was that Roman I heard?" asked Mary. "I didn't hear his entourage arrive."

"He's alone," said Mike. "Not sure what's going on."

The door opened and Roman stepped in, followed by an older blond man of medium height with a thin build. Roman pointed over his shoulder.

"Tom Dempsey. Tom's the lead agent on my Secret Service detail. Also, a damn fine chopper pilot."

Roman walked over to the counter and hugged Mary Thurston, who then walked over and shook Tom's hand, as did Mike.

"Pleasure to meet you folks," said Tom.

Mary held up a large blue mug that said BEST GRAMMA EVER in large black letters. "Tom, coffee?"

"Yes, ma'am."

Mary filled the mug and handed it to him. She filled

two more mugs and handed one to Mike and one to Roman.

"Wouldn't have any of that world-famous strawberry rhubarb pie lying around?" asked Roman.

Mary looked at him and sneered. "You see any strawberries growing under that snow? I made a cherry pie. Will that do?"

The president sat on one of the kitchen chairs looking properly chastised. "Yes, ma'am. That would be great." Everyone laughed as Mary cut three slices of pie and put them on the plates on the table.

Mary Thurston was somewhere north of eighty, but she'd never admit it. Short, with long gray hair and a strong physique, she never complained about the occasional aches and pains that came with age and running a working horse ranch. The ranch in northern Colorado had been in her family for a hundred and fifty years and at one time produced some of the best quarter horses in the country. Now, in her waning years and with her children and grandchildren spread all over the country, it was more of a hobby ranch.

Mary had married United States Supreme Court Justice Elliot Thurston while they were still in college at the University of Colorado in Boulder. The older law school student had swept her off her feet after a friend introduced them. They married the following spring and, sixty years later, had seven children, fourteen grandchildren and nine great-grandchildren.

She also had one adopted child—well, not legally adopted, but part of the family nonetheless. Mike Branik was eleven when he showed up at the back door one winter day, wearing sneakers, ripped jeans and a filthy T-shirt. He was half frozen and starving, and Mary took him in, fed him and gave him a place to sleep. The next morning, fed and warm, Mike told her that his mother had been involved in an accident and had driven off the snow-covered road about five miles from the ranch. Mike had spent two days walking in the snow until he smelled the smoke from the ranch house's fire. Elliot found out through various sources that Mike's mother was running after she got word that there was a warrant for her arrest for drug distribution. She had grabbed Mike and her meager possessions and headed for the mountains.

The following day, the sheriff found her car in a ravine. She had been dead for a couple of days. When he offered to turn Mike over to social services, Mary looked into those big brown eyes and told him he was welcome to stay with them for as long as he liked. That was a long time ago, and now it was just Mike and Mary and a couple of horses.

Mary refilled their coffee mugs and tapped Tom on the shoulder. "Let me show you around the ranch house." She and Tom disappeared through the door, and Mike picked up his cup and headed towards the back of the house, followed by Roman. Mike stopped at a heavy wood door and placed his hand on a palm reader that blended in perfectly with the wood paneling. There was a quiet click, and Mike pushed open the door.

They stepped into the room, and Mike pointed towards one of the big leather armchairs that sat in front of his desk. He pushed a button on the side of the desk and a gas fire ignited in the fireplace. Mike sat and looked at the president.

"You didn't fly out here for a piece of pie and a mug of coffee. What's going on?"

Roman laughed. "I was in the neighborhood."

Mike laughed too, and Roman continued. "I actually was. I was at a meeting in Denver. The meeting was a cover so I could sneak out, grab the chopper and fly here. I have a concern, and I need your help."

Mike leaned forward.

"There's a lot of talk going around Washington that several militia groups are going to hold a massive rally in front of the Capitol on January sixth and may try to seize the building and its occupants to prevent the certification of the election. Certification is mandated as part of the peaceful transfer of power and has never been prevented from happening. I am damn sure not going to let it happen on my watch. I have already issued orders activating the National Guard units in Virginia and Maryland to protect the Capitol. I have additional units on standby. Once we see how large a crowd gathers, I can move people and materials as needed.

"The Capitol and the metro police will barricade the building and will back up the guard units. The problem is that Stevenson has a lot of friends in the guards, and the last thing we need will be units dropping their weapons and stepping aside or turning around and joining the rioters to attack the building. I am working on contingency plans in case something like that happens."

"Sounds like you have everything in hand," said Mike. "What do you need my help with?"

"I've heard rumors, and at this point it's just rumors, that there might be a threat against the president-elect. An action that could put Stevenson in the White House."

"I'm sure they get death threats all the time. Why is this different, and why can't the Secret Service and the FBI handle it?"

Roman tented his fingers in front of his face, then looked at Mike. "Death threats come with the job. My problem is I'm not sure who I can trust. I've got less than two months left in this job, and I don't want to see this country thrust into a civil war. There is some concern that there are a lot of folks in the Secret Service and the FBI who believe the election was stolen. Many of those folks may hold high-ranking positions. Information they may receive might never get to the president-elect. It could also prove out to be just rumors and nothing else."

"Why would Stevenson become president if something happened to Baker? Wouldn't Hanford become president since she would be next in line?" asked Mike.

"According to the Succession Act, that's true depending on when it happens. The worst-case scenario is that something permanent happens to both. We've never had a situation like that in this country before. This country is a powder keg right now, and every right-wing group is threatening with some kind of action. I was told there was a podcast on one of the right-wing media sites and that some noted legal scholar suggested that the country would be best served if both Baker and Hanford disappeared, then Stevenson could be elected president by Congress. The guy supposedly said that live on the air. A few years back, that would have been unthinkable. Now it's a reality."

"You're not just talking about both becoming unqualified, you're talking about them disappearing or dying. That's a huge undertaking to get rid of both people, and besides, Stevenson lost by a huge margin. How could Congress just up and make him president?"

"That's part of the problem, Mike. With the Republicans taking the House and Senate and controlling the Supreme Court, no one knows what will happen, but trust me when I tell you. Whatever happens will not be good for this country, and neither will an Oliver Stevenson presidency."

"Could Stevenson be behind this?" asked Mike.

"Good question, Mike. He's been busy suing everyone under the sun and losing every case so far, but who's to say? Desperate people do desperate things. Personally, I don't think he's smart enough to pull off something like what we are talking about."

"Have you told the president-elect about the threat?"

"That's the other problem, Mike. They are prepared for any contingency, but so far, there is no actual threat, just rumors and my gut feeling. We've beefed up their protection detail, but, again, we don't know if members of the detail have similar feelings as the militia groups. There's only so much we can do."

Mike leaned back in his chair and looked at Roman. "I would trust your gut over anything else. That feeling in the pit of your stomach kept us alive, more times than any of us can count. It's always been good enough for me. What do you want me to do?"

"My best guess, and based on a couple of people a lot smarter than me in constitutional law, is that whatever is going to happen will happen between the certification of the election on January sixth and the inauguration on January twentieth."

"Why then? Why not before?"

"Baker will not be the president-elect, officially, until the vote certification. If something happens before that, the job will fall to the current Speaker of the House. If it happens after the certification, the VP-elect would become president. If they are both unable to take the job, then all bets are off, and most likely the House would vote on a new president and the Supreme Court would back them up. Stevenson is their likely pick."

"Sounds like a nightmare any way you look at it," said Mike.

"It's basically a silent coup, and whatever happens will be a legal nightmare." The president sat back and sipped his coffee.

"Okay, Rome. Let me do some digging before I pull in the team. I would hate to pull them away from

Christmas with their families. If I find something actionable, what are the rules of engagement?"

The president set down his coffee mug. "There are none, Mike. The goal is to protect the president- and vice president–elect, no matter what. Failure could mean the end of our republic as we know it."

Mike pushed a button on his desk, and the office door unlatched. They stood and pushed through it. Tom and Mary were back in the kitchen, sitting at the table and talking like old friends. Mike called it the Mary effect. No one ever walked away from Mary as a stranger. Tom and Roman shook hands with Mike and Mary and thanked Mary for her hospitality. Mike grabbed his coat and hat and followed them out the door. Tom ran ahead to get the chopper fired up.

Roman stopped short of the landing pad and turned to Mike. "We've been through some hairy shit together, and I've placed you in danger more times than I can count. Watch your six, Mike." They hugged, and Roman climbed into the chopper and took the pilot's seat.

Mike stepped back and watched as the chopper lifted off in a whirl of snow and headed south. He walked back to the house, entered and took off his coat and hat.

Mary looked at him. "It's bad this time, isn't it?"

Mike, who had never lied to Mary about anything, nodded. "Yeah, it could be." He picked up his coffee mug, filled it and headed for his office. He had a lot of work to do, and the clock was ticking.

Chapter Nine

Robert E. Lee Richardson parked his Mercedes in the parking garage and stepped over to the elevator. He swiped his key card across the card reader mounted to the wall and stepped into the elevator, pressing the top floor button. At the top, he stepped through the door and entered an amazing suite of rooms, with an incredible view of Washington, DC, on three sides. The butler, waiting near the elevator, stepped up and took his coat and hat.

"Your guests are in the sitting room, sir." He turned and disappeared down a hall towards the back of the penthouse.

Richardson walked past the kitchen, stopping at the bar to pick up his nightly glass of bourbon that was waiting for him, and stepped into the massive living room. He stopped to look at the view of the Capitol in the distance. This was his home away from home and the place where he did most of his business dealings. From this penthouse he ran his media empire, a multibillion-dollar business that saw Richardson become one of the nation's wealthiest men before he hit forty. That was a long time ago.

It was also where he wined and dined politicians and dignitaries from around the world. Anyone he could wield influence over. The entire penthouse was wired for sound and video, and he had numerous young and talented men and women on speed dial to deal with any of his guests' special needs or proclivities. He once told a friend that if he chose to, he could destroy the federal government with one wave of his hand and the release of several hundred if not thousands of videos and audio clips. This was most likely why no one investigated his businesses or the militia group he ran. One of the largest in the country. If civil war ever became a reality, Robert E. Lee Richardson could raise an army one hundred thousand strong with a few phone calls.

He sipped his drink and walked over to his guests.

“Gentlemen, so glad you could make it.” He shook hands with Oliver Stevenson and Paul Grayson, congressman from the great state of Virginia and the current Speaker of the House.

Paul had won re-election in November and would be elected to the speakership once again, during the next session of the House of Representatives, starting on January 3. He was young by Washington standards, forty-two, but was the face of the new Republican party, and if Richardson had his way, Paul would be the Republican candidate in the next presidential election, four years down the road.

Paul stood and stepped over to Richardson with his hand extended. “Mr. Richardson, how nice to see you again.” They shook hands.

“Paul, how many times do I have to tell you that you can call me Lee in private? Thanks for coming.” He looked at Oliver. “Oliver, how are you this evening? Please give my regards to your wife.” They shook hands.

Paul Grayson, six foot two with brown hair and hazel eyes, picked up his drink from the table and stepped over to the full-height windows. "Amazing view from up here," he said, sipping his drink.

Richardson ignored him and sat in a plush leather recliner. "Gentlemen, we have a lot to discuss and little time to implement. Let us begin."

Stevenson was already seated, leaned in. Paul took a seat opposite Richardson.

"A revolution is underway, gentlemen, and in a few short weeks we will control the entire government. The election has given us control of the House and the Senate. We already own the Supreme Court, and following Inauguration Day, we will own the presidency."

Paul looked surprised. "But Mr. Richardson, Oliver lost the race."

"Yes, Paul, he did, which is why I have invited you here tonight. I have it on good authority that the president-elect and the vice president–elect will be unable to serve their terms and will not be inaugurated on January twentieth. Towards that end, we need to make sure that we have legislation in place in both your chambers to make our friend Oliver here the next president. You will both need to call for a vote on that legislation as soon as it is announced that the president- and vice president–elect could not meet the qualifications for their offices. The nation will be surprised, and you will need to move quickly to grab control of the government and do what is needed to make sure this happens. There will surely be a fight, as we will be stepping into uncharted waters, but I am sure that your staffs, working together, will come to a joint resolution that will stand under the highest scrutiny."

"Mr. Richardson, it sounds like you are talking about a coup," said Paul. "I cannot be a party to something illegal."

Richardson held up his hand. "Paul, no one said anything about anything illegal. We are preparing for a situation that could prevent this country from seeing the peaceful transfer of power and we want to make sure you are ready to step in and prevent that from happening. That's all."

"Sir, I don't know. If both Baker and Hanford are not qualified to assume their elected positions, why wouldn't we have known about this before the election?"

Oliver stood up, stepped over to the bar and poured himself another drink. "Paul, for fuck's sake, get a grip. No one is asking you to do anything illegal. All we need from you is to make sure that you have legislation already written, making me the president when it comes to light that Baker and Hanford will not be able to serve. That's all."

Paul leaned back in his chair and looked at Oliver and then at Richardson. "What are you two planning?" asked Paul.

"Nothing you need to worry about, Paul," said Richardson. "It's a contingency plan, that's all. You want to protect this country, don't you, and you want to make sure that Republicans take control of the entire government, right?"

"Well, sure," said Paul, "but the people voted, and they chose a divided government. We can't just make that go away with a flick of our wrists."

"The people are stupid, Paul," said Richardson. "Selecting who runs this country should never be left to the common people. They have no idea how things should work, and they obviously made a mistake in not electing Oliver to the presidency. We want to fix that mistake before that cattle rancher has time to destroy what we are trying to build. Am I right?"

Paul stood and walked to the window. "No one will get hurt by this, right? And all I have to do is craft legislation with Oliver and put it to a vote?"

Richardson laughed. "Of course, no one will get hurt, Paul. We are not barbarians or communists, but we have an obligation as the leaders of this great nation to make sure she lives up to her God-given potential. We are not talking a few years here, Paul. We are talking the next hundred years of Republican control of the government."

"What about the certification on January sixth?" asked Paul.

"The certification will go off without a hitch," said Richardson. "Oliver will see to that, and as long as you are both ready on January twentieth, then we will have no problems."

Paul walked back to the sitting area, and they clinked their glasses. "To the beginning of the thousand-year American Reich," said Richardson.

"God bless America," said Oliver.

The butler was standing next to the bar.

"Gentlemen," said Richardson. "If you will follow Halston, he will take you to your rooms, where your night's entertainment awaits. Please enjoy this early Christmas gift."

Oliver and Paul finished their drinks and followed the butler. Richardson finished his drink and stepped over to the window. The lights outside twinkled in the frosty night air. He turned, walked to the bar, poured himself another drink and walked to his office on the other side of the suite. Once inside, he sat behind his desk, clicked a few buttons on his laptop and watched as the multiple monitors along the walls lit up. He activated the cameras, sat back and watched his guests enjoy themselves.

Christmas had come early this year.

Chapter Ten

Mike parked his rental SUV in the parking garage of the River One apartment building and made his way on foot to the upper level of the garage where the VIP parking was. Getting past the digital card scanner that protected the VIPs from the rest of the riffraff was easy, and he now found himself safely ensconced in the heated garage, behind a couple of luxury SUVs. He spotted all the security cameras and avoided them. He sat on the concrete floor and waited.

He needed a place to start his investigation, and he thought that the best place to start was with Senator Oliver Stevenson, since everything revolved around him. He had parked down the street from the senator's Washington brownstone and had prepared to settle in for a long night when the senator walked out of his townhome and slid into the back of a black car service.

Mike followed at a safe distance and slowed as the car turned into the parking garage for River One. When it opened just over a year ago, River One had become the place to live in Washington. The client list read like a who's who of the political and business elites, and it offered the well-heeled business and political leaders all the amenities one would need to lead a luxurious life. But most important, it offered privacy.

Mike followed the car into the garage but lost it when it entered the VIP area. He took the stairs and got through the security system in time to see the car pulling away from the private elevator.

Mike had Googled the building while he sat and waited and found several articles speculating about how many secret business dealings were conducted behind the closed doors of the enclave. With all the rich and famous living in the same building, the press was cut off from asking impertinent questions.

He had put his phone back into his pocket when another car pulled up next to the elevator and another member of the Washington elite slid out, pushed the button on the wall panel and entered the private elevator.

"Hmm," said Mike. "I wonder why the Speaker of the House is here?"

Mike sat back and waited. Fifteen minutes after the Speaker arrived, another black SUV stopped at the elevator. Mike pulled out his camera and took several pictures of the older gentleman as he exited the car and, using a pass card, accessed the elevator and disappeared. Mike looked at the pictures. He had two good pictures that he could use for facial rec. Since the older guy had a pass card, Mike assumed he was the owner of the penthouse. That would be easy enough to check. He wondered to himself if any of these rich people who were so concerned with their privacy ever realized how easy it was for a trained professional to access their lives. Might make them change their minds about how much they spent on security and anonymity.

Mike had sat back when another car pulled into the parking area. He pulled out his camera and snapped some pictures of two young people, one male and one female, who were in the car. They looked like teenagers, but they certainly didn't dress like they were. The young woman wore a short leather coat over a red dress that barely covered the crack in her ass, and her black shoes had six-inch stiletto heels. She had blond hair and bright red lips. The young man wore skintight black pants and a white shirt open to his navel and had several chains around his neck. His hair was blond and choppy, and it looked like he had black eyeliner on. Mike snapped a few more pictures and wondered what these two were bringing to the party inside. They were buzzed into the elevator, and the car left.

Mike sat back. He had learned a long time ago to eat and sleep whenever he could. He pulled a protein bar out of his pocket, washed it down with water and closed his eyes.

He was awakened by a noise at four A.M. and looked between the cars. Both Stevenson and the Speaker walked off the elevator and slid into separate cars that were waiting for them. The cars left the garage, and Mike waited. A few minutes later, the young man and woman exited the elevator, looking a little less put together than they had when they arrived. They slid into another car that left the garage.

The owner walked out of the elevator and slid into the back of another car and left the garage. Mike stood and stretched. He pulled out his phone, dialed up the security system and, with the push of a button, shut down the cameras. He stepped to the elevator, held up his phone to the palm reader and pushed several buttons. The light on the panel turned green, and the elevator doors opened. He covered his head with a ski mask he had pulled out of his pocket and waited as the elevator rose. He pulled his pistol from his holster, attached the silencer he had removed from his coat pocket and waited to the side of the doors.

The elevator slowed to a stop, and the doors opened. Mike looked out and stepped through with his pistol leading the way. The doors closed behind him. He stopped in the foyer and listened. Not hearing anything, he moved farther into the penthouse, checking each room as he went until he located the office. He slipped into the room and holstered his pistol. The room was a man's office, with dark paneling and polished wood floors. The desk was burled wood and shined like glass. He looked around, pulled out his phone and took pictures of everything he could find. It was odd. For an executive's office, there were no family photos, certificates on the walls or papers on the desk. He checked the file drawers, and they were all empty.

This was a front. A fake office. No one lived or worked here. He was about to leave when he spotted a scratch on the floor in front of the middle of one wall. He checked the wall panel, pushed and heard a click. The panel popped open. Inside the small space, there was a laptop and several monitors.

He stepped over to the laptop, opened it and looked at the password box. Since he had no idea who the owner was, he decided not to crack the password now. He pulled a small USB drive out of his pants pocket and plugged it in. There was a small red button on top of the drive, and he pushed it. After five minutes, the button turned green, and he removed it. The Trojan horse would activate the minute anyone turned on the computer, and as soon as they logged in, he would have full access to everything. He pocketed the drive and headed back to the elevator.

Once back in his rental, he pulled left out of the garage and headed for his hotel. He needed to download the pictures he had taken and start a search for names to match the faces.

Chapter Eleven

Mike woke to the sound of banging on his door. He reached over, looked at the clock on the nightstand and saw that he had crawled into bed three hours before. He wiped the sleep from his eyes as the banging started again. He grabbed his pistol off the nightstand, threw off the covers and stepped up next to the door. He knew better than to look through the peephole. That was a great way to get shot in the head. He flipped off the security latch, grabbed the knob and whipped open the door. He lowered his pistol when Ronnie pushed into the room.

"What the fuck are you doing here, and do you know what time it is?" he asked.

She looked at her watch. "Yeah. It's eight fifteen in the morning. What are you still doing in bed, and would you mind putting on some pants?"

Mike walked into the separate bedroom and slipped on his jeans and a flannel shirt. He holstered his pistol and walked into the adjoining room.

"How the hell did you find me, and why are you here?"

Ronnie threw her coat on the couch, poured some cold coffee from the carafe and stuck the cup in the microwave. She waited for the ding and pulled out the cup. She took a sip.

"Fuck. How old is this stuff?" she asked. "I was bored at home. Christmas is going to be a real buzzkill this year, and I needed to leave before one more person asked me why I looked depressed. So, I called Mary. She said you were in Washington following up on a couple of leads, so I decided to join you. You got a problem with that?" She plopped down on the couch and sipped more of the two-day-old coffee.

"So, what are we working on?" she asked.

Mike picked up the room phone and dialed room service. He ordered two full breakfasts and a carafe of fresh coffee. He sat in the chair opposite Ronnie.

"Roman came to visit me."

"In Colorado?" she asked. "I didn't think he ever left the White House." She leaned forward and waved her hand for him to continue.

"He's worried there's a plot to kidnap the president-elect and the vice president–elect. Something about if they don't show up for the inauguration, then Congress will make Stevenson the president.

"Can they do that?"

"I guess, although he indicated that it's never been done with two missing people, but they will try."

"How good is his information?" she asked. "I'm guessing people in those positions get death threats all the time."

"He wouldn't give me his source, said he was concerned that the threat was real and he didn't know who in the Secret Service or the FBI he can trust. That's why he came to me."

"Were you gonna call us in?"

"After the holiday. Whatever happens needs to happen between January sixth and the twentieth. I didn't want to ruin anyone's Christmas, so I figured I'd head out here and do a little snooping around."

"Well, don't keep me in suspense. What have you found out so far?"

Mike filled her in on his late-night surveillance and his search of the penthouse. By the time he finished, there was a knock on the door, and the room service waiter wheeled in their breakfast and coffee. Once the waiter left, they grabbed their plates and fresh coffee and sat at the small table by the window overlooking the Potomac River.

Ronnie finished first and put her plate on the cart. She poured another cup of coffee and returned to her seat.

"So, you have no idea who the fat cat or the two kids are, but you think the kids might be professionals?"

She grabbed her backpack off the floor, opened it and pulled out her laptop. She lifted the lid and entered her password.

"Send me the pictures you took and let me see if I can identify them. Go grab a shower and a nap. You look exhausted and you smell."

Mike raised his middle finger and waved it at her. He picked up his phone, pulled up his secure email and sent her the pictures he had taken. He finished his coffee, stood and stepped into the bedroom, closing the door behind him.

Ronnie opened her email and downloaded the

pictures Mike had sent her. She logged into another server and uploaded the pictures. She sat back while the server ran through millions of social media posts. She had to run one picture at a time, so she started with the young girl, figuring that she might post more than the young man.

Five hours later, Mike opened the bedroom door and smelled a fresh pot of coffee. "I ordered more," said Ronnie. "Well, you don't look any better, but you sure smell better." She laughed.

Mike poured a cup of coffee and stood behind her. "Any luck?"

She didn't look up from the keyboard. "Tons. You awake enough to listen?"

Mike poked her on the arm and waved his hand. She turned and faced him.

"The kids—and that's what they both are—were easy. Ashley Parker and Austin Randolf III. She's sixteen and he's seventeen. Both go to Devonshire Academy in Alexandria. Devonshire is a school for the top one percent of the top one percent. Very exclusive. I also found their nest on the dark web. They are solicited through a site called Nimble Nymphs. When I finished scrolling through the site, I wanted to jump in the shower. It's pervertsville in moneyland. The website is full of teens from wealthy families selling themselves, and not for cheap either. Big bucks. I also think it might be a honeypot with a little blackmail on the side. The site is run by a douchebag named Aristotle Windom. I tracked him to an address in Brooklyn, New York. He must be raking in half a mil a month.

"I've grabbed all their social media accounts plus the accounts belonging to their family members. I got the addresses for the two from the party the other night. Should we pay them a visit?"

"No, whoever hired them is too sophisticated to let them in on anything that's going on. They're just candy." Mike thought for a minute. "Out them all to their family and friends. Every kid on the site. Put them on their school websites, churches, anyplace you can find. Cover every social media site. Send the website to the FBI and NYPD pervert squads and crash his site. Get your friend at the NSA to hit the client list and out them as well. For the moment, I want you to hide any info on the senator or the Speaker of the House. We're gonna need that later."

"Are you sure you want to out the client list? Lot of big names on there."

"Yeah. It was their choice to fuck kids. Burn them down. And make sure you get it on all the media websites. What about the guy who owns the penthouse?"

She laughed. "Fuck, Mike. You were only asleep for five hours."

"What did you find?"

"Okay, the penthouse is owned by a dozen different LLCs. I'm working backwards through the list. Give me a few more hours and I'll find him."

Mike looked at his watch. "Five hours. And then we're gonna hit the penthouse and tear it apart.

Somebody pays the staff and the limo drivers. There must be a trail."

Mike picked up the room phone and ordered two dinners and more coffee. They had a lot of work to do. He sat back in his chair and laughed.

Ronnie looked at him. "What?"

"Aristotle. Who names their kid Aristotle?"

Chapter Twelve

Jimmy Bronson had left Richardson's house that night with a plan, and he knew he needed to move because time was not on his side. He spent the next day calling twelve men he knew he could trust. Men who had put themselves on the line and had proven their worth in combat. But more important, these twelve men were also part of the brotherhood, and he knew they hated the current administration and the newly elected president and vice president. He knew if he could get these guys on board, he wouldn't have to vet them to make sure their beliefs fell in line with the others'. These were men who would kill to protect the country they loved.

The meeting place was another part of the plan that had been carefully thought out. The bar owner was an old friend of his family, and when he told him he needed a spot where the government couldn't listen to their conversations, the bar owner was more than happy to offer his place. The bar was secluded, had a specific clientele and didn't cater to strangers. As a matter of fact, their presence was discouraged.

More important, because the bar owner believed in every conspiracy theory that came down the road, he had the bar swept for electronic listening devices every morning before he opened. He was a man who could be trusted, despite the fact that everyone who knew him thought he was crazy. But that worked for Jimmy.

The CLOSED sign on the door stopped anyone who was looking for a drink at six A.M., and so far, Jimmy had had to get rid of three early-morning drinkers, who were pissed, but by the time they came back in the afternoon, they would have forgotten all about it.

Jimmy met each man at the door and hugged them like long-lost brothers. Some were local and had seen Jimmy within the last couple of weeks, but others came from as far away as Texas and Idaho. It was a mixed bag of heights, weights, hairstyles and lives, but each man had one thing in common with the others. They had lived together and watched their friends die, fighting for what they believed in. If a civil war started, these were the men you wanted on your side.

Jimmy had sent the bar owner to his apartment above the bar as soon as he had finished scanning for bugs and told him not to listen in to what was being discussed.

With the bartender gone and the handshaking and backslapping complete, it was time to get down to business. Jimmy looked around the room.

"Fellas, we've been called upon by our savior Jesus Christ to strike a blow for liberty and freedom and thank you for answering his call. We are going to be the tip of the spear to break the backs and the spirit of the radical left and return this country to the values and morals of our Christian forefathers."

"Amen, brother." A shout came from the back of the room. Heads nodded, and small conversations started. Jimmy held up his hand for silence.

"Before I tell you our assignment, I need to swear you all to secrecy. What I am about to tell you cannot be shared with your parents, friends or siblings. Too much depends on our success to let a loose lip sink this ship. Please stand and face the flag of our great nation and swear that what you hear this morning will not be revealed to anyone and that you will give up your life to protect our freedom."

Each man faced the flag as Jimmy watched and, to a man, they each swore allegiance to secrecy and the flag. They all sat.

Jimmy walked around the room between the tables and looked at each man. "Guys. Our orders are to capture and kill the president-elect and the vice president–elect."

A low murmur moved through the room as men looked at one another, some smiling, some concerned, but everyone interested to hear more.

"I know you all want to be home with your families on Christmas, and our plans should not interfere with that. We have a very specific time frame to abide by. No action can be taken prior to the certification of the election on January sixth, and we must complete our goal before noon on January twentieth. This is very important, so keep those two dates in your head." Jimmy let the dates sink in for a bit before he continued.

"I am awaiting confirmation on information I received last night that the targets will be huddled together at Baker's Montana ranch until the night before the inauguration. Becausc of security concerns, their teams feel it will be easier to keep them safe the longer they are away from Washington. We are going to prove them wrong. Our plan, once we receive confirmation, is to hit them at the ranch."

Jimmy got a serious look on his face. "Men, we are going to get bloody on this one, and some of us may not make it out alive. We will go up against trained protection agents whose job it is to protect these people at all costs, even if it means giving up their own lives. Your sacrifices will be immortalized in song and verse before a grateful nation once our candidate becomes the president. Your sacrifice will not be forgotten. One thing you should know is that we have people on the inside who will help us with this mission."

"Hoorah," came shouts from the men. Jimmy smiled. He felt like General Patton standing in front of his men. His daddy would be proud if he knew what he was about to do.

Jimmy held up his hand. "We are a little over three weeks out from our January sixth date, and we have a lot to do, but for most of you, that time will be spent with your families, awaiting orders. I have chosen two of the men who don't have families to head to Montana with me. We will surveil the ranch and put together our plan of attack. Those two men are Earl Slocum and Barry Crane. While we do that, Will Hutchins and Frank DeLuca will gather the weapons and materials we will need from our brother militia groups. The rest of you are free to leave following this meeting, but plan to return two days after Christmas to train for the upcoming battle. Once we start to train, there will be no contact with our families until we have completed the mission. Make sure your families understand that, but share nothing else about our mission." Jimmy looked out over the room.

"Gentlemen, the bar is open."

Jimmy stepped behind the bar and started pouring beers and shots for his team. This would be their last celebration together until after the mission was completed.

Scott Wiley stood at the end of the bar and sipped the draft beer that had been set in front of him. His mind was racing with the thought that they were planning to stage a coup and murder the people who had been legally chosen to lead this country. He wondered who had put this crazy idea into Jimmy's head.

Chapter Thirteen

Mike turned on the local eleven P.M. news and smiled at the lead story. The reporter on the scene was trying to get a comment from the headmaster of the prestigious Devonshire Academy regarding internet activity showing several of his students involved in a sex-for-hire scandal. Parents of many students were seen slamming their doors in the faces of other reporters. They reported that the same thing was happening in several other cities at other private academies.

He looked at Ronnie. “Nice job. Anything on the owner of the penthouse?”

“Nothing definitive. I’ve gone back through a dozen different corporations and I still haven’t reached the bottom. Whoever this guy is, he’s careful.”

“Let’s go see if he’s home and introduce ourselves.”

Ronnie stepped into the second bedroom and came out a few minutes later, dressed all in black. Mike had done the same thing earlier in the evening. They checked their pistols, grabbed their backpacks and left the room.

Once outside, they zipped up their black jackets and slid into Mike’s rental. Mike pulled out of the parking lot and headed for the apartment building. The city of Washington sparkled in the crisp, frosty night air, and the decorations along the streets made everything look festive. Mike and Ronnie were not in a festive mood.

Mike pulled into the garage entrance and headed for the top level, where he parked his car. They slid out, and Mike opened the trunk. He opened the duffel bag and made sure the extra weapons were ready to go, then lifted the bag. Anyone watching would have noticed two travelers carrying their heavy loads into the hotel that occupied the first ten floors of the high-rise. He closed the lid, and they entered the elevator lobby.

Making sure no one was around, he placed his phone over the palm reader on the emergency door and watched as the red light turned green. He pulled open the door and held it for Ronnie to pass through. He let it close behind him, and they raced up the stairs and entered the heated private parking area for the penthouse.

They pulled down their ski masks and stepped into the garage. Mike waited until the camera was facing away from them before racing to the door next to the elevators. Using his phone, he undid the lock, and they slipped into the stairwell. They ran up the private staircases and twenty floors later reached the door to the penthouse.

Mike opened the duffel, and they grabbed a ballistic vest and an AR-style rifle. He bypassed the door lock, and they slipped into the penthouse lobby. They stopped to listen for a minute. It was as quiet as it had been the night before.

They did a quick search and found that the place was empty. Two of the bedrooms were made up; the rest of the rooms except for the office and the living room were devoid of any furnishings. There was no food in the refrigerator, but the bar was stocked.

"I don't think anyone lives here," said Ronnie. "I think it's a front. The owner must use it just for business. It's all for show."

"I think you're right," said Mike. "I'm gonna set up some cameras. Why don't you head into the office and see what you can find behind the hidden door?"

Ronnie headed for the office, and Mike opened his backpack and removed a box full of miniature cameras and audio bugs. He walked around the penthouse and placed them in inconspicuous places. He covered the bar area, sitting area, dining room and two bedrooms.

He stepped into the office and found Ronnie tied into the laptop that was sitting open on the desk. She was feverishly clicking keys as line after line of code raced across the screen. He took out two cameras and two microphones and placed them in the office. He pulled out his phone and checked all the feeds. Everything was active.

"Any luck?" he asked, sticking his head into the closet-sized room.

"I'm into the system. Guess these guys weren't concerned about anyone breaching their system. The encryption sucks." She clicked a few more keys. "Want to see what the possible next President of the United States was doing last night before you arrived at the party?"

She turned the laptop so he could see the screen. After five minutes, he had seen enough.

"There're six hundred eighty-seven individual folders. Each folder belongs to a different person, and each one contains multiple audio and video files. This is a honey trap all right, but on a huge scale."

"Anything about who might own this setup?" asked Mike.

"Nope. This is a library. Nothing more."

"Okay," said Mike. "Let's pack up and get out of here."

They grabbed their gear and stepped through the door. Mike heard the sound at the same time Ronnie did, and they pulled their pistols. Someone was in the penthouse, and they were talking into a throat mic.

They pulled out their silencers and screwed them onto their pistols. Mike indicated for Ronnie to move off towards the two bedrooms while he circled around through the sitting area. With no curtains on the floor-to-ceiling windows, the sitting area was lit up like a carnival, and there were few places to hide.

Mike worked his way behind the leather couch and froze when he saw a shadow coming from the kitchen. A tall white guy with a shaved head dressed all in black stepped into the room, swinging his silenced pistol from side to side as he scanned the area. He spotted a shadow behind the couch and fired a three-round burst.

Mike had left his backpack behind the couch and had scooted away on his belly. He lined up his shot under the couch and fired a bullet into the foot of the assailant. The guy yelped and danced around, covering his mouth with his hand. Mike jumped up from behind the couch and shot him in the head, and he fell back and slid down the face of the bar.

Mike heard the telltale sound of another silenced weapon, and then he heard a muffled scream. Ronnie stepped into the room, dragging assailant number two, and dumped him next to his buddy. She wiped her knife on his sleeve and put it back into the sheath on her belt.

She reached down and frisked each man and looked up at Mike.

"Nothing," she said. "Who the fuck are these guys?"

"Good question." Mike pulled out his phone and took a full-face picture of each man. He put the phone away. He pulled the throat mic off the guy he shot.

"This is high-end stuff. I wonder who's paying these guys?"

"I don't know," said Ronnie. "But I think we'd better get out of here before someone else shows up."

They picked up their gear and exited the way they entered. Once they reached the stairs for the private garage, they hesitated. Mike held his phone against the palm reader and heard the lock click. They pulled their pistols and prepared to move.

Mike pushed open the door and caught the driver off guard as Ronnie put a bullet through his left ear. He fell across the seat of the SUV. They checked the vehicle, but all the documentation had been removed. Mike pulled out his phone and took a picture of the license plate, and they headed for the emergency exit, bypassed the palm reader and ran down one flight of stairs to the resident's and visitor's garage. They pulled off their ski masks and held their pistols at their sides as they walked across the garage and slid into the rental car. Mike pulled out and headed back to the hotel. They needed to figure out who those guys were and who sent them.

Chapter Fourteen

Robert E. Lee Richardson stood in the middle of the sitting area and looked at the two bodies sprawled on the floor. He walked over to the bar and poured himself a drink and stood looking out the window at the Capitol. The rainy weather matched his mood.

"Do you think they're onto us, whoever they are?" he asked over his shoulder.

"Can't say for sure, sir. Could have been a simple B and E, but these guys were three of our best."

"What were they doing here?"

"Someone tripped one of the laser beams. These guys came to investigate."

"I don't like it. Not one bit," said Richardson. "After what happened with the website last night and the embarrassment it caused all those families finding out what their rich little angels were involved in, this reeks of someone messing in our lives. We've got too much going on right now to risk this kind of exposure. Clean up this mess, strip everything out of here and sanitize the place."

He picked his coat and hat off the couch, walked to the elevator and pushed the down button. Someone had cost him a lot of money over the last twenty-four hours, and he was determined to find out who they were and make them pay. He stepped into the elevator and exited at his private parking level. His driver was waiting for him, and he walked past the body in the SUV and slid into the back seat of his limo.

On the way to Dulles International Airport, he made some calls and set up a meeting at his house at nine. He had no idea if the break-in and the killing of the security team were related to the plan regarding the inauguration, but it was too coincidental not to be. He also wondered if the B and E team had gotten into his other computer files and what information they might now have in their possession. That information could cause a tremendous amount of embarrassment to his business partners and clients.

He was glad he was flying out of a private terminal and didn't have to put up with the Christmas rush that was well underway. His car dropped him off at the entrance to the terminal. He walked, was cleared at the desk and walked onto the tarmac and onto his plane. He pitied those poor suckers who had to fly commercial during the holidays.

He landed at the John C. Tune Airport just outside of Nashville, and his car was waiting right outside the terminal. No cranky adults or unruly kids to deal with.

He arrived home, greeted his wife with a kiss on the cheek and stepped into his office. Calvin Mace, Warren Turlock and Harold Wahls were seated around the small conference table. Richardson dropped his coat and hat on his desk chair, poured himself a bourbon and sat.

"We may have a problem," he said. The three men at the table were partners in the penthouse and the escort service. They weren't aware of the video recording he had been making, so he would leave that part out.

"Someone broke into the penthouse last night. Three security guards were killed." He sipped from his glass.

"What would they be looking for? There's nothing there to steal," asked Wahls.

"I had a meeting the night before with Stevenson and Grayson. It's possible someone followed them and was looking for information," said Richardson.

"Was the website exposed?" asked Mace.

"Yes. Every one of our escorts was outed. Luckily, we don't keep client records at the penthouse, so whoever breached the property didn't get those, but the business is now shuttered until we can regroup. I'm surprised you didn't see it on the news today. It's a huge story in Washington. This is going to cost us a lot of money."

"Does this have anything to do with our latest project?" asked Wahls.

"I don't know, but I have people looking into it. Whoever broke into the penthouse knew what they were doing. We had the most sophisticated security system money could buy, and they got through it without triggering any alarms. It was just by luck they triggered a laser beam, otherwise we might have never known about the breach."

"What about Stevenson? Does he know?" asked Turlock.

"I had to call him. Both he and Grayson were

entertained earlier in the evening. I had to let him know in case this was related to his move into the White House. We will need to be on high alert until after the twentieth."

"I received an update from Jimmy. He has surveillance on both Baker and Hanford. They split up for the holiday, so he had to activate a second team. He's in Montana with a team, and he now has a team in San Diego, covering the VP-elect. He has picked up some intelligence that shows they will be hunkered down after the holidays on the ranch in Montana until the inauguration."

"Good," said Richardson. "Stevenson told me he lost two more lawsuits this week. That makes over forty failed lawsuits. I tried to tell him to stop wasting his money, but you know how he gets once he sets his mind on something."

They all laughed. Richardson stood and walked over to the bar. He carried the crystal decanter to the table and filled all the glasses.

"Gentlemen, I won't keep you any longer. Enjoy Christmas with your families, and we will talk in a couple of days."

They finished their drinks and made their way into the foyer, where Mrs. Richardson was holding their coats and hats. They wished one another a merry Christmas and headed out into the night.

Chapter Fifteen

Gilbert Grant never worried about where the next story for his investigative news podcast would come from. He had figured out a while back that there was a whole host of lonely single women who worked for powerful people, and all they needed was a little alcohol and a little sex and they would happily reveal their best-kept secrets. The one caveat to that was that he never revealed to them what he did for a living. He would introduce himself as a stockbroker or insurance salesman; his favorite was college professor. It was amazing how many young women had a fantasy about sleeping with their college professor.

His conquest for the evening was a twenty-something who worked in the office of Senator Oliver Stevenson. She had graduated from Georgetown with a degree in journalism and took the first job she was offered, the chance to work for the Senate majority leader on his public relations team. It had been speculated when she took the job that he would run for president, and Ashley Grimes, as part of the campaign, had gotten an incredible education in politics.

Ashley walked through the door of Randi's, a K Street hangout filled with power brokers, politicians, and lobbyists. It was the place to be seen if you were an up-and-comer, and Ashley wanted to be all that. Gil watched her as she approached. She had short blond hair and blue eyes and a substantial chest. The minidress she wore showed enough thigh to keep Gil interested, since she wasn't overly pretty and was rather plain, but that was okay with him. He had found that when he put on the charm, the plain ones were easier to get into bed.

They had met a week ago at a Republican fundraiser for some guy who had just been elected to his first seat in Congress and had hit it off, especially when he found out she worked for Stevenson. He had tried on several occasions to hook up with someone from the senator's staff but hadn't had much luck until he met Ashley.

He waved her over to his table, stood and gave her a hug and a peck on the cheek.

"Have a seat," he said over the noise in the bar. "You look great. I'm glad you could make it."

The server came over, and Ashley ordered a margarita with no salt. She had to be careful about her weight. After the drinks arrived, they made small talk about family, their lives, how they came to be in Washington and plans for the future. The more Ashley drank, the more talkative she became, and by the third margarita she would have given away our nuclear secrets.

"It's so weird," she said.

"What's weird?" asked Gil.

She leaned closer and whispered, "I probably shouldn't say anything." She finished her third margarita.

"Yeah, it's weird," she said, slurring her words. Gil looked at her; his first glass of whiskey was half gone.

She leaned in again, resting her boobs on the table

and giving him an impressive look down her bra. She indicated for him to move closer by waggling her finger.

"The other day." She looked around to make sure no one was listening. "The other day, my boss stepped away from his computer for a minute and I saw what he was working on. It was an inauguration speech for the senator, accepting the presidency. Is that weird or what?"

Gil's brain went into high alert. "That is weird."

"I know, right," she slurred.

She reached across the table and grabbed his shirt and pulled him closer. "Buy me another drink and then take me home and fuck me."

Gil called the server over, ordered another margarita and looked at her. He thought about what she had said, and he wondered why they would write an inauguration speech. He wondered what they were planning, but he knew as soon as he was finished with Ashley, he needed to find out. Something didn't make sense.

Gil watched as she pounded the drink, and then he helped her up, wrapped her in her coat and walked her to the door. First thing in the morning, he had some phone calls to make, but first he was going to have some fun.

He woke to the sun shining through his bedroom curtains. Ashley was sprawled naked on his bed, and he was glad it was a Saturday morning, because she was in no shape to go to work. He figured she was down for the count, so he slid out of bed, put on a pair of sweats and headed for his office. His mind had been racing during the night with thoughts of why the losing presidential candidate would write an inauguration speech. He opened his laptop and pulled up the Constitution. He pulled up a blank Word document on his second monitor and added notes as he read. He stopped when he read Section 3 of the Twentieth Amendment. He sat back.

The links led him to the Presidential Succession Act of 1947, and for the next hour, he bounced all over the internet. He sat back and read his notes, and a crazy thought entered his brain. "Somebody is planning to kill the president-elect and the VP-elect." That was the only reason he could come up with for Stevenson writing an inauguration speech.

He checked on Ashley, who was sound asleep, and left a note on the nightstand telling her that there was coffee in the kitchen and that he had a wonderful time, but he had to go to work. He dressed, threw his laptop in his bag and left the apartment. He had some sources he needed to hit up to see what fell from the trees. He left his apartment and headed for his car. He never saw the two men sitting in the coffee shop across the street who observed him as he left.

They finished their coffee, left a tip on the table and walked across the street. The building wasn't a secure building, so they entered the lobby and pushed the button for the third floor. The elevator door opened, and they walked down thc hall until they were in front of apartment 3F. They looked around. One man pulled a lockpick tool out of his coat pocket and in five seconds they were inside the apartment. They closed the door and walked into the bedroom and looked at Ashley sleeping. They walked down the hall to the office and looked around. There was nothing on the desk to show why the reporter had left the pretty young woman lying naked in his bed and run out the door. They checked the rest of the apartment and walked back into the bedroom.

One man pulled a syringe out of his pocket, removed the cap and stepped to the side of the bed. He stuck the needle in Ashley's arm, and she stirred. He pushed the plunger, removed the syringe and covered her up with the blanket that was lying at the foot of the bed. They had to wait a few minutes for the massive dose of ketamine to end her life. He dropped the syringe and the cap onto the floor, and they stepped into the living room. He pulled out his phone and pushed the button.

"She's done," he said. "The reporter booked out of here in a hurry. What do you want us to do?"

The Southern voice on the other end of the phone said, "Track down the reporter, see what he knows and make sure he can't report it to anyone." The call disconnected.

They made one more sweep of the apartment and stepped into the hallway. They took the elevator to the first floor and pushed through the door into the street. The office of Sundance Media was about ten miles away, so they slid into their SUV and pulled away from the curb.

Chapter Sixteen

Mike sat in the corner booth in Chubby's Jazz Club and picked at his cheeseburger and fries. He watched the crowd, a mix of young and old folks with one thing in common. They all liked Missy Swan's voice. Missy was a tall, thin Black woman in her mid-sixties who had a voice like velvet. She sang songs by the jazz greats from the forties, fifties and sixties. She didn't seem to have a favorite. She covered everyone, male or female. It didn't matter.

She had stepped off the stage to take a break when a shadow crossed in front of Mike and sat on the seat opposite him. Willie Mitchell hadn't changed since the last time they saw each other, which was behind a burned-out building in a small town in Afghanistan. He was trim, medium height and well-muscled, with wavy dark hair and a mustache.

Mike reached across the table, they shook hands and he called over the server. Willie ordered a beer and a cheeseburger and fries and looked at Mike.

"So, what brings you to Washington—you working or relaxing?" asked Willie.

"Working, which is why I called. I need some help identifying a couple of guys."

Mike opened his phone, pulled up the photos and slid the phone over to Willie. Willie picked it up.

"These guys don't look so good," said Willie. "Your handiwork?"

"Yeah. Line of duty," said Mike.

"What'd they do that got them in this condition?"

"Surprise attack. They responded to an alarm that might have gotten missed. Any idea who they might be or who they work for?"

Willie smiled. "It makes me sad that Mike Branik might have missed an alarm. I guess we're all getting older, huh?"

"Yeah. The place was a honey trap. Used a bunch of well-off kids to playhouse with their guests."

"Wait a minute. The escort site that got outed and some dude in New York who got busted. That was you guys?"

Mike nodded. "Yeah, they were working out of a penthouse suite at River One. The place was clean. Lots of names you'd recognize on the client list."

Willie sat back. "Was this your assignment?"

"No, happened by accident, but you know how I feel about people using kids. Couldn't let it go."

Willie and Mike had spent four years as part of a Delta Force team. They had worked in some of the shittiest and most hostile places on the planet. Mike knew that besides his own team, if there was one person in the world he could trust, it was Willie. It also didn't hurt that Willie worked for the Naval Criminal Investigative Service. NCIS was the criminal investigation arm of the United States Navy. Willie had accepted a position at NCIS after he recovered from the wounds he got working on his last field case with Mike. No one came away from that operation unscathed, but they got the job done. Willie spent a couple of months in rehab and then opted for a cushy office job in Washington. That was many years ago.

Willie looked at the pictures a second time. He tapped one of them. “This guy here. Jimmy Tancredo. Good marine back in the day. Pulled the pin a few years back. Last I heard, he was working private security for a firm out of Atlanta. Guy was tough when I knew him. Not easily surprised. Guess everyone’s getting a little older. Advanced Services or something like that. Big outfit. Picks up ex-military with clean records. If you ran into him, then someone with deep pockets is covering the bill.”

“What about the other guy?” asked Mike.

“No idea on contestant number two.” He picked up the phone, opened the email app and emailed the picture to himself. “I’ll run facial rec through the military databases and see if he pops.”

Willie ate his burger and sipped from his beer glass. “You want to tell me what’s going on?”

“Can’t just yet, but once I figure it out, we’ll grab a beer, and I’ll tell you all about it.”

“How are the kids?” asked Mike. He was the godfather to Willie’s oldest, William Jr., but he hadn’t seen them in years. Willie’s wife had died in an auto accident a few years back. Hit by a drunk driver, so Willie was raising the two boys with the help of his mother, who lived with them. Mike had been on an assignment and hadn’t gone to the funeral. He always felt bad about that, but Willie told him not to.

Willie put down his burger and smiled. "They're doing great. Billy started high school this year and is quarterback of the junior varsity football team. Danny is learning to play the saxophone for the middle school band and is getting straight As. I guess he got all that smarts from his mom. Sure didn't get it from me."

"You used to be plenty smart enough," said Mike. "Maybe not book smart, but you had it where it counted. How's the admiral doing?"

Willie's father had been a rear admiral until Alzheimer's interrupted his career. He was one of the most decorated flag officers in the navy and had never been afraid to look death straight in the eye. He always came out on top.

Willie looked up from his plate. "Dad is Dad. You remember how he was. Old guts and glory. He's been in a memory care home for the past three years. He once commanded a fleet, and officers and sailors jumped when his booming voice would shake the walls. Now he can't tie his own shoes or brush his teeth."

Willie wiped a tear from his eyes. "Sorry, man," said Mike. "Maybe when this is all done, I'll run by and see him. He might not remember me, but who knows?"

"He'd like that. Maybe I can get tickets to a football game, and we'll take the boys. Make a day of it. I know Mom would enjoy seeing you. She always asks me where you are and, of course, I usually can't tell her."

Mike's phone chimed with an incoming text. He

read it and frowned.

"Everything okay?" asked Willie.

"Not sure," said Mike. "I need to run. Take your time, the bill's taken care of, and let me know if you track down the other guy for me. It was good seeing you, man."

Willie stood and hugged Mike. "Whatever you're working on, watch your six."

Mike put on his coat and headed for the door while Willie sat back down to finish his dinner. As always, he was worried about Mike, but he knew he had a good team backing him up. He hoped whatever he was into, they were enough.

Chapter Seventeen

The offices of Sundance Media were in one of the seedier sections of Washington, DC, in an old tool and die company that had gone out of business in the seventies. They had gotten the old building dirt cheap, but at the time they were a startup, and no one had any idea that they would last fifteen minutes, let alone fifteen years. Most of their success was because of Gilbert Grant and his popular podcasts covering everything from crime to politics and everything in between.

The two guys who had been watching Ashley Grimes had parked a few buildings down and watched the front of the building. Not seeing anyone around on this early Saturday morning, they slid from the car and walked towards the door. There was a simple doorbell camera next to the door, and one guy placed his thumb over the camera while his associate pulled out the lockpick tool and unlocked the door. They pushed through and checked around the small entry for a security panel but didn't see one.

They pulled silenced pistols from under their coats and slipped into a larger lobby area with a small reception desk, which was unoccupied. They pushed open the door to the left of the desk and entered a space filled with cubicles that were empty, all in neat rows. They paused, listened and heard music coming from somewhere in the building. They walked towards the sound.

Jason Radovich and Stephanie Varney were sitting

in one of the recording studios along the back wall and were working through a script for a story on the death of a woman who was killed in her kitchen when the local cops raided the wrong house. According to their chief, the officers mistook the forty-eight-year-old Black woman for a thirty-four-year-old white meth head who had been wanted for distribution and assault. It was a big story, and Radovich and Varney had gotten several exclusives from the parties involved and were in the process of taping their next podcast.

They turned off the recorder and sat back to review their script. They felt like they were missing something but weren't sure what it was; they felt like the story lacked punch. They were rewriting a couple of lines when the recording studio door flew open and two men in dark trench coats stepped in and pointed guns at them.

"Hey. What the fuck?" asked Radovich.

"We're looking for Gilbert Grant. Where is he?"

"How the fuck should we know, asshole? We're not his keepers. Now, get the fuck out of here before I call the cops." Varney reached for his arm to pull him back as he stood and confronted the two guys.

The sound from the silenced pistol, not as quiet as the television shows made it out to be, was absorbed by the soundproof walls as the bullet passed through Radovich's chin and blew out the top of his head. The second bullet hit Varney below the right eye and blew out the side of her head. They were dead before they hit the floor. The men left the recording studio and walked into another man, who stopped and stared at the carnage. He turned pale, and they could smell urine as a stain appeared on the front of the man's pants.

The man stuck the end of the silencer against the man's chest. "Who are you?"

The man sputtered, and spittle ran down his chin. He gained a little composure. "D . . . D . . . David Reubens. This is my . . . my company."

"David, we're looking for Gilbert Grant. Do you know where we can find him?"

David pointed down the line of cubicles. "End cubicle on the left." He stared at the dead bodies.

"Well, David. He doesn't seem to be there, so where would he be?"

David shrugged as tears rolled down his face. The bullet tore through David's chest, and he slammed into a desk in the cubicle behind him and slid to the floor. The second bullet hit him in the forehead.

The men stepped over his legs and walked to the end cubicle. They ransacked the desk but found nothing that would lead them to Gilbert's location, so they holstered their weapons and left the building. They slid into their car, and one man pulled out his phone.

"Not at his office," said the man.

"Okay," said the Southern voice on the other end, "go hole up somewhere and I'll see what we can do from here. Stay ready."

The call disconnected. The car started, and they pulled onto the street.

Gilbert watched the two men exit the office of Sundance Media, and he ducked behind a dumpster that sat in front of the roll-up door for a small manufacturing company next door. He watched as they slid into the car and drove away a few minutes later. He waited until they were out of sight and then hurried across the street. He waved his pass card over the card reader next to the doorbell camera and heard the door click. He pushed through, making sure the door was latched before he moved into the main reception area and then stepped into the main office space.

The first thing he noticed was the mess that was once his cubicle. Everything that had been on the desk and in the drawers was on the floor. He looked around and wondered what the hell had happened. As he looked around the rest of the space, he noticed that none of the other cubicles had been touched. Whatever those two guys were looking for, he was their center of attention.

He looked down the center aisle and noticed two legs protruding from the last cubicle. He walked down the aisle and choked back a throat full of bile when he saw his boss, David, sprawled on the floor with blood covering his chest and his head. He couldn't hold back the bile when he saw the two bodies in the recording studio, and he puked all over the floor next to the body of his boss. His head was swimming, and he pulled a chair from the opposite cubicle and sat down. He put his head in his hands. His body was shaking, and he wiped tears from his eyes.

"Fuck! Oh fuck! What the hell happened here?" he said out loud. After the scene at his desk and now this, the only conclusion he could come up with was that they were after him, and had he arrived at the office ten minutes sooner, he would be dead on the floor as well. But the question still lingered. "Why?"

Gilbert jumped out of the chair. He needed to get away before the two guys came back. He needed to find a place to hide until he could figure out what they were after. He wiped his face with his coat sleeve, picked up his backpack and headed for the door. He thought twice about going out the front door in case they were outside waiting for him, so he headed for the door to the alley behind the building.

He pushed open the door and looked up and down the alley. Confident no one was around, he pulled out his phone and dialed 911. He reported multiple murders, gave the operator the address and disconnected the call when she asked for his name. He let the door shut behind him and headed for the parking garage three blocks over, where he had parked his car.

He slid into his car and sat for a minute, trying to get his hands to stop shaking. He didn't know what to do, but he needed to do something. He still couldn't come up with a reason someone would want to kill him. None of his podcasts for the past couple of weeks were controversial. The information about the senator was the best thing to drop into his lap in weeks, but he hadn't even started working on it. He closed his eyes to think.

Gilbert could hear sirens in the distance and figured the cops were on their way to the office. He knew it was time to go, but he had no idea where to go, so he decided to head out of Washington, towards Baltimore; he would figure it out when he got there. His investigative journalist brain was locked on the story about Senator Stevenson, and he figured he needed to do some digging to see if he was right. He slowed at the exit from the parking garage as three police cars drove past him.

Gilbert pulled forward as a dark SUV stopped across the exit, blocking him in. Two men exited the SUV and walked towards his car. They raised silenced pistols and fired through the windshield hitting Gilbert multiple times. One man walked to the passenger door, opened it and lifted the backpack off the seat. They put their pistols away, slid into the SUV and drove away. Gilbert's car drifted down the exit ramp and was hit by another car, which pushed it up on the sidewalk where it continued to roll until it stopped against a light pole.

Chapter Eighteen

Mike had parked three blocks away from the warehouse because of all the emergency vehicles in the street in front of the building. He badged his way into the security area and stopped next to Ronnie, who was talking to a short Hispanic woman with a Washington, DC, police badge hanging from a lanyard around her neck.

"Hey, Mike." She pointed towards the detective. "Detective First Sally Hernandez, Mike Branik. Mike, Sally."

They shook hands. "So why are we here?" asked Mike.

"Sally and I were having lunch when the call went out. Triple homicide at a digital news media office. She invited me to tag along."

"Okay, but why does a triple homicide interest us?" he asked.

Sally turned and faced him. "The call came in anonymously, but shortly after the first units arrived, the editor, Mack Bergen, showed up. Let's step inside."

They followed Sally and entered the building, pushing through into the cubicle area. The first thing Mike noticed was the mess around one desk. He pointed at the desk.

"This the only desk like this?"

Sally nodded. "According to Mr. Bergen, this desk belongs to Gilbert Grant. Grant has a popular podcast and has exposed many people doing bad things over the years."

She walked forward, and Mike gave Ronnie a curious look. She nodded and followed Sally, as did Mike. Sally continued the tour.

"The first body is that of the owner of Sundance Media, David Reubens. According to his wife, he was coming by the office this morning to pick up some documents. She had no idea what the docs were for, but he said they were important."

"Important enough to kill over?" he asked.

"Not sure. We found a packet of legal documents on his desk, but they were for setting up a charity. Not worth getting dead over. Anyway, he was shot twice. Looks like a hit."

She stepped over to the recording studio and pointed inside. "Jason Radovich and Stephanie Varney. They were working on a podcast that was to be released this coming week. Each shot once in the head."

Sally stepped away from the studio door. "These all look like the work of a pro, except for the mess at that one desk. Whoever did that didn't care if it got noticed or not. I got Grant's number from his boss, and it goes right to voice mail."

"Mike," said Ronnie. "Whoever did this was looking for something, and this guy Gilbert was targeted. What got my attention was that Mr. Bergen mentioned Grant was on a date last night. The date was with a young woman who works in Senator Stevenson's office."

That got Mike's attention too. "Do we know where this Grant fella lives?"

"Yeah," said Sally. "I've got a unit heading over there to check it out and see if he's home. If not, then we can conclude that he's running, and someone's chasing him."

"Does his boss know what he was working on?" asked Mike.

"That's just it," said Ronnie. "His boss said he wasn't working on anything right now, but I'm wondering if he got a tip about something at the senator's office."

Sally's phone chimed, and she answered it. "Yeah."

She nodded a few times and disconnected the call. She looked at Mike and Ronnie. "We need to go. There's another dead body in Grant's apartment. A young blond woman."

They followed Sally; she offered to drive them since parking was always a bitch, and they slid into her unmarked Camaro. Sally hit the lights and siren as soon as they got past all the emergency vehicles, and she hit the gas.

The drive was short, and they pulled in behind more DC police cars. Sally badged them past the security cordon and walked into an old brownstone. They climbed the stairs to the third-floor unit and pushed inside.

Sally talked to a detective at the door and then they stepped into the bedroom. The body, according to the first officer on the scene, was naked on the bed and covered by a blanket.

Sally put on rubber gloves and walked around the bedroom. Ronnie walked over and kneeled next to the bed and looked at the body. She pointed to her arm, and Mike and Sally stepped closer.

"Little tiny blood spot near her shoulder," she said. She stood and looked at them. "Someone gave this girl a hot shot. Could be fentanyl, liquid cocaine or maybe ketamine. That's very popular amongst the jet-set crowd."

"I'll get the lab to do a full tox screen. We'll know soon enough," said Sally.

Mike had stepped away and wandered into an office next to the bedroom. There was no laptop or desktop, but there were three large monitors. He sat in the desk chair, went through the drawers and looked at everything on the desk. There were no notes anywhere.

Ronnie entered the office, and Sally stopped at the door. "Anything?" asked Ronnie.

"Nope. Whatever made this guy want to leave that young woman in his bed and go to the office must have been damn important."

He stood, reached into his pocket and handed the detective a business card. "Please email me the tox results as soon as you get them."

She looked at it and smiled. "All your card says is

‘Mike’ with an email address. What exactly do you do for the government? I know Ronnie was a badass, because I was one too, but the marines were a long time ago. What do you guys do now?”

Mike looked at her. “Whatever we have to do.”

Sally led them back through the apartment and out into the street. They slid into her car and headed back towards the first crime scene. She dropped them off out front and headed inside, following a forensic tech.

“What do you think?” asked Ronnie.

“I think we need to have a chat with Mr. Grant. That young woman is dead because she told him or showed him something she shouldn’t have seen. Something someone wants to keep quiet. We need to know what that was. Do me a favor. Head back to the hotel and run a check on a company called Advanced Services or something like that.”

He pulled up the picture on his phone and handed it to her. “I sent you this guy’s identity. My contact says he works for a big security firm, hires only former military. See what you can find and then background this guy, Gilbert Grant.”

“What are you gonna be doing?” she asked.

“I’m gonna shake the trees and see what falls out. Stay by your phone. I’ll call you if I need you.”

“You gonna call the rest of the team?” she asked.

“Let them have Christmas tomorrow with the family. I’ll get them up here the day after.”

He buttoned up his coat and headed for his car. The

wind had picked up, and the humidity was high. Washington, DC, might wake up and have a white Christmas. Mike walked three blocks to where his rental was parked and noticed the guy on the roof of the warehouse across from the crime scene who had been taking pictures of everyone entering and leaving the scene. Mike pulled onto the street and drove off at the same time the guy on the roof was sending his picture to someone else.

Mike's phone chimed and he hit the talk button. "What's up, Ronnie?

"Sally Hernandez just called me," said Ronnie. "Gibert Grant is dead. He was shot pulling out of a parking garage a couple of blocks from his office."

"Fuck," said Mike. "It would have been nice to know what he was working on. All right. Let's move on as planned."

"Yeah," said Ronnie.

"Follow up on the other information and we'll connect later. Mike disconnected the call and shook his head. He hated days like this.

Chapter Nineteen

Senator Stevenson's phone chimed as he was opening the gift from his six-year-old granddaughter. She'd spent all day yesterday coloring Christmas scenes on white paper and then wrapping this gift with her homemade wrapping paper. She stood in front of him, beaming as he removed each piece of tape so as not to damage the paper. He let his phone go to voice mail.

Inside the colorful paper was a small box, and inside the box was a bracelet made of red, white and blue beads with her name, Eva, spelled out in the middle. He put the bracelet on and gave her a huge hug, then kissed her on the top of the head. He excused himself and headed towards his office down the hall. He closed the door and pulled out his phone. He recognized the number, and he knew there would be no voice message.

He hit redial, and the phone on the other end was answered right away.

"We may have a problem," said the Southern voice on the other end. "There seems to be a player involved that we can't identify. Two of them. A man and a woman. They weren't with the DC metro police, yet they were given access to two crime scenes. That might affect us."

"Federal?" asked the senator.

"That's what we're thinking, but if they are, they don't show up in any databases, and we have access to them all. Can you send their pictures to anyone in the military chain of command who might help, or maybe someone with the CIA or NSA?"

"Yes," said the senator. "Email me the pictures and I will get them to the right people. It might take a day or two because of the holiday."

The senator's phone chimed with an incoming text, and he opened the attached photos. "Okay, leave it with me."

He disconnected the call. Opened the text and forwarded the photos to a number in his phone. Being the highest-ranking senator came with several perks, and one of them was having contacts in all the right places. He put his phone down and headed back to the rest of the family.

Mike had called Mary to check on the ranch and wish her a merry Christmas. The family members who lived in Colorado were coming to spend a couple of days with her, so she was feeling good. Mike told her he should be back before the New Year and hung up. He slid over to Ronnie and looked over her shoulder.

"Any ID on the cameraman on the roof?" he asked.

"Yeah, found him in the military database. Low-level sailor. Spent four years in logistics in the navy."

"Any idea who he's working for?"

Ronnie looked up at him. "Shit, Mike. I just found him. How about giving me a few minutes to track him down?" She laughed.

"You worried he got our pictures?" she asked.

"Nah. We're not in anyone's database, so even if they can identify our pictures, they can't access our files."

"I hope that's enough. So, what happened after we split up yesterday?"

"I drove out to Alexandria and got a look at the senator's house. He's got a lot more security than the government is providing him. Lot of ex-military types walking the property. I got to within fifty yards of the house, but the inside perimeter is tight."

"Mike, do you honestly believe that the Senate majority leader would be involved in a plot to disrupt the peaceful transfer of power? I mean, the guy is at the top of his game, and he's young enough that he can run again in four years."

Mike thought for a few seconds. "Yeah, he could run again, but that would be his third attempt, and each time he has lost by more votes than the previous time. The party can't seem to shake this guy. I think his ego won't let him accept reality."

Ronnie's laptop chimed, and she opened the notification. "Got an address for the photographer. Want to pay him a visit?"

"Yeah," said Mike. "Nothing else to do, so let's see what he's willing to tell us."

They stood, grabbed their coats and backpacks and left the room. The hotel was quiet, and they left without seeing anyone in the lobby. The fact that they were photographed yesterday meant that someone was interested in what they were doing. It could have been a random encounter, but Mike didn't think so. Now it was time to find out.

The little white house on Maden Street in Fredericksburg, Virginia, needed repair. The roof had been patched with different-colored shingles, and the front porch sat tilted on a couple of cement blocks. The lawn, or lack thereof, needed some fertilizer and some water. While many of the houses on the street had bright Christmas displays, the little white house sat dark and isolated.

Mike parked one house over in front of a house that had no lights lit. The family was probably off visiting relatives for the holiday. At least he hoped that was the case. They sat for a minute and watched the neighborhood. The cold evening and the holiday spirit seemed to have kept most people inside. A damp, cold mist hung in the air. It was a miserable day but a good chance for folks to stay inside and enjoy time with family and friends.

Mike checked his pistol, snapped off the safety and holstered the weapon as Ronnie did the same thing. They exited the rental car and walked along the sidewalk to the narrow driveway. They looked around, walked up the driveway to the backyard, pushed open a broken chain-link gate and stopped to listen. Not hearing any dogs, they walked to the back door and tried the handle.

While Mike stood guard, Ronnie pulled out a lockpick gun and unlocked the door. Mike pulled his pistol and pushed open the door. He could hear a television on somewhere in the house, and he stepped into the kitchen, the smell of garbage and grease filling his nostrils. Ronnie moved ahead into the next room and cleared it. The living room contained an old torn couch, a small end table and a big-screen TV hung above a fake fireplace heater. She pointed down a hall and Mike moved, checking in each room he passed.

The second-to-last door contained a desktop computer and several large monitors. There were cameras of all types hanging on hooks on the wall. They would come back to this space in a few minutes.

At the last door, Mike could hear faint voices on the television, and as he cracked the door, he saw the room was lit by an ever-changing blue light. Mike pushed open the door and stepped into the room. The blue light came from the television screen, the porn movie running until Mike switched the TV off.

George Colletti was crashed out on the bed. His clothes were disheveled, and his hair looked like it hadn't been washed in days. The bed was covered with empty tequila bottles, and empty beer cans were scattered all around the bed.

Mike looked over at Ronnie, who walked into the kitchen and found a pitcher in one of the cabinets. She filled it with cold water and carried it back to the room, where she dumped it on George's head. George jumped up, startled.

"Wwwhaat the fuck?" he asked, trying to sit up.

Mike grabbed him by the shirt and dragged him off the bed. They hauled him to the computer room and plopped him into the desk chair. While Mike held him down, Ronnie pulled some long black wire ties out of her backpack and secured his hands and feet to the chair. George shook his head, trying to clear the cobwebs, and stared at his two visitors. Mike put his hand on George's chest and leaned forward, pushing the chair until it banged into the computer desk.

"Hi, George. Remember us?" said Mike.

George shook his head and was about to say something when a look crossed his face, and his pale skin turned almost white.

"I can see by your reaction that you recognize us, George. That's good. We can skip a lot of the formalities then, okay, George?"

"What do you want?" asked George.

"You were taking pictures at a crime scene earlier today, and you took some of us. We'd like to know where they are, George."

"Fuck you," said George.

Mike laughed. "Now, that's not very nice, George. We drove all the way down here just to introduce ourselves to you, and you seem to want to turn this encounter into something unfriendly. Why is that, George?"

"I got nothing to say to you, so fuck off. I know people," said George.

Mike leaned in closer. "Is that so, George? You know people, huh? Well, you'd better look around, George, because none of those people are here now, but we are."

While George was trying to be macho, Ronnie had been working on his computer. She looked at Mike. "This is disgusting. Who has this much porn on their computer? Gross!"

She started deleting files one at a time as George watched and tears rolled down his face. "Stop, please," he said.

"Sure, George," said Mike. "Just as soon as you tell us where our pictures are."

George sneered. "Top row, last file on the right."

Ronnie opened the folder and pulled up the photos. There were a hundred and ten pictures in the folder.

"George, that's a lot of pictures. What was your assignment?"

"Fuck you," yelled George.

Mike laughed, grabbed a sock off the floor and shoved it into his mouth. He pulled a knife out of his pocket and snapped it open. George's eyes got wide. Mike held the knife against George's crotch and pushed it until he heard the material tearing.

"Now, one more time, George. What was your assignment?"

George shook his head, and Mike pulled out the sock. George spit in the air. "You can't do this. You're cops."

Mike and Ronnie both laughed. "Oh boy, George. You couldn't be further from the truth. We're not cops."

"But you were at the crime scene," said George.

Mike pushed the knife a little harder. "Now, how about we stop the bullshit, and you tell us what we want to know or I'm gonna cut your dick off. Okay, George?"

George looked defeated. "What do you want to know?"

"What was your assignment? Who paid you, and where did you send the pictures?" asked Mike.

"They'll kill me," said George.

Mike smiled. "George, I'm holding a knife against your crotch."

"Okay, okay. I was told to go to the crime scene and take pictures of everyone there. That's all."

"Who paid you, George? And don't give me that anonymous-over-the-internet bullshit."

"I was paid by a guy I know who works for some big security outfit. I sent him the pictures, and he made a deposit into my account. That's all I know, I swear." Sweat ran down his head.

Mike pulled back the knife. Ronnie tapped him on the shoulder, and he looked at the screen. "Lots of kiddie porn on here. Can't say if any of it is local, but the metadata suggests that the pictures were taken with his cameras."

Mike looked at George. "So, you're a pervert, huh, George?" He grabbed his head and shoved the sock into his mouth. George struggled, but it was a losing effort.

Ronnie grabbed one of George's cameras off the hook, made sure the battery was charged and took several pictures of George bound to the chair. She connected the camera to the desktop and downloaded the pictures. She looked up two addresses on Google, opened George's email app and composed an email to the Virginia State Police and the Virginia attorney general. She attached George's picture and several of the porn files. She also forwarded the email George had sent to his friend with their pictures to her email and hit send on both emails.

Mike folded the knife and put it away. He leaned closer to George. "We know who you are, George. If we find out you contacted the guy who ordered the crime scene pictures, we'll be back, and it won't be as pleasant the next time."

They grabbed their backpacks and coats, bundled up and left the house. Mike started the car and looked at Ronnie. "Were you able to track his friend?"

She reached over and punched an address into the dashboard nav system. Mike looked at the information.

"No time like the present. Call Jeff, give him the address and ask him to sit on it until we get there."

Ronnie nodded and pulled out her phone. He put the car in gear and headed for the interstate.

Chapter Twenty

Mike pulled into the motel outside Jonesboro, Georgia, and parked next to Jeff Halsey's pickup truck. The door to room seven opened, and Jeff stepped out onto the sidewalk that ran in front of the building. He holstered his pistol as Mike and Ronnie slid from the rental car. They shook hands, entered the room and closed the door. Mike plopped down on one of the twin beds and let out a sigh. The drive from Fredericksburg had taken a little over nine hours, and he was beat.

He sat up and looked at Jeff. "Any luck?"

"Yeah," said Jeff. He pulled a small notebook out of his back pocket and flipped the pages until he found what he was looking for.

"Jake Twindell, former army Green Beret. Did several tours in Afghanistan. Bronze Star and two Purple Hearts. He mustered out two years ago and went to work for Advanced Services. It looks like mostly protection work. No police record. Married, two kids, nine and eleven. He lives here in Jonesboro. Nice house, fat bank account. Living the good life between gigs."

"Sounds like a model citizen," said Ronnie as she poured herself and Mike a cup of coffee from the machine on the bathroom counter.

Jeff smiled. "Maybe not quite. House sits on a wooded lot, so good cover for surveillance, but the streets are narrow and kind of rural. The kind of place people notice things like strange cars. Anyway. I watched the house for a while and at about nine P.M. Jake left the house and headed to a motel on the other side of town. Met a busty bleach blonde and was there about two hours. I think he might be stepping out on the Mrs."

"I hate the idea of taking him around the family. Think we can take him at the motel?" asked Mike.

"Might be an option. He was kind of wary. Looked around a lot. Good situational awareness skills. There's a narrow, wooded road he has to head down to get to the motel. Traffic interdiction might be the best approach."

"That's risky," said Ronnie. "If he's armed, which there's no reason to believe he's not, we could end up in a shoot-out."

Mike sipped his coffee. "Let's keep an eye on him for a couple of days and see if an opportunity presents itself. In the meantime, we need to find some other people we can look at. Advanced Services seems to be ground zero, so let's see who else is on their payroll that we can grab."

Mike lay back on the bed and closed his eyes. He was out in seconds. Ronnie grabbed her laptop and started running an internet check for anyone who might work at Advanced Services.

Jeff decided to take the more direct approach, so he grabbed his coat and headed for his truck. He was going to stake out the headquarters building of Advanced Services and take pictures of everyone entering or leaving. He hoped he might see someone he knew, either from the service or locally.

Mike woke with a start, reached over and lifted his pistol off the nightstand. He looked around the room. Ronnie was sound asleep on the floor, covered with a blanket. Something had caused him to wake up. He lay there for a few minutes not moving and decided that it must have just been the wind or something. He rested the pistol on his chest and put his head back on the pillow.

The next time he heard the noise, Ronnie was next to him on the floor with her pistol in her hand. Whatever woke Mike had also awoken her. She raised a finger to her lips and pointed towards the door. Mike nodded and rolled off the bed on the opposite side.

Ronnie scooted back until she crossed over the threshold to the bathroom and kept low, moving into the space between the door and the shower. She aimed her pistol at the door.

Mike moved into the opposite corner of the room in line with the front window and the door. He stood and peeked along the edge of the drapes. Two men stood outside the door. They were wearing black fatigues and had balaclavas over their heads. Each was armed with a White Manufacturing 9mm SPEC Machine Pistol with an extended clip. They could do a lot of damage with that if they got the chance. Mike wasn't willing to give them the chance.

Mike moved to the side of the room and aimed at the door. He held his pistol straight and steady and took a couple of deep breaths.

There was a loud crash as one of the two guys

kicked in the door. Mike and Ronnie fired. The first guy through the door went down fast, and because of where Mike had positioned himself, he had a perfect view of the second guy off to the side of the door. His bullet impacted the side of his head and slammed him into the post, holding up the overhang.

Mike looked at Ronnie, and she gave him a thumbs-up sign. She stood and, leading with her pistol, walked towards the front door. Mike covered her as she kneeled next to the first guy. She put her fingers on his throat but found no pulse; she walked over to the second guy and just nodded. The bullet from Mike's .45-caliber pistol had blown a huge hole through the back of the guy's head. There was no doubt he was dead. She kicked their weapons to the side.

Sirens could be heard coming from several directions, and Mike and Ronnie holstered their weapons, pulled their federal badges and hung the lanyards around their necks. They stood under the overhang next to the light and waited.

Three sheriff's department SUVs pulled into the lot and shut off their sirens. They pulled to a stop behind Mike's rental car and exited their SUVs with guns drawn.

Mike and Ronnie had their hands in the air and made sure their badges were visible.

"Freeze," yelled one of the deputies. "On the ground."

Mike, with his hands in the air, said, "I don't think so. Federal agents. We are armed, our weapons are holstered and our hands are raised. We are no threat." He said that because he assumed they would have their body cameras running, and he wanted his statement on the record.

The deputies glanced at each other and weren't sure what to do. Another deputy yelled over. "Drop your weapons."

Mike repeated the same thing a second time. He looked at the first deputy. "Please call your watch commander and ask him to report to the scene. Tell him two federal agents on the job were attacked and had to use deadly force to protect themselves."

The deputy spoke into the mic on his shoulder and lowered his weapon. "Sergeant is on his way. What agency you with—FBI, DEA?"

Mike smiled. "We'll explain it all to your sergeant. We are going to lower our hands, but we will remain next to the light so you can see us." He and Ronnie lowered their hands and waited.

Another sheriff's SUV pulled into the lot, and a heavyset white sergeant slid out of the SUV and spoke with the two deputies who had remained near their vehicles. They holstered their weapons. The sergeant walked to the closest deputy and put his hand on his weapon and pushed it down to the low ready position. He approached Mike.

"Sergeant Prentice. Can I see some ID?"

Mike pulled out his wallet, slipped out a card and handed it to the sergeant. The card contained a phone number with an area code for Washington, DC. The sergeant looked at it.

"Sergeant," said Mike. "Please call that number."

The sergeant, more curious than anything, pulled out his phone and dialed the number. There was a surprised look on his face when the phone was answered, and he pulled back his shoulders and stood at attention. The sergeant identified himself and explained the situation. He described Mike and Ronnie and listened.

"Yes, sir, I'll let them know. Thank you, sir." The sergeant hung up, handed Mike back the card and pocketed his phone. He told the deputy next to him to holster his weapon. He looked at Mike.

"I have to tell you, that's a new one on me. I've worked with a lot of Feds over the years, but none of them had the president's cell phone number on them. He asked me to tell you that the next time you get in a shoot-out, do it after the sun comes up."

Mike laughed. "Sounds like we woke him up." Ronnie smiled.

"Sergeant, I'm assuming you called the local medical examiner? While we wait, I'd like to lift the balaclavas and see who these two guys are. Okay?"

The sergeant nodded, and Mike stepped over to the first guy they shot, kneeled and lifted the face mask to his forehead. The second guy's mask needed a little coaxing, since his brains were sticking to the fabric. Mike pulled it up. He looked at Ronnie and stood.

"Don't know this guy," he said, pointing to the first

guy, “but we had this guy,”—he pointed to the other guy—“under surveillance since yesterday.”

“What’d they do, if you don’t mind me asking?” asked the sergeant.

“It’s not what they did, it’s what they might do. This fella here was being watched because he posed a threat to the president.”

A black van pulled into the parking lot and parked next to where they were all standing. A crowd had gathered in the parking lot as people stood by their rooms and watched the spectacle. The sergeant turned and asked his deputies to get out some crime scene tape and to move the crowd of onlookers back.

The county medical examiner, a short, bald man with thick glasses, walked up and kneeled next to the first body. He checked for a pulse and did the same to the second man. While he did that, Mike took several pictures of the assailants. The ME looked at the sergeant.

“Merle, they’re both dead. We’ll load them up and head for the morgue.” He waved over his assistant, who walked over with two folded body bags. He laid one out on the concrete, and they rolled the body into the bag and zipped it up. They did the same with the second body. The sergeant asked the deputies to give them a hand getting the bodies into the van, and once done, the ME and his assistant slid into the van and drove from the lot.

The sergeant looked at Mike. “Don’t suppose you’d let us run a ballistic check on your weapons, huh?”

"Not gonna happen, Sergeant. If you get in a jam, call the local FBI office and tell the agent in charge what you need. They'll take care of it, and Sergeant, you might want to delete that phone number from your call log."

The sergeant laughed, pulled out his phone, opened the call log and pushed delete. He showed the screen to Mike.

"Thank you, Sergeant."

Mike shook his hand and stepped into the room. He and Ronnie gathered up their things. He pulled out his phone and called Jeff to meet them for breakfast. They slid into their rental car and backed out of the lot. The sergeant was standing off to the side talking with the deputies, and he tapped the brim of his hat as they drove by. Ronnie waved.

Chapter Twenty-One

Robert E. Lee Richardson closed his office door and picked up his phone.

"Good morning, Senator. Hope you had a nice Christmas."

"I did, Lee, I did. I have a name for you."

"By all means, Senator, go right ahead."

"My source says the big fella is Mike Branik. His service record might as well be a blank page for all the black ink on it. He's some kind of hotshot operator. No one seems to know who he works for or how he gets paid, but he's connected to the government. My source thinks he was a tier one operator back in the day. Now he seems to be a troubleshooter. I hope that helps because I had to call in a couple of huge favors and make some promises I hope I can keep."

"Well, I appreciate the information, Senator. Please give my regards to the Mrs., and enjoy the New Year, if we don't speak before then."

He disconnected the call and stared at his phone. He wondered how this guy got onto his operation, but he was bound and determined to find out.

He picked up his phone and dialed a secure number and relayed the senator's information to the voice on the other end. He hung up and walked into the kitchen, where the chef was just setting out breakfast.

Jimmy Bronson hung up the phone. He called his small team together.

"We have an immediate mission. There's a guy named Mike Branik trying to stop us from completing our mission. We need to stop him. He's some hotshot government guy and might have been an operator some time back. Towards that goal, I need you all to reach out to people you worked with. Someone in the community must know this guy. Let's find him so we can stop him."

His guys pulled out their phones and laptops and went to work. Jimmy was confident they could find this guy. They had two weeks left at the farm before they needed to hit the road.

The farm, near Murfreesboro, North Carolina, had been in Jimmy's family since the early 1800s and was the perfect place to set up a training facility. The nearest neighbors were more than two miles away, and the farm had an enormous barn that was no longer used for cows. Jimmy and a crew of believers had spent a year rebuilding the barn into a state-of-the-art training facility, a match for anything the government had, that included soundproof walls and a tactical shooting range that could be reconfigured in minutes to any layout needed for the mission. Jimmy was proud of his space, and his team felt at home.

They had all the luxuries of a fine hotel at their disposal and never had to leave the property for anything. There was also a computer lab staffed with some top black hat hackers that Jimmy had recruited and vetted. Jimmy ran a first-class operation, and his team were some of the best-trained militia members in the country. They were the first group called whenever the Free America movement needed help.

Jimmy had planned to have the team run different entry scenarios for the president-elect's Montana property. His computer team had pulled maps from Google Earth and various for-profit satellite companies that Jimmy paid for, and they had created a full mockup on the mission board. Today he was going to arrange the moveable panels to replicate the inside of the president-elect's house. He had secured the plans from a friendly inside the Secret Service.

Instead, they needed to focus on this outside player who could gum up the works. Jimmy hated loose ends, and this guy could be a serious loose end if the information they received was correct. They had to work fast; the clock was ticking.

Jimmy's phone rang, and he looked at the number. "Yeah, who's this?" Jimmy listened.

"I don't know you," he said. "How do I know this is real?"

The caller disconnected, and Jimmy pulled up a search app. One of his team stood next to him.

"What's up, Jimmy?" he asked, looking over Jimmy's shoulder.

Jimmy read two articles. "Fuck."

"Who are Twindell, McCall and Tancredo?" asked the teammate.

"They were members of our group. They were on two assignments the day before yesterday. Now they're dead. All it says is Twindell and McCall were killed by federal agents at a motel in Jonesboro and Tancredo was killed in an apartment in Washington,

DC. Shit."

"Were they part of our thing?" asked the teammate.

Jimmy looked up from his phone. "They were doing a side gig. Not directly a part of what we're doing but connected. They were family." Jimmy hauled off and kicked over a small desk covered with papers. The desk slammed against the wall, scattering papers everywhere.

"God damnit," he yelled.

Three more members of the team who were nearby ran in with guns drawn. They stopped and looked at the mess on the floor and then at Jimmy, whose face was bright red. They stood and waited.

"Twindell, McCall and Tancredo are dead," he said. "Killed by unnamed federal agents. I want those fucks dead. Now!"

"You think it was the same Feds who were at the crime scene?" asked one man.

"Had to be. Somehow, the Feds got onto them, and they killed them." He looked at his men. "Find me someone who knows this fuck."

"What about Guffy? Any word on him?" asked another man.

"The article said there was also an unknown male found at one of the scenes. Has to be Guffy," said Jimmy.

They all left the room, leaving Jimmy to run things through his head. He had sent those guys on their assignments. He hadn't lost any men under his command since his second tour in Afghanistan. He didn't like the feeling.

Jimmy righted a chair that fell over along with the desk, sat and dialed a number.

"Sir, we may have a problem."

The Southern voice on the other end responded, "What's going on?"

"I just got an anonymous call that Twindell, McCall, Tancredo and Guffy are dead."

The person on the other end interrupted, "How did they die?"

"Sir, Twindell and McCall died at a motel in Jonesboro, and Tancredo and Guffy died in Washington."

There was silence on the phone, and Jimmy stood by, knowing better than to interrupt.

"Jimmy," said the voice. "This is not good. Tancredo and Guffy were supposed to protect the penthouse. What were Twindell and McCall doing?"

"Not sure, sir. They had completed their assignment at the news company, and I told them to lie low for a bit. They must have got onto something, or they wouldn't have been at a motel."

"I'll see if I can find out any more information about the shootings. Any luck finding our elusive Feds?"

"Working on it, sir," said Jimmy.

"Good. When you find them, kill them." The call disconnected.

"It will be my pleasure," said Jimmy to the quiet phone in his hand.

The door to Jimmy's office pushed open, and one of the newer members of the team, Jessie, leaned in.

"Sir, I may have something."

Jimmy waved him in. "What have you got?"

"It might be nothing," said Jessie.

Jimmy scowled. "Out with it."

"Well, sir. I have an old contact who served for a lot of years in Delta. He remembers a guy named Branik, but it was also a long time ago and his memory ain't what it should be. Well, anyway, he said this young guy Branik was a real hotshot. Volunteered for every crazy mission."

Jimmy looked at him. "Okay."

"Well. He thinks he remembered the kid came from Colorado. Someplace way up the north end, big ranch or something. I did some checking, and I found a large ranch belonging to a former Supreme Court chief justice and his wife. He's long dead, but his wife is still listed as the owner of the property. Big spread, but way too big for some old lady to run by herself."

"Good work. Who do we have up that way?"

Jessie set a piece of paper on Jimmy's desk. Jimmy picked it up and looked at it.

"The Poudre River Rangers. Hmm. Local outfit, aligned with the big militia out of Denver."

"Yes, sir. They have some tested guys on their team

and could be there in a couple of hours," said Jessie.

Jimmy picked up the paper and raised his phone. He dialed a number, and when the phone was answered gave a password. The voice on the other end was gruff and sounded older than Jimmy. Jimmy explained the situation.

"Yes, sir," said the voice. "I got me a good team. We can be there before dawn. What's the rules of engagement?"

"Burn it to the ground and kill anyone you encounter."

"You can count on us."

Jimmy disconnected the call and placed his phone on the desk. He'd wait to call the boss until he heard from Colorado.

Chapter Twenty-Two

Mike, Ronnie and Jeff sat in a small office in a hangar in Missouri. Their MATS flight from DC back to Colorado was grounded due to weather, so they had a bit of time to put their feet up and kick back. Mike had looked outside a few minutes ago and seen that the morning sun was having a hard time breaking through the snow squalls. He had just poured himself a coffee when an alarm sounded on his phone.

He opened his phone and kicked Ronnie in the foot. She shook the sleep out of her eyes and looked at him.

"Just got an intruder alert at the ranch. Multiple hostiles in the woods south of the house."

Ronnie jumped up and grabbed her laptop, while Mike speed-dialed a number.

"Hi, Mike," said Mary.

Mike cut her off. "Mary, listen carefully. You've got intruders on the ranch. I need you to head for the safe room, now."

Mary knew the drill. She disconnected the call, grabbed her coat and headed for the barn. She pulled the big door open, slipped through and pulled it shut. She disconnected the rope and dropped the big beam in place across the door brackets. She stepped into the middle stall and hit the button, and the floor of the stall opened, revealing a metal hatch. She hit a second button at the back of the stall and the hatch opened. She climbed down the ladder, hit a button and the hatch sealed back up. Nothing in the stall looked amiss. She took off her coat and dialed Mike. As she waited, she pulled two shotguns off the rack, made sure they were loaded and placed one in the middle of the room and one at the far end. She had plenty of places to hide in case the room was breached.

Mike answered. "All good?"

"Good to go. Who are these folks?" she asked.

"Not sure, but Ronnie activated all the countermeasures. You sit tight and don't worry."

"Go get' em, Mike." Mary hung up. Mike knew his countermeasures were good, but he was still worried about Mary.

He looked at Ronnie. "All set?"

"All countermeasures are live. Whoever these guys are, they're sitting ducks."

"Yeah, but it only takes one to get through."

"Don't worry, boss, I got this."

Mike stood behind her and watched the cameras in the woods. She had a dozen small screens open on the laptop, and she was tracking eight different intruders. They watched as the intruders stopped at the edge of the woods. Ronnie looked up.

"Looks like some militia types," she said.

The heavyset guy in the middle circled his finger over his head and pointed towards the house, and his unit moved forward. Ronnie sat with her fingers on the controls. Her face was solid, and she looked ready to fight.

When they were fifteen feet from the woods, Ronnie pushed a button on her laptop. On the screen, eight claymores buried under the snow exploded. Steel balls flew through the air and ripped through the line of men and the trees behind them. The devastation was surreal. They could see arms, legs and heads separate from the bodies that were torn apart by the shrapnel. The heavyset guy was the first to die.

Ronnie turned her attention to two men who had come around the left flank and were firing into the logs of the house. Ronnie pulled up a target reticle, took aim and pushed a button. A door on the side of the house opened, and a mini gun slid forward and opened up. The two guys disappeared, leaving a pink spot in the snow where they had once stood. There wouldn't be enough left of them to put in a sandwich bag.

Ronnie scanned the rest of the property, checking all the cameras, and was convinced that they had taken out all the intruders. She wondered who these guys were and if they realized, when they took the assignment, what they were up against.

Mike picked up his phone and called the local sheriff.

"Mike, what can I do for ya?" asked Sheriff Paul Wooster. Paul and Mike had gone to school together and were good friends. Paul also knew better than to ask what Mike was involved in.

"Hey, Paul. I need a favor. We had an encounter with some intruders on the ranch. I'm stuck and can't get there for a couple of hours, and Mary is in the safe room. Can you hook up with her and make sure she's good? Probably some great coffee and a piece of pie in it for ya."

Paul laughed, then got serious. "How many body bags am I gonna need?"

"Well," said Mike. "You can probably put what's left of them in a gallon freezer bag. There's a couple of pickup trucks pulled into the woods, just off the entrance road. Might help you figure out who these guys are."

"Okay, Mike. Rest easy. I'll take care of Mary until you get back."

"Thanks, Paul." Mike disconnected the call. "How the fuck did they find out about us?"

"I'm working on that," said Ronnie, clicking keys like a madwoman.

Jeff had woken up during the melee and was now looking at Mike.

"What the hell happened?" he asked.

"Intruders. Looks like the militia guys have a better network than we thought. Somehow, they found out about the ranch."

"Shit, Mike. Is Mary okay?"

"Yeah, she's fine, but we need to find out how they found us."

"What are you thinking?" asked Ronnie.

"I think we need to talk to Senator Stevenson. We know the guys we killed in Washington and Jonesboro were militia. We know the militia backed Stevenson and are preparing a huge rally on January sixth in Washington. He's got the connections as the Senate majority leader to get information from sources that might be closed off to others."

"But how would he have found out about the ranch? That's not in any of our files," said Jeff. "I've seen my file. It doesn't even have my picture in it, let alone any information that's worthwhile."

"If there's a plot to overthrow the government, then it has to center around Stevenson," said Ronnie. "I agree with Mike. I think we should have a talk with Stevenson."

"It's not going to be easy," said Mike. "I think the best first step might be for us to pay him a visit. I'll see if the president can get us an interview."

Mike pulled out his phone and dialed a number.

"You guys okay? I just received a report on an attack at your ranch."

"Yeah. We're good. We're stuck in Missouri at an air force base due to the weather," said Mike.

"Do I need to get some people up there to take care of Mary?"

"No. I've got that covered. What I need is an appointment to talk to Senator Stevenson. Can you help?"

"I can set that up. How do you want to go in?"

"We'll use our Homeland Security covers. Ronnie and I will go as soon as the weather clears. I'm sending Jeff to Montana. We need to get eyes on the president-

and vice president–elect and make sure they're covered."

"Okay. Call me when you get to Washington and I'll get you set up. Mike, how did they find out about the ranch? No one has that information."

"Not sure, sir, but we're gonna find out."

The phone went dead, and Mike looked at the others.

"Jeff, take a look around in Montana. Stay off the radar," said Mike.

"No problem."

"Ronnie, grab the base commander and let's shift our flights. Looks like you and I are heading back to Washington."

Chapter Twenty-Three

Mike pulled the rented SUV up to Senator Stevenson's gate and was stopped by two guys carrying assault-style rifles. One man stepped to the driver's door while the other one stood in front of the SUV looking menacing. Ronnie, sitting next to Mike, chuckled. She thought about the fact that he would get run over if they charged forward. Mike rolled down the window.

"Help you, sir?" said the man.

"Sure can," said Mike. "You can open the gate so I can get through."

"I need to see some ID," said the man.

Mike held up his Homeland Security Department ID. The man reached for it, and Mike pulled it back.

"You can look at it, but you don't get to touch it."

The security guard was taken aback. "Sir, I need to see your ID."

Mike held it up again. "Here it is. Take a look and then call the house. We have an appointment with the senator, and I would hate to keep him waiting."

"What about her?" asked the guard.

Mike smiled. "She has an appointment too."

"I need to see her ID," said the guard.

"Why?" asked Mike. "She's with me, and I've shown you my ID."

"Sir, it's procedure. I need to see her ID, or I will have to ask you to turn around and leave."

Ronnie laughed and held up her ID. The guard looked at it but made no attempt to reach for it. He checked his digital notebook, walked into the shed and pushed the button to open the gate. Mike waited for the other security guard to move, then he drove through the gate.

"Did you have to provoke him?" asked Ronnie.

Mike looked at her and smiled. "Why, yes. Yes, I did." They both laughed as they pulled under the Porte cochere and stopped by the stairs.

They slid out and approached the door, which opened. Two more security guards blocked their way.

"You'll need to leave your weapons locked in your vehicle," said the guard.

Mike moved closer, and he backed up a step. "Not gonna happen," said Mike, his voice level but sharp as a knife. "Now, let's quit the dance and tell your boss that we're here."

A voice from down the hall called out. "It's okay, boys. Let the agents in, please."

The guards looked at each other and stepped aside. The man they met in the hall was tall and well built, with close-cropped gray hair. He wore a shoulder holster over his crisp white button-down shirt.

"Welcome, folks. Don't mind the boys, just doing their job. Please follow me. The senator is waiting."

He turned sharply, and they followed him to a door

at the end of the corridor. He pushed open the door and stepped aside. Mike and Ronnie stepped into the room.

Senator Stevenson was sitting behind a huge wood desk, looking at some papers. He pushed the papers aside and rose from the chair. He looked up at Mike and froze. He recovered, but Mike and Ronnie had both caught the moment of recognition.

The senator reached Mike and Ronnie and shook their hands.

"What can I do for Homeland Security today?" he asked, covering his surprise by turning and heading back to his desk.

Mike walked over and took a seat in front of him. Ronnie stood next to the desk and casually placed a small listening device under the lip of the desk.

"Sir, Homeland Security has been hearing rumblings that there is going to be an attempt on the lives of the president- and vice president–elect. We know you have a lot of supporters all over the country, and we were wondering if you or your security team had heard anyone discussing an operation like that?"

The senator looked uncomfortable. "Are you accusing me or my supporters of wrongdoing, agent?"

"Absolutely not, sir, but since you were the other candidate in the race, we wanted to make sure you hadn't been threatened. Our goal is to protect you. If there is a plot to overthrow the legitimate government and interfere with the peaceful transfer of power, we wanted to make sure that you were safe, sir. We don't know how deep this might go, and we would hate for all the candidates for president to be attacked at once."

The senator paused for a moment, deep in thought. He looked up. "I see your point, agent. If something terrible were to happen to the president- and vice president–elect, the country would need someone to step up and take their place at a moment of crisis. I appreciate you looking out for me, but I can assure you, we have not heard of anything related to your information, and my security staff is top-notch." He stood. "Now, if there's nothing else, I have a meeting to attend. Thank you for coming and thank you for your service to this great nation."

Mike and Ronnie stood, shook his hand and walked to the door, which opened as they approached. They were escorted to the front door and walked to their SUV. Once inside, Ronnie opened an app on her phone, and Mike pulled away from the house.

"What's the range?" asked Mike.

Ronnie, pushing buttons, said, "Couple of hundred yards."

They passed through the gate, and Mike turned onto the highway. He pulled to the side of the road, out of sight of the mansion, and waited.

Ronnie looked up from her phone. "Did you see his reaction when he saw you? It was like he was looking at a ghost. Guess that answers one question. We know how they found you."

Mike looked at her and she held up her finger. She pushed a button on the phone and set it on the console. Mike could hear ringing. Then, the senator's voice came on the line. They couldn't hear the other side of the conversation.

"It's me. That Branik guy you had me check out was just in my office. ID says he works for Homeland Security. What the hell is going on? I thought he was supposed to be dead."

Silence.

"Well, you had better fucking handle it, because he was asking about a plot to take over the country and kill the president- and vice president–elect."

Silence.

"I don't give a shit about your excuses. This guy has me in his sights, and you need to fix this."

Silence.

"Then send another team. We have hundreds of thousands of friends. Send an entire fucking army if you have to, but fix this now!"

They heard the phone slam into the desk and then the door opened. Someone walked into the room.

"Yes, sir."

"Those agents that just left might be trouble. Increase security here at the house and lock the place down. If we don't know them, they don't get in. Clear?"

"Yes, sir. I'll take care of it personally."

They heard footsteps walking away and then silence. They could hear ice dropping into a glass and the lid being removed from a glass decanter. Liquid poured into the glass.

Mike put the SUV in gear and pulled onto the highway. They had gotten what they came for. Now they needed to react to it.

Chapter Twenty-Four

Jeff Halsey pulled his truck into the snow-covered parking lot of Tiny's Café and Bar on the outer edge of Bozeman, Montana. As he drove through the lot, he noticed a lot of pickup trucks and SUVs with STEVENSON FOR PRESIDENT signs still attached to their doors and bumpers. He figured this would be a good place to start.

Bozeman, Montana, was about twenty miles from Thomas Baker's ranch. Baker, the president-elect, had been the governor of Montana for eight years before running for president. With his running mate, Elizabeth Hanford, they had created a massive coalition across the country, which led to a huge win at the polls in November. The problem was that with their victory, they couldn't bring Congress along on their coattails.

Their victory was more of a stop-Stevenson movement than anything else. Stevenson, as a U.S. senator, had come across as someone unhinged during the campaign, and many of his ideas turned off even seasoned Republicans. Much of the country trusted their congresspeople, so even though Baker won by double digits, he would face a hostile Congress for the first two years of his administration.

The ranch in Montana had been in his family since the beginning of the state. His twice-great-grandfather had settled the land before most people back east had even heard of the Montana territory. It was just the old man and the Native American tribes he had taken the land from. When gold and silver were discovered on the land, the Baker family was rolling in money. Now, under the former governor's reign, they raised cattle and horses and farmed corn and wheat. It was a place where the governor felt safe, but it was also a place where dislike for Baker ran high.

Jeff parked his truck next to a truck that had four Stevenson flags hanging off it. With the election being almost two months ago, this seemed odd, but then Stevenson's followers had done a lot of strange shit during the campaign. Some would have called his followers a cult. Jeff thought it was worse than that.

Jeff picked up his beat-up STEVENSON FOR PRESIDENT hat off the seat, put it on and slid out of his truck. He checked to make sure the gun in his back waist holster was accessible and walked to the entrance. He opened the door, and loud music filled his ears. The bar was packed. Jeff strode towards the bar like he owned the place, nodding to several tables as he passed. He found an empty seat and ordered a draft beer from the bartender. He turned to face the room and looked around. The bar looked like a Stevenson for President field office. These were hardworking and hard-looking people out for a good time on a Friday night, and the seven waiters and waitresses he saw couldn't keep up with the demand.

Jeff took a sip from his beer and was about to turn when two guys approached and stopped in front of him.

"Ain't seen you around here before," said the shorter one, who slurred his words as he puffed out his chest.

His taller partner nodded.

Jeff stared at them. He noticed the bartender reach under the bar and pick up a small wood billy club. He held it at his right thigh.

Jeff turned and took another sip of his beer.

“Hey, pal,” said the tall guy. “My friend here is talkin’ to ya.”

Jeff turned and faced the tall guy. “Just passin’ through, pal. Saw some signs in the parkin’ lot said this might be a nice place to stop for a beer with some like-minded folk.”

The shorter guy stepped up. “How we knows you ain’t some gov’ment spy?” Spit rolled down his chin.

“You get a lot of government spies in here, do ya?” asked Jeff.

“Hey, you sassin’ my friend?” asked the tall guy. He pushed his hand into Jeff’s chest.

Jeff looked over his shoulder at the bartender. “You know I’m about to beat these two into the floor. You come after me with that club and I’m gonna shove it up your ass so far it will take the doctor a week to find it.” Jeff smiled.

The two guys looked at each other and then at the bartender.

“You two, back the fuck off,” said a voice behind Jeff. “I can see from the looks of this fella that you are about to get your shit handed to you. Charlie, put that club back under the bar.”

The bartender put the club back on the shelf. Jeff turned to see who was doing the talking. The two guys backed up.

"Sorry about that, friend. Rudy and Barnes can get a little uppity when they've had too much to drink." He held out his hand. "Mitch O'Toole. This is my place. Let me get you another beer." He signaled to the bartender, who placed another glass of beer on the counter.

Jeff shook his hand. "Mark Goodson. Pleased to meet you."

"What brings you to town?" asked O'Toole.

"Just passin' through. Been working in Washington and heading home to Pennsylvania for the holidays. Haven't seen my kids in over a year. Looking forward to it."

"What do you do?" O'Toole asked.

"Whatever I can. Been working as a lumberjack most recently."

"When did you leave the service?" asked O'Toole. "You look like you can handle yourself."

Jeff smiled. "I do all right. I wouldn't have hurt those guys too bad. Been out about five years."

"You see action?"

Jeff laughed. "Oh, yeah. Plenty. Nothing I can talk about though."

Now it was O'Toole's turn to smile. "Yeah, thought that might be the case. Well, listen, enjoy your beer and stay as long as you want. Lots of these folks sleep in their cars on Friday and Saturday nights. Cops won't bother you." He shook Jeff's hand and stepped away.

Jeff turned back to his beer. He spent the next two hours listening to various conversations happening throughout the bar. He didn't want to overstay his welcome, so he decided to move on. He finished his beer and paid his tab.

He walked across the parking lot and was about to get into his truck when two shadows approached. He spun, pulling his pistol and pointing at the first shadow. The guy raised his hands and took a step back.

"Easy there, fella, just want to talk," he said. He was a medium-height white guy wearing jeans and a long-range coat. He had a beanie on his head. The second guy was shorter but built like a fireplug. His muscles were clear under his puffy coat, and he wore a STEVENSON FOR PRESIDENT ball cap.

Jeff held the pistol steady. "Talk," he said.

"We've been watching you, and it's clear you can handle yourself. We might have a spot for you," said the taller guy.

"Not lookin' for a job," said Jeff. "Heading back east to see my kids for Christmas."

"I can respect that, but we've got something going down soon that could change the world. You might want to be part of it."

Jeff holstered his pistol. "What would I have to do?"

"Give me your number," said the tall guy. "We'll call you in the morning and meet someplace to talk."

“Someplace cheap around here I can get a room?” asked Jeff.

“Yeah,” said the short guy. “About two miles down this road on the right. Little motel. Tell Mary that Barry sent you.”

Jeff turned and slid into his truck and headed for the motel.

Chapter Twenty-Five

Robert E. Lee Richardson disconnected the call and sat back in his chair. He didn't appreciate Senator Stevenson calling him at home and climbing up his ass. He stood, walked to the bar and poured himself a glass of bourbon. He walked back to his desk and sat. The last conversation he'd had with Jimmy Bronson was clear and concise. Find this Mike Branik guy and kill him and anyone with him. It sounded simple enough to him, and since he hadn't heard from Jimmy in the past two days, he figured everything had been fine, and that they had gone radio silent while preparing for the mission.

Richardson picked up his phone and dialed a number.

"Yes, sir," said Jimmy as he answered the phone.

"What the fuck happened?" asked Richardson.

"About what, sir?"

"About what?" Richardson asked incredulously. "That Branik guy just left the senator's home in Virginia. He's supposed to be dead. That's about what."

"I'm trying to piece together what went wrong. We found out where this Branik guy lives, and I recruited a local crew out of Colorado to handle it. These guys were all veterans. Top-notch guys. They were planning to hit the place early yesterday morning, and I couldn't reach them. I assumed they were finished and lying low, but your call changed that. I told them to call me when it was done with an update. That's why I've been trying to get their leader. Tried calling the sheriff's office up that way, but they have no information. I'm not sure what the hell happened."

"This is not good, Jimmy. How much exposure do we have?" asked Richardson.

"We shouldn't get any blowback. The Colorado guys were given no information other than the guy's whereabouts, so nothing can come back on you."

"Jimmy, you need to handle this. I don't want the senator calling me again about this. By the way. He said the guy had Homeland Security credentials. I thought you checked him out."

"I did," said Jimmy. "My guy at Homeland couldn't find anything. Is the senator sure he works at Homeland?"

"How the fuck do I know?" said Richardson. "That's what he told me, and I'm not gonna question him about it. Fuck, Jimmy, get this handled."

"Yes, sir," said Jimmy.

"Hey, before you hang up. What's your status?"

"We're good, sir. The team is assembled and on-site, and we are running simulations drills. There should be no trouble. Some of the boys wanted to attend the rally at the Capitol on January sixth, but I told them no. We are going to go radio silent as of tomorrow. If you need to get hold of me, you know how; otherwise, we're going dark and won't resurface until we're in Montana."

"Good," said Richardson. "Good luck, Jimmy."

Richardson disconnected the call and took a sip of his bourbon. He didn't like that this Branik guy had showed up at the senator's house. He hoped the senator had kept his cool and not let anything slip. Things were moving too fast for any hiccups.

He picked up a paper from his desk. It was the copy of an email that he would send to invite all the militia people to show up outside the Capitol on January 6. The certification vote was to take place at noon, and he wanted all parties in place so they could storm the Capitol at eleven A.M. to stop the vote. His email and social media posts did not specifically tell his followers to bring weapons, but he made it clear that the purpose of this march was to spill the blood of tyrants. He figured everyone would get the message.

He was expecting a million militia members to show up. More than enough to tear down the fences and overtake the National Guard and the police. He knew that Senator Stevenson had huge support among the Washington, DC, Metro Police and that the members of the National Guard would join the assault as soon as it started. And if some senators or representatives were hurt or killed, well, that was the price of freedom.

Richardson picked up his phone and called his office. He asked to be patched through to Jerry, one of his most loyal IT techs.

"Yes, sir," said Jerry.

"Jerry, I looked at the text. Have the department

send out the emails and let's cover social media. I want this on every site, no matter how obscure, and I want it posted hourly. We'll bury social media, like we are going to bury the Capitol."

"No worries, Mr. Richardson. I'll get everyone mobilized."

"Thanks, Jerry. Let me know if you run into any problems."

"Shouldn't be any problems, sir. You own most of the sites, and for those you don't own, your people have already spoken with those owners and everyone is on board."

Richardson disconnected the call. His call to arms to the white Christian militias would be heard far and wide, and nothing would stop the takeover of the Capitol. If they could stop the certification, then all would be good, but if they couldn't, then Jimmy and his team would stop the inauguration cold. Either way, January was going to be a huge month for the Stevenson for President team, and the help from the militias would be heralded in songs and literature. January 20 would be the day White America reclaimed their country.

Chapter Twenty-Six

Mike and Ronnie spent Christmas Day on the ranch restoring the defensive countermeasures and adding some new ones. The attack on the ranch had been short-lived, and the devices had done their job, but Mike wanted to increase the firepower around the ranch.

Mary had weathered the storm fine, but she kept a loaded shotgun in the kitchen and in her bedroom, and she kept a switch pistol in the pocket of her vest.

While Mike tinkered around the ranch, Ronnie sat at the kitchen table and worked on her laptop. Mike walked in and shook off the snow from his jacket. The weather report had called for an additional foot of snow overnight, and it looked like the forecasters were right. Mike took off his jacket and gloves and rubbed his hands together. He walked over to the counter, poured a cup of coffee and held the cup with both hands.

"Any luck?" he asked.

"Yeah, some," said Ronnie. "I got a friend at the NSA to do a cell tower dump around the senator's house. He made the one call we heard after we left. That call went to a burner phone, and my friend is trying to track it, because it's still active."

Ronnie's laptop chimed with an incoming message. She clicked on the message.

"Cell tracks to an address in Nashville. I'm running

a property search right now."

She clicked a few keys and pulled up a satellite image of a sprawling property. "Property belongs to Robert E. Lee and Dorothy Richardson. I'll run a quick background check."

Mike stopped her. "Don't bother. Richardson is a billionaire media mogul. He is the founder and CEO of Patriot Media Enterprises. He controls most of the right-wing media in this country, and he's tapped into a dozen different militia groups."

"Have you run into him before?" asked Ronnie.

"Yeah, years ago. If there's a plot to kill the president-elect, then you can bet he's behind it or he's financing it. He's a big fan of Senator Stevenson."

"What are we gonna do?" she asked.

"The FBI has a full file on him. Pull that up and let's look at his associations and see who might have the muscle and the talent to pull off an attack on the president-elect. Have we gotten anything back on their schedules yet?"

"I tried, but the Secret Service is keeping everything close to the vest. I sent a message to the president to see if he can shake something loose. So far, no one seems to be aware of any serious threat to the elects. Maybe we're chasing ghosts and there is no plot. They'd have to be nuts to kill both."

"Okay, keep trying. Have you heard from Jeff?"

"Not since yesterday. He texted me he was in Bozeman and thought he might have connected with a couple of locals. Was supposed to meet with them sometime today."

"I'm worried about him being up there alone," said Mike.

He pulled out his phone and dialed a number. Arnie Stern answered on the first ring.

"Hey, Mike. Merry Christmas."

"Hiya, Arnie. The same to you," said Mike. "Listen, Arnie, I hate to pull you away from Christmas, but Jeff's doing some surveillance in Bozeman, Montana, and I'm concerned. Can you pull away from the family and head up there to back him up?"

"No problem, Mike. The kids have already opened their gifts, so yeah. I can head up there later today. I'll get a flight out this afternoon and let him know I'm coming. Anything I need to know?"

"Yeah. We may be looking at a potential attack on the president- and vice president–elect. He's up there shaking the trees to see what kind of nuts fall out."

"You serious, Mike? You think someone wants to kill them?"

"Yeah. That's the only way to stop them from being inaugurated. They have to disappear after January sixth but before January twentieth in order for Stevenson to be appointed president by Congress."

"Fuck, Mike," said Arnie. "Do we know who's involved?"

"Might be militias. The president is concerned that some members of the Secret Service might be compromised, but there's not much he can do, other than reassign agents, but that might make things worse since he doesn't know who to trust."

"So that's where we come in," said Arnie.

"Correct. For the next couple of days, we need to keep this low-key and see if the threat is real, then we'll know how to respond."

"No worries, Mike. I'm halfway to Bozeman."

Mike disconnected the call and dialed a second number. Bill Rogers answered the call.

"Hey, Mike. Merry Christmas."

"Same to you, Bill. You doing anything right now?"

"Sitting on my ass waiting for a football game to come on the TV. Spoke to the kids this morning. They got the gifts I sent; they were heading for the beach. What's up?"

"I need you to head to Nashville and do a little recon," said Mike. He gave Bill the same information he had given Arnie. "Need to stay low-key. Ronnie will send you the name and address of the guy I want you to watch. I'd like to get some electronic surveillance on him. Also see if you can pick up any local chatter about a potential plot. As soon as I can get hold of Stosh, I'll have him hook up with you. These guys are dangerous, Bill, so keep your head on a swivel."

"No worries, Mike. I'll get rolling and should be there by nightfall."

"Thanks, Bill."

Mike disconnected the call and dialed one more

number. Gregory Stoshakowski answered.

"Hiya, Mike. What's up?"

"Hey, Stosh, you ready to go back to work?" asked Mike.

"Fuck yeah. Sitting in a bar in Fort Lauderdale at noon on Christmas Day. What a life. What are we working on?"

Mike filled him in, and Stosh was quiet on the phone for a few seconds.

"This Richardson guy. Didn't we run into him a couple of years back? Gunrunning and human trafficking, if I remember right. Got off scot-free because his lawyer was some big deal."

"That's the guy," said Mike. "Want another shot at him?"

"Fuck yeah," said Stosh. "Where am I going?"

"Ronnie will send you what you need to know. Call Bill and figure out where to meet up."

"No worries, Mike."

Stosh disconnected the call, and Mike looked at Ronnie. "Well," he said. "The troops are rolling. Let's grab some lunch and then dig into the FBI file and start looking at all Richardson's contacts."

Chapter Twenty-Seven

Jeff Halsey parked his truck in the parking lot of the Blue Sky Diner and walked through the fresh snow to the door. The six inches of snow that fell overnight made everything feel quiet and fresh. The sunlight poking through the clouds was warm but had trouble cutting through the below-zero morning. Jeff pushed open the door and was engulfed by the smell of bacon cooking. He stepped inside and spotted his two friends from the night before sitting at a table in the corner.

Earl Slocum and Barry Crane shook his hand as he sat in the open seat, and a server named Molly brought over a cup of coffee and a menu.

"Mary able to take care of you last night?" asked Barry. He picked up his coffee and took a sip.

"Yeah," said Jeff. "Got me a nice room and some good sleep after a long day on the road yesterday."

The server came back and refilled their coffee cups, and they ordered breakfast. Jeff put his cup down.

"So, what you fellas want to talk about?" he asked.

Barry looked at Earl. "I like this guy already. Gets right down to business."

Jeff looked at Barry and smiled. "Just tryin' to beat the next storm so I can get home sooner than later."

"I appreciate that," said Barry. "So, we'll cut to the chase. From the way you responded in the bar last night, you can obviously handle yourself. We're like the marines. We're looking for a few good, like-minded men for a special project. Can't tell you much about it right now, but it's gonna happen in the next three weeks, and the pay. Well, the pay will knock your socks off."

The server came by and set down three huge platters of eggs, bacon, sausage, pancakes and hash browns. It was enough to feed an army. Jeff took a few bites.

"What kind of money we talkin'?" he asked.

"Hundred grand each," said Barry.

Jeff stopped eating and looked from Earl to Barry.

"Hundred grand. What do I got to do, kill the president?"

Barry pushed back from the table. "What made you say that?" he asked, a scowl on his face.

Jeff laughed. "Just jokin', fellas. I ain't never seen that kind of money. Seriously, what I got to do to earn that?"

Barry looked at Earl, then back to Jeff.

"When you figuring you'll be coming back through here after you see your kids?" asked Barry.

"First part of next week. Boss gave me two weeks off. Figure I'll be home in two days, weather permitting, couple days with the kids and then three days to get back to Washington."

Earl handed Jeff a card with a phone number on it. "You get back in town, you give us a call. You help us out and you sure as hell won't need that plumbing job in Washington."

Jeff smiled. "Lumberjackin'. That's what I been doin' in Washington. Lumberjackin'."

Earl and Barry finished their meals, and Earl pulled a big roll of cash out of his pocket, pulled off a couple of twenties and laid them on the table.

He reached out his hand, and Jeff took it. "Breakfast is on us. Safe travels, and don't forget to call when you get back here."

They stood, grabbed their coats and nodded to the server as they left. Jeff finished his breakfast and asked the server for a refill on his coffee. He sat for a minute, running their conversation through his head. He felt a tingle up his spine, and he wondered what was going on. He had the feeling he'd said something wrong, but when he ran back the conversation in his head, he couldn't think what it was, unless it was the comment about killing the president. Maybe that went a shade too far.

He needed to be on high alert, so he finished his coffee, grabbed his coat and headed for the door. The light snow that was falling made everything look like a picture postcard, and he pulled up his collar.

Jeff had unlocked the truck and pulled open the door when he was struck from behind. He fell onto the front seat as someone punched him in the kidneys. He was stuck on the seat and getting pummeled.

Barry grabbed him by his back collar and pulled him from the seat, spun him around and punched him in the face. Blood splattered from his nose as he tried to get to his feet.

"What are you, some kind of cop?" he yelled. He hit him again as Earl kicked his legs out from under him, and he flopped onto the snow, wedged up against the open door.

Jeff reached under the seat and pulled out a small expandable baton, flipped it and caught Earl across his knees just as he was about to kick him again. Barry punched him on the side of the head, and he felt like he was going to black out. Earl was lying on the ground, holding his knees and screaming in pain. Barry reached under his coat just as an arm wrapped around his neck and pulled him backwards. Whoever grabbed him kicked him in the back of his knee, and he fell to the ground. His pistol fell out from under his coat and hit the snow. He reached for the gun, but a boot crashed down on his wrist. The snap as his wrist bones broke could be heard on the other side of the parking lot. Barry screamed.

Arnie Stern grabbed Barry by the collar, lifted him up and smashed his fist into his face. Blood splattered. The second time he did it, Barry collapsed and didn't move. He turned his attention to Earl, who was trying to stand. He kicked Earl in the right knee, and as he fell forward, he drove his knee into Earl's face. Earl flew backwards and hit the side of Jeff's truck. As he was sliding down the side of the truck, Arnie grabbed his collar, jerked him up and smashed a powerful right hand into his face. The fight went out of Earl, and he lay unconscious on the ground.

A crowd had gathered on the sidewalk in front of the restaurant, and people had their cell phones out taking videos, which would be online before the first cops arrived. Sirens could be heard in the distance, and two county sheriff SUVs pulled into the lot.

Arnie was helping Jeff to his feet when the first deputy jumped out of his SUV and looked at the mess on the ground that was Barry and Earl. He pulled his pistol and pointed it towards Arnie.

"Hands in the air!" he yelled.

Arnie had Jeff under the arms and was sitting him on the driver's seat. He looked over his shoulder.

"Call an ambulance," he said.

The deputy, now backed up by a second deputy, also aiming his pistol, yelled again.

"Hands where I can see them!"

Arnie yelled back, "This man is hurt. Get a fucking ambulance."

The second deputy spoke into his shoulder mic. The first one repeated his command a third time. Arnie stood up, turned and looked at the deputy. He was about to move when the server stepped forward, holding up her cell phone.

"Toby," she said, talking to the first deputy. "We all have it on video. That guy jumped in to help the other guy who was getting the shit beat out of him by those two on the ground." The second deputy walked over and watched the video. He looked away and keyed his mic, said something so the crowd couldn't hear and walked over to the first deputy.

"Lower your weapon, man. The two guys on the ground are the ones who jumped the other guy. This guy jumped in to help."

The first deputy, looking unsure, lowered his weapon. A siren grew louder, and an ambulance pulled into the parking lot, followed by a third sheriff's department SUV. The sheriff, a tall thin man with brown hair and brown eyes, slid out of his SUV and walked over to the two deputies.

"What have you got?" he asked.

The second deputy walked him over and they looked at the video. The sheriff walked past the first deputy and approached Arnie.

"That video says you're a hero. Why'd you step in to help this fella?"

The paramedics were walking Jeff over to the ambulance, and a second ambulance pulled into the lot. The sheriff turned and faced his deputies. "When they get these two in the ambulance, make sure you cuff them to the gurney."

He turned back to Arnie. "Where were we? Oh, that's right. You were about to tell me why you got involved."

Arnie smiled and pointed to the flag on the sheriff's collar. "Where I come from, that still means something, and you don't leave a fallen comrade behind."

He then pointed at the sticker in the back window of Jeff's truck that said ONCE A MARINE, ALWAYS A MARINE.

The sheriff smiled. "The country needs more folks

like you. Thanks for your service. We'll need a statement, if you don't mind stopping by the office."

"No problem, Sheriff. Happy to."

The sheriff walked away to confer with the two deputies, and Arnie pulled out his phone and dialed Mike.

"What's up?" asked Mike.

"We got a problem," said Arnie.

Chapter Twenty-Eight

Mike hung up the phone and looked at Ronnie. "Pull everything you can find on the two guys that jumped Jeff, and let's see if they're connected to this thing." He picked up the phone and dialed a number.

"Mike. What's up?" asked the president.

"Sir, Jeff was jumped by two guys who told him they were planning something big in Montana in the next two to three weeks."

"Is Jeff okay?" asked the president, interrupting Mike.

"According to Arnie, he'll be okay. I need a favor, sir. Can you pull some strings and get me a federal warrant for sedition and have the two prisoners turned over to me?"

"What are you going to do with them, Mike? Or don't I want to know?"

"It's better you don't know, sir. We'll handle them with kid gloves."

The president laughed. "Yeah, that's what I'm afraid of. You going to use your Homeland IDs again?"

"Yes, sir."

"Okay, Mike. Sit tight and I'll get back to you."

"Thanks, sir."

Mike clicked off the call. "Ronnie, call our friends in Cheyenne and let's get a flight to Bozeman."

Ronnie picked up her phone, and while she was calling the air force base in Cheyenne, Wyoming, Mike was flipping through some pages Ronnie had uploaded to his laptop. Robert E. Lee Richardson had long arms that reached all the way to several seats of power, both state and federal. The FBI had an extensive file on him and his cronies—he was suspected in several murders related to militia activities, and he had been charged several times with sedition, gunrunning and human trafficking—but nothing they could make stick. He had some of the best constitutional lawyers in the country working for him, and he had the money to push off any prosecution indefinitely.

Mike was looking for a connection between Senator Stevenson and Richardson when he spotted something and sat back in his chair. Ronnie had hung up from the air force and looked across the table at him.

"What's up?" she asked.

"Richardson invests in a lot of causes and organizations. Some religious, some not. He's always careful to disclose his contributions because he knows his lawyers will fight like hell to make sure nothing blows back on him. He thinks he's untouchable. One of his contributions year after year is to the Conservative Christian Action Team."

"Yeah, and?" asked Ronnie.

"The CCAT is run by a guy named Jimmy Bronson. He's a real religious zealot. Thinks God controls everything in our lives and believes he and his militia members have been ordained by God to work on his behalf here on earth. Has a following of maybe a hundred fanatical followers. Last I heard, he had been unceremoniously discharged from the army. No reason given, but there was scuttlebutt that he was involved in a series of weapons thefts from several Southern bases. They couldn't convict him because they didn't have the evidence, but they had enough reason to discharge him from the military. He promised retribution and revenge on anyone who wronged him.

"In 2018, two members of the military tribunal that heard his discharge case were found murdered in their homes. Both lived off base, so the crimes were investigated by the local authorities with assistance from Army CID. The CID investigator was my late wife, and her life was threatened several times by Bronson or his followers. She couldn't get anything to stick, and when she took a medical discharge, I thought it was all over, but several unexplained incidents happened at our house, and she was accosted once at her car at the grocery store. When she died, we received a bouquet of dead black roses that were sent to the funeral home. I always believed it was Bronson's doing but could never prove it."

"All well and good, Mike, but what does that have to do with our investigation?" asked Ronnie.

"Bronson's crew are some of the best-trained militiamen. They would be the equivalent of the Navy Seals in the Christian militia world. Get this info off to Bill and Stosh. We need to know where Jimmy Bronson is and what he's doing."

Ronnie opened an encrypted email and sent the information to Stosh and Bill. Her email clicked with an incoming encrypted email. She ran it through the encryption program and sent it to the printer.

"Warrant's in. The president came through."

Mike looked at the warrant coming off the printer and smiled. "He got a Supreme Court justice to sign the warrant. Great. Let's head to Montana and pick up our prisoners."

They grabbed their gear and stopped in the kitchen to let Mary know where they were heading.

"You two be careful," she said as they headed for Mike's SUV. They had a two-hour drive to get to Cheyenne.

The MATS flight to Bozeman was quick, and they grabbed a government SUV from the military motor pool. They drove to the Gallatin County Sheriff's Office and pulled into a visitor's space near the front door. They slid from the SUV and pushed open the door. A deputy on duty at the front desk asked how he could help them. They presented their Homeland Security IDs and asked to speak with the sheriff.

After a few minutes of waiting, Sheriff Caleb Winslow stepped through a side door and approached them.

Sheriff Winslow was in his forties and was trim and fit. He stood about six feet tall and had brown hair and brown eyes. His badge sparkled as the light hit it.

"You the folks from Homeland Security?" he asked as he extended his hand.

Mike introduced himself and Ronnie, and they shook hands.

"What can I do for Homeland today?" asked the sheriff.

Mike pulled the arrest warrant out of his pocket and handed it to the sheriff.

"Sheriff, you've got two men on ice: Earl Slocum and Barry Crane. We'll be taking them off your hands."

The sheriff read the warrant and looked at the signature. "This is signed by a justice of the Supreme Court. Mind if I ask what these fellas did to warrant that kind of attention?"

"Sedition," said Mike. "They're wanted for their part in a domestic terrorist plot to attack the president. An attack that killed two Secret Service agents. We've been looking for these guys for a while. Just curious, but what did they do to end up in your jail?"

"They picked on the wrong guy. Jumped a guy in the parking lot of a diner. A guy they just had lunch with. Patrons got the attack on their phones. They beat the guy up pretty good before another guy pulled into the lot, saw the altercation and got involved. Guy was former military and, well, let's just say that when he was finished, they looked like they had gone a couple of rounds with Joe Louis. Follow me?"

The sheriff led them through the door he had come out of and down a long hallway to the jail section of the justice center. He handed the paperwork to the jail supervisor and turned to face Mike and Ronnie.

"He'll bring your prisoners right out. If you want, pull your car into the sally port and we'll get them loaded for you."

They shook hands, and the sheriff walked away. Ronnie took the keys from Mike and headed for the entrance to get the SUV. She pulled it into the sally port and waited with the door open and the heat on.

Two jailers, leading the two prisoners, waited for the gate to be opened and approached Mike.

"Where you want them?" asked one of the jailers.

Mike looked at the two prisoners. Both men had bruising on their faces, and they walked slowly. Mike almost felt bad for them. Arnie had muscles he hardly used, and if he let loose on these guys, they were lucky to be alive. Barry looked up at Mike.

"Who the fuck are you?" he asked with a scowl.

Mike held up his ID. "Homeland Security. You're being transferred into our care."

"For what?"

"You're being arrested on federal sedition charges," said Mike.

"What the fuck," said Earl. "We haven't done nothing. This is bullshit. We ain't going. We know our rights."

Mike laughed. "You can tell it to the judge when we get you back to Denver."

Mike led the way down the hall, followed by the guards and the prisoners. He had the guards put one in the back seat, Ronnie sliding in next to him after they used the seat belt to secure him, and the other one went in the front seat, next to Mike. Mike thanked the guards and signed the release. As the door to the sally port rolled up, Mike pulled forward and turned onto the highway fronting the prison. Instead of turning towards the airport, Mike turned west and headed for the mountains.

Barry and Earl were quiet for the first part of the ride, but then they started to fidget.

"Where you takin' us?" asked Barry, concern on his face.

"Someplace we can talk," said Mike.

"Talk about what? We ain't done nothing. Had a local beef with some guy, but last I checked, that wasn't federal."

Mike looked over at him. "So, what are you, a constitutional scholar?" He laughed, as did Ronnie, who got a sideways look from Earl.

They drove for another twenty minutes and then pulled onto a dirt road that led to a log cabin along a stretch of frozen river. Mike pulled to a stop, and the front door to the cabin opened and Arnie stepped out onto the porch.

Barry's eyes got wide, and he looked at Mike. "What the fuck is this? We want our lawyer."

Mike smiled and opened the door. He walked around as Ronnie and Arnie opened the back door and yanked Earl out, pulling him by the leg shackles. His back slammed into the doorframe and then onto the hard-packed snow. Arnie grabbed him by the handcuffs and lifted him. Earl let out a yell as his arms pulled straight back. Arnie dragged him into the cabin. Mike followed, pulling a twisting and turning Barry, who was shouting vulgarities at him. They sat the two men on the chairs in the middle of the open room about ten feet apart and wire-tied them to the chairs. The chairs were sitting on a large blue plastic tarp, and both men fought the restraints.

Earl, wide-eyed and sweating, looked at Mike and then at Arnie.

"You can't do this. You're cops?"

Mike laughed. "You are so sadly mistaken. We can do whatever we want. No one knows we're here. The nearest neighbor is five miles downriver, and he only comes up in the summer. So, you can scream all you want. No one will hear you."

"What the fuck is this about? And why is this asshole here?" He pointed towards Arnie.

Arnie smiled. These guys were panicking, and they hadn't even started yet. That was a good sign.

Arnie gagged each man and put black hoods over their heads with noise-canceling headphones, and Mike turned out the lights. They headed for the kitchen. They could hear Barry and Earl taking deep, shaky breaths.

Chapter Twenty-Nine

Bill Rogers and Stosh sat in Bill's pickup truck and looked at the house behind the gate. They were surprised when they pulled up. Since this guy was a billionaire, they expected something bigger and grander than an old farmhouse with clapboard siding and a wraparound porch. The house had a lot of Southern charm, but it didn't look like the kind of place a media mogul would live in.

The sun had set two hours before and they watched as lights came on throughout the house. The black Cadillac Escalade pulled to the front gate and waited. The gate rolled back, and the car proceeded through. There was no sign of a guard anywhere near the front gate, so they assumed there must be cameras, or the car had a remote control for the gate. They settled in to wait to see who might visit Robert E. Lee Richardson. They didn't have to wait long.

Three cars, all expensive models, approached the gate, one after the other, and each time the gate opened automatically. Stosh watched the driveway through a 300-millimeter lens attached to an SLR digital camera. Each picture he took was uploaded to the cloud and directly to Ronnie's laptop. With luck, he'd know who was visiting Richardson before dinner was over. He reached for a piece of cold pizza and sat back, waiting for something to happen.

So far, the laser microphone that Bill had focused on the kitchen window hadn't picked up anything other than common kitchen noises. He moved the mic to what he assumed was the dining room window.

"How do we know his guys were captured?" asked a deep Southern voice.

The laser microphone did an amazing job using the glass window as an amplifier. The voices were as clear as if they were sitting in the same room. Bill turned on the recording app on his laptop and listened.

"He hasn't had any contact in a day and a half. They were supposed to check in every four hours. He can't raise them on their phones, and the owner of the motel they were staying at said the rooms hadn't been slept in. Something's wrong," said the voice.

"What does that do to our timetable?" asked a different voice.

"I think we're okay, Senator. I don't want to panic yet. We've got two weeks before we have to make our move, and we have a thirteen-day window to get it done. If something doesn't feel right, we'll pull the plug and move to an alternate plan."

"Do we have an alternate plan?" asked one of the voices.

"Robert," said a woman's voice. "I hate interrupting, but dinner is ready. Shall I serve?"

"Yes. Thank you, dear," said Robert. "Gentlemen, we'll resume this conversation after dinner."

Bill could hear china and glassware being moved around and the sound of food landing on plates. He hoped they were having something good as he grabbed the last piece of cold pizza and took a bite.

An hour later, he could hear the plates and glasses being cleared from the table and a chorus of *thank you*s and *that was wonderful*s were followed by the closing of a door.

“Getting back to my original question, Robert. Do we have an alternate plan?” said a voice.

“Yes, Judge. Of course we do. I’m not going to go into the details now because we are still working some things out. But the plan will be ready when we need it.”

“How are the plans coming for the Capitol rally?” asked one of the other men.

“Everything is in play. We’ve sent out emails to our brethren, and we are hammering the message on social media. My office has received thousands of calls wishing us well. I also heard that there has been a serious uptick in the purchasing of assault-style rifles and large-caliber handguns. I was talking to the owner of our local gun store, and he can’t bring in ammunition fast enough. We’re putting the ammo shortage on social media and blaming it on the current administration.”

Another voice spoke. Senator Oliver Stevenson, barked, “Judge, where the hell do we stand? These lawsuits . . . ?”

A cruel laugh, sharp as shattered glass, sliced through the silence. "Exactly where I predicted, Senator. The courts are spitting these pathetic filings back in our faces faster than a rabid dog can bite. Without a shred of tangible evidence, without a single verifiable instance of election fraud, your campaign is nothing but a monument to . . . well, let's just say monumental stupidity."

Stevenson's voice cracked, a raw tremor betraying the carefully constructed façade. "But I won. Fair and square."

Robert slammed his fist on the mahogany desk, the sound echoing the thunder of Stevenson's collapsing world. "Oliver," he spat, the name dripping with contempt, "stop your pathetic charade. You lost by twenty million votes. A landslide. We filed these ridiculous lawsuits because of . . . sentimentality. Friendship, even. But from the outset, I told you it was a fool's errand. A desperate gamble with reality itself."

Stevenson's voice, strained and desperate, whispered, "But the illegals . . . the millions of illegal votes . . ."

Robert's chair scraped back, a harsh metallic screech that mirrored the agonizing sound of Stevenson's crumbling delusion. "God in heaven, man! Listen to yourself! You sound like a deranged parrot squawking conspiracy theories. There weren't twenty million illegal votes. There wasn't even one, not in a way that could remotely impact the result. You. Lost. Period.

"And now, because of your insatiable ego, we're on the precipice of something illegal, something utterly reckless. Something that will land all of us in a place far worse than political oblivion."

Stevenson roared, "How dare you? Thirty years I've served this country! The White House is my rightful place!"

Robert's voice, low and dangerous, cut through the senator's bluster. "Shut up, Oliver. We've been burning the midnight oil, hemorrhaging resources on these lawsuits. I warned you, but your ego wouldn't allow you to hear reason. The only path left, the only sliver of hope, rests with Jimmy. His plan is audacious, and bordering on insane, but it's our one shot. He has people in place, dark horses ready to spring into action. But for now, go back to Washington. Keep your head down. Act normal. Pretend this . . . charade . . . never happened."

The taste of defeat was bitter, acrid, a poison consuming him. But the faintest spark of a reckless, impossible gamble still burned within him. He was not satisfied. Not by a long shot.

"Where is Jimmy?" asked Stevenson. "He should be here."

"Jimmy has gone dark," said Robert. "His team is ready and waiting to be deployed. As soon as we make sure none of his people have been compromised, he will set off for Montana. Gentlemen, it's getting late. I suggest we say good night."

Bill heard chairs sliding and the dining room door open, each man saying good night to Robert's wife as they left. He watched as the front door opened and saw Robert shake hands with the men. He noted that Robert held back the judge and closed the door.

Bill listened closely.

"Judge, I'm worried about Stevenson. Every time

we meet, he sounds like he's gone around another curve."

The judge laughed. "Tell me, Bob. Why did you back him?"

Robert laughed. "Because that cowboy from Montana is bad for the country."

"Okay," said the judge. "Oliver is a placeholder. We'll need a strong vice-presidential nominee to put before Congress, and not that loser he had on the ticket. We need someone who in, say, six months can take over and run this country the way we want it to run. That means we will also need a strong cabinet of people who feel like we do. Start putting together a list of people who are loyal to us, but not necessarily to Oliver. Understand?"

"No problem, Judge. I'll get started on that as soon as I get back from talking to Jimmy. I'm heading to North Carolina in the morning. I'm concerned about his two missing guys. It's not like his guys to go dark without a damn good reason. All our plans moving forward depend on him and his team."

Bill heard the door open and the men walking down the hall to the front door. The judge left without another word, and Bill heard the front door close. He pulled off his headphones and put down the microphone. He looked at Stosh.

"Send Mike a text. It looks like we're heading to North Carolina in the morning."

Chapter Thirty

After six hours of waiting, Mike felt it was time to see what their two guests had to say. They walked into the great room area and noticed the smell of urine. Both men, naked, were sitting in puddles of urine, and it ran down the chair legs and onto the plastic tarps. Both men were shaking.

Mike walked over and closed the patio door that had been open the entire time. The temperature in the room was uncomfortable. Jeff, recovering from his injuries, helped Arnie drag in a heavy leather-covered bag, and they hung it from a thick rope tied to the beam above. Arnie put on a pair of training gloves and got ready.

Since neither man could hear or see anything, it wasn't until Mike removed the headphones that the men knew they weren't alone. Mike stood between the men.

"Here's how this is going to work," said Mike. "We are going to soften one of you up. You won't see a thing, but you will know if you are the one getting beat on. When one of you is ready, we will start on the other. At some point, one of you will tell us what we want to know."

Arnie took his stance in front of the heavy bag and landed a massive right. The bag thudded, and both men jumped, each man thinking the other one was getting the tar beat out of him. Arnie threw a few more punches, and Mike could see that both men were visibly upset. If you were sitting in the dark, the sound would be enough to make you think your partner was being pummeled. Arnie hit the bag, working up a sweat. Earl's bowels let go, and he shook. Mike held up his hand, and Arnie stopped hitting the bag. Mike walked over to Earl leaned next to his ear.

"Something you want to tell us?" asked Mike. Earl shook his head.

Mike stood, and Arnie hit the bag again. Each time he hit the bag, Barry jumped, thinking the worst was happening to Earl. Mike held up his hand after another ten minutes. Arnie was exhausted, but a few sips of water were enough to revive him.

Mike stood behind Barry and whispered, "Barry. Are you ready to help us out?"

Barry nodded, and Mike signaled Arnie to take a breather. Mike stepped over to Earl and put the headphones back over his ears, and Earl squirmed and groaned.

With Earl secure, Mike raised the hood enough to clear Barry's mouth and removed the gag. Barry sucked in some air and asked for water. Mike held a bottle of water up and let him sip it. Then he took the bottle away.

"Is Earl all right?" asked Barry.

"Nothing a few weeks in a hospital won't fix," said Jeff. Tears dropped from under the mask and landed on Barry's legs.

"Barry. We're gonna keep this simple. What is the plan to stop the inauguration and make Stevenson president?"

"I don't know," said Barry. "Jimmy was keepin' that shit close to the vest. All I know is that he has a small team, and whatever they are planning is going to happen in Montana."

"What was your job? You and Earl."

"We were up in Montana to recruit some local help. Lots of militia folks up that way, so we just had to pick to make sure we had the right people. We were the backup plan."

"How many people did you recruit?"

Barry was quiet for a few seconds. "Not many. We were just getting started. We were gonna spend a few days hitting some of the local bars, spread some money around for drinks and talk to folks, then we would choose who to approach. Jimmy wanted at least twenty people, but they had to be like-minded people who believed in the cause. We were going to be the first line of defense if the government fought back."

"Barry. What cause are you talking about?" asked Mike.

"You know. People who think the woke government has overstepped its bounds. People who want to return to an America where everyone knew their place."

"So, a white, Christian America," said Mike. "Where everyone follows your rules."

"White people were bred to be in charge. We have the intelligence and the drive to lead those less fortunate."

Barry sat quietly. Mike looked at Jeff, who shook his head and frowned.

"How is Jimmy going to get to the president-elect?"

Barry shook. "We have people on the presidential security team. I don't know who, but Jimmy said it would be easy when the time came."

"Barry, where is Jimmy now?" asked Mike.

"Don't know. That's the God's honest truth. I know he has a place in North Carolina, but I don't know where. It's like a training base for his team. Real hush-hush stuff."

"Barry, do you know any of the members of his team?"

"No. No one ever uses names. Jimmy said that way the government can't hurt us if they grab one of us."

Mike gave Barry another sip of water, put the gag back in his mouth and pulled the hood down. "Barry, we're gonna have a talk with Earl. If he corroborates what you told us, we'll see about sending you on your way." He put the headphones back over his ears.

"What do you think?" asked Jeff.

"I think Barry and Earl are hired guns. Not privy to the inner workings of the group. We have their phones. We'll see who they've been in contact with and try to put together a picture of this first line of defense. Let's get a message to Stosh and see if they can track down the North Carolina training camp."

"What about them?" asked Arnie, who had stepped back into the room sipping from a bottle of beer. "You think he believes that crap he was just spewing, or is he just parroting shit he heard?"

Mike looked at both poor excuses for human beings, wallowing in their own shit and piss. They didn't look superior to anyone.

"I think deep down inside, they believe what they've been fed. The sad part is, if history is any indicator, the people in charge will fuck them over as fast as everyone else and they'll never see it coming."

"So, what do you think the plan is, Mike?" asked Ronnie, stepping into the great room from the kitchen. "Is this gonna be a straight-up snatch and grab?"

Mike sat on the arm of the leather couch. "I don't know. What bothers me is that they have people on the presidential security team. That leaves them a lot of options."

"You don't think they'll try to assassinate the president-elect, do you?" asked Arnie.

Mike pondered the question. "If they did, then the VP-elect would take over. That doesn't sound like it would get them what they want."

"What if they killed them both?" asked Ronnie.

Mike's phone chimed. He read the note and dialed a number.

"Stosh, how much of the plan did you overhear?"

"Hey, Mike. Lots of talk about putting Stevenson into the White House. They didn't talk about the plan. Only that this Jimmy Bronson guy was running the show and he's gone dark. We're gonna follow the big guy to North Carolina in the morning and see what else we can get."

"Okay, Stosh. You guys stay safe."

Mike walked around the room for a minute. He stopped and looked at the group. He looked at Ronnie.

"That's interesting. When Roman flew to the ranch, we had that same discussion. The president elect and VP-elect have to be alive on January sixth so the election can be certified. If they die before that, then a special election is called for, but after January twentieth the Speaker of the House becomes president until the election. Once the election is certified, then all bets are off. They would need to die before January twentieth, and then Congress could select a president. So, the only way Stevenson becomes president is if the president and VP-elect die between January sixth and January twentieth. The closer to the twentieth, the better for Stevenson."

"If Rome already thought about this, why doesn't he just tell the FBI and the Secret Service and let them deal with it?" asked Arnie.

Jeff stood up and looked around the room. "Too much division in this country. Rome doesn't know who he can trust other than us. If the security details are compromised, then all bets are off." He looked at Mike. "That means we are going to be facing off against our own people."

"Absolutely," said Mike. "We've always been square with each other. This could get hairy, and we're not gonna have much cover if Rome is right and the FBI and the Secret Service have been compromised.

We're gonna be pretty much on our own. We're gonna have to work in the shadows without a net. Give me your thoughts."

Jeff stepped to the fireplace and faced the group. "I've never backed away from a fight and don't plan to back away from this one. The president has asked for our help to save our country. I'm in."

Mike nodded at Jeff and looked at Arnie, who stood and moved next to Jeff. "We've faced shitty odds before with a lot less at stake. Count me in." Jeff and Arnie bumped fists.

Ronnie set down her coffee cup, walked over to the fireplace and took her place next to Arnie and Jeff. "We're a team. Where one goes, we all go. Let's save the country."

"Okay," said Mike. "Let's see what info Bill and Stosh get tomorrow, and then we can work out a plan. We're gonna have a brief window to do whatever we need to do, but all we can do is all we can do."

Jeff pointed to their hostages. "You realize we can't let them go. All we have going for us is surprise, and we can't have them fucking that up."

"Rome told me that this time there were no rules of engagement," said Mike. "The people we are going up against are American citizens who are trying to take over the government by force. We are going to get dirty. Anyone have an issue with that?"

No one said a word. Arnie walked over to his backpack sitting on the kitchen counter, pulled out a pistol and silencer and threaded the silencer on the end of the barrel. He walked behind Earl and Barry and shot each man once in the head. They jerked in the chairs and their heads slumped forward.

Mike looked at his team. “Looks like we’re all in. Ronnie, see if you can get into the presidential transition website and let’s see if we can figure out where the president and VP-elect are going to be between January sixth and the twentieth. It looks like from what Barry told us, whatever is going to happen will happen here in Montana, but I don’t want to count on that. We need to figure out when and then come up with our counterplan. Jeff, pull up everything you can on the president-elect’s ranch here in Montana and see what you can find on the VP-elect’s house in California. I want two different contingencies. Arnie. Looks like you and I have some cleaning to do.”

Everyone headed in a different direction to work on their assignments. Arnie cut the wire ties on the two dead men and lowered the bodies to the plastic. The masks over their heads had contained a lot of the mess, so he and Mike wrapped the plastic around the bodies and duct-taped the bundles. All their clothes went into the fireplace, and Mike and Arnie carried the bodies to a greenhouse at the back of the property and buried them in the soft earth.

It was time to prepare for war.

Chapter Thirty-One

Robert E. Lee Richardson filled his thermos with coffee, thanked his wife for the breakfast she made with a peck on the cheek, put on his coat and headed for the detached garage behind the house. He opened the garage door and slid into his 1985 Ford F-150. The truck had been a project car for him and his oldest son while he was in high school, and now Robert drove it whenever he didn't want to be recognized. The red-and-white truck had a full eight-foot bed, wide all-terrain tires and a Confederate flag decal on the back bumper next to the NRA bumper sticker. He turned onto the highway just as the sun crested the trees to the east and headed for the interstate and the five-hour drive to North Carolina.

Robert valued these free days, as he liked to call them, when he was on the road, alone with his thoughts. Today his thoughts were on the confrontation they'd had last night with Oliver Stevenson. The other members of the group were right to be concerned. Stevenson was heading for a collision with reality, and no matter what they did or said, he was stuck on the idea that twenty million illegal votes were cast for his opponent. Last night after dinner, he'd sounded like a man who had let a conspiracy theory get into his head and carve out a spot to live in. He was concerned that Stevenson would not make it to the inauguration.

Robert decided he was going to work on a contingency plan to replace Stevenson if the man became unmanageable. He had spent most of the night after dinner sitting in his office making lists of people to fill various roles. He had a potential vice-presidential pick, and he had made a good start on his list of cabinet secretaries, but he was having a hard time coming up with someone to replace Stevenson.

They had been grooming Stevenson for the presidency since the first time he showed up at a Republican Convention, thirty years ago. He was a bright, spirited campaigner, and the people liked his comfy, backwoods charm. He had the right touch for a Southern politician: charming, sophisticated, handsome and easily manipulated. With the help of Robert and his friends, Stevenson had no problem winning that first Senate run and was soon on his way to being the heir apparent for the presidency.

The luster had gone off the shiny penny, and over the years, Stevenson lost more and more of his political friends, all the while strengthening his base. His folksy style was no longer the draw it was for the Republican money people, but the regular folks ate up his down-home style of retail politics. He was the representative of the everyman, and that connection to the base had forced Robert and his friends to back him in two presidential elections, all lost by increasing margins.

If they walked away from Stevenson, the base would turn ugly, and he would be hard-pressed to find another candidate who appealed to the base and the donor class. He saw the next couple of months as a lose-lose for everyone involved.

Robert pulled onto the interstate heading north and never noticed the pickup truck following him at a safe distance. Stosh had laser-marked the old truck, and if at any point they lost him, they could launch a drone and pick up the laser signature.

After two hours, Robert turned off the interstate and headed northwest into the hills of western North Carolina. Traffic was lighter along the two-lane backcountry roads, so Bill slowed and they switched to laser tracking. It was a beautiful day, so the tracker was working fine.

At one point, Robert pulled into a roadside gas station, filled up the truck and grabbed a couple of cold bottles of water from the convenience store. Bill had pulled over just before the parking lot, and they waited for Robert to resume his trip. After ten minutes, a relieved and no longer thirsty Robert E. Lee pulled out and continued north.

They were four hours into the drive when Robert pulled to the side of the road into a small rest area along a thin ribbon of a creek and parked next to a large black SUV. The windows of the SUV were heavily tinted, so Bill and Stosh couldn't see how many people were in the vehicle. They pulled onto a small farm lane and watched through the long lens of the camera.

Robert slid out of the old pickup truck and locked it. He had his thermos in one hand and his coat in another. A tall, well-built white guy wearing camouflage fatigues slid from the SUV and walked to Robert. He had a pistol on his hip and wore ballistic armor over his shirt. The shirt had no insignias, so identification was pointless. Stosh had gotten a few pictures of the guy, but they knew facial recognition would be difficult at this distance.

The big guy approached Robert and said something, to which Robert raised his arms and extended them to the sides. The guy ran a wand over Robert and then held out his hand. He pulled his phone out of his pocket and handed it to the driver. The driver walked back to Robert's truck, clicked the unlock button on the key fob and left the phone on the front seat before locking the truck. Robert slid into the back seat of the SUV, and the driver placed a loose-fitting hood over his head. He buckled Robert's belt, climbed into the driver's seat and headed away from the rest area. Whoever Jimmy Bronson was, he was careful.

Stosh used the laser tracker to target the SUV, and they continued their steady drive through northwestern North Carolina. The SUV slowed as it approached a small farm road with a solid metal gate, a metal cattle guard and two guards carrying assault-style rifles who materialized at the sides of the gate. The SUV was waved through the gate, the gate closed and the two guards disappeared into the woods.

Bill continued along the two-lane road for about a half mile and then pulled the pickup truck onto a small pullout on the side of the road. They sat back, ate some snacks and waited for dark. Stosh pulled up the pictures he had taken as they drove by the gate, and when he enlarged them on his laptop, he noticed several cameras along the road leading to the gate. He slid the laptop towards Billy.

"Looks like a lot of security. I count at least eight cameras, and those are just the ones I can see in the photos. We're gonna have to be extra careful tonight."

Bill flipped through the pictures and looked at Stosh.

"Yeah, those two guards materialized like ghosts. Wonder where they are hiding when they're sitting back waiting for a car to show up."

Bill looked at his watch. "We should have full dark in two hours. Let's rest up."

They sat back in the seats and closed their eyes. Two hours later, their internal alarm clocks went off, and they sat up and rubbed the sleep out of their eyes. A couple of more hours of sleep would have been great, but they had a job to do. They slid from the truck, slipped into their black pants and shirts, strapped on ballistic vests and loaded up their weapons. They were traveling light because they had no idea how much distance they would need to cover, so they each carried an assault rifle with a folding stock and a sidearm in a thigh holster. Donning black watch caps, they locked the truck and stepped off into the woods, disappearing into the dense forest. Most of the leaves had fallen off the deciduous trees, but the forest was an equal mix of pine and spruce trees, so cover was excellent.

The going was slow as they searched as they went for booby traps or cameras. After two hours, they spotted a clearing ahead and slowed their approach. Finding cover in the trees, they pulled out two spotting scopes and scanned the area. They cleared the area and were about to move when Stosh spotted something in the middle of the field. A bush rustled even though there was no wind. Stosh focused the spotting scope on the bush and watched. He spotted the movement right away. Whoever was hiding in the bush wasn't used to sitting still for long periods of time. Stosh pointed to the bush, and Bill focused his spotting scope. He scanned away from the bush and spotted a second oddly placed bush. Bill tapped Stosh on the shoulder and pointed. Stosh scanned the second bush and nodded.

Bill pointed to the left, and they backtracked the way they came and followed the edge of the clearing away from the two bushes. They circled the clearing and moved deeper into the woods. Another mile led them to a large barn and what looked like a small motel. There were security guards posted at each end of the motel structure.

Stosh pointed to a dense bush, and they slid behind it and set up their surveillance. They didn't have to wait long. The side door to the barn opened, and Robert E. Lee Richardson stepped out and zipped up his jacket. A well-built younger man with a shaved head stepped out behind him, and they walked towards the SUV.

Bill had the microphone out and aimed at the two men. They listened.

"Okay," said Robert. "As long as you're comfortable that those two in Montana are just off the grid, we'll keep moving forward, but I will tell you, Jimmy. I'm not comfortable with this."

"I understand, sir," said Jimmy. "If they don't get in contact by the end of the day today, we'll look at the plan and adjust as needed. We've spent too much time on training and gear to pull the plug now. Once we kill the president and VP-elect, we'll roll up everything and disappear, but I want to see this through."

Robert nodded. "Okay, Jimmy, but I want to know by the end of the day if these two guys are still missing."

They shook hands, and Robert walked to the SUV and slid into the back seat. The driver covered his head with the loose hood, slid into the seat and drove away. Jimmy stood for a minute when the barn door opened, and a tall fair-haired man stepped next to him. He was dressed like Jimmy in black fatigues and had a pistol strapped to his waist.

"Looks like our friend's getting nervous. What do you want to do?"

Jimmy looked at him. "Get hold of our contacts in Montana and see if anyone has seen those two motherfuckers. We'll probably find them shacked up in some whorehouse, but whatever, I want them found and I want them dead."

Jimmy stepped back into the barn, and the fair-haired man headed for the motel. He walked over to an old metal triangle hanging from one of the beams of the covered walkway and, grabbing a small metal rod, beat on the triangle. Lights came on in the rooms, and within fifteen minutes, a dozen men stood in formation in front of the structure.

Jimmy stepped through the barn door and addressed the men. "We are going to push up the timeline. The certification of the election is in a little over a week. Once that happens, we can move forward with our plans. We'll spend two more days here in camp and then we'll reconvene at the base in Montana. Today I want to run through the scenario for the house in California. Grab your breakfast and then reconfigure the shoot house for the VP-elect's residence. We still don't know their exact plans, but I want to be ready."

The men disappeared into the barn. Stosh would have liked to get a look inside the barn, but they knew that would be pushing their luck. They had gotten pictures of most of the men, so now they needed to get them to Mike and let him know what they saw. They'd scooted deeper into the bush when they heard a noise coming from their left. The two men froze.

One of the bushes from the field was walking straight towards them. He led with his rifle and looked like he was stalking them. Bill slid away from Stosh and disappeared behind a large oak tree. The bush kept coming, and Bill pulled out his KA-BAR knife and crouched low. Stosh had his silenced pistol in his hand and was ready to move. They had hoped to escape the woods without being noticed, but that now seemed unlikely.

The bush got within fifteen feet of the two men, stood and scanned the area with his rifle. He turned ninety degrees and headed towards the barn. Bill and Stosh breathed a sigh of relief. They waited until the guard entered the barn, and then they backtracked the way they had come and headed for the truck, arriving just as first light broke over the trees. They slid into the truck and headed down the road until they reached the interstate and headed back to Nashville. Stosh uploaded the pictures to their secure cloud server and sent Mike a quick encrypted report on what they had seen and heard. Halfway back to Nashville, they pulled into a small motel, got two rooms and grabbed a couple of hours of sleep.

Chapter Thirty-Two

Certification Day

The morning of January 6 dawned cold and snowy as members of Congress arrived at their offices to perform their constitutional duty of certifying the election. The president had ordered the Virginia and Maryland National Guard to surround the Capitol building and make sure only legislators entered the space. Things were quiet at first.

By late morning, a large crowd had gathered in front of the Capitol. At first it was speeches and cheering. When Senator Oliver Stevenson arrived at the Capitol, the crowd erupted. Stevenson, never one to miss an opportunity, stood on the steps of the Capitol with a bullhorn in his hand and spoke to the crowd that had now reached several thousand. His ego wouldn't let him accept defeat, no matter how hard members of his family and staff tried to convince him otherwise.

Stevenson wasn't a scheduled speaker since he was supposed to be inside the Capitol, voting with the rest of the electoral college to certify the election. Never one to walk away from a crowd of the faithful, he borrowed a bullhorn from one of the cops guarding the fence and waded into the crowd. His speech followed the same pattern as all his speeches had since the election. He never considered how his speech would affect all those people who had come, many armed, to stop the certification.

"My fellow Americans," he said. "As the legitimately elected president-elect of the United

States, I call upon you to make sure that this travesty goes no further. Our opponents have tried to hide the truth, but we will not be silent. Twenty million illegals voted for my opponent, and the news media and members of the legislature who work in this building know the truth. Right now they are preparing to certify this past election, which will be a lie and will cause a constitutional crisis the likes of which this great country of ours has never seen. It is incumbent upon you people to protect and defend the Constitution when our elected leaders fail in their responsibility. My team and I have filed lawsuits in every county in this country that had questionable election results, and we will prevail in the courts, but in the meantime, we cannot let this certification go on. It is a travesty and a slap in the face to all the decent folks who legally voted. As your president-elect, I am asking you to step up and do the right thing. It is time to shed some blood to protect our country from tyranny. Stand with me and fight."

Stevenson's team ushered him into the building as the crowd surged towards the Capitol steps. Signs proclaiming Stevenson the winner were replaced with weapons—pistols and rifles—and the crowd destroyed the first barrier.

As they approached the National Guard units, many members of the guard lowered their weapons and stepped aside. Several turned their weapons on their fellow guard members and disarmed them, passing out the weapons to the charging mass of humanity now heading up the steps. The Capitol Police and the Washington, DC, Metro Police barricaded the doors, but it was fruitless. Shots rang out, and pandemonium became the rule of the day as the crowds charged over the police and swarmed into the building.

The crowd was cheering and dancing like it was a big party, and then things took an ugly turn as the crowd turned on the police officers and attacked with anything they could get their hands on. The crowd surged towards the House chamber and, using statues as battering rams, smashed through the door. They found the chamber empty. Infuriated, they moved en masse towards the Senate chamber and, after smashing their way through the doors, found that chamber empty as well. They took their anger out on the police officers and guard members who continued to fight back, many of whom suffered devastating injuries.

The crowd, led by various militia leaders, was dismayed, and they turned and exited the building, leaving destruction and injured bodies in their wake. The damage they had caused to the building and the people who had gotten in their way was incredible, and it had all been seen live by millions of Americans. The negative comments filled the internet, but the question that was on everyone's minds was, where were the legislators? Even Senator Stevenson, now barricaded in his office in the Senate office building, was confused.

"Where the fuck is everyone?" he asked his staff, who stood around dumbstruck. "Did we stop the certification?"

No one on his staff knew what to say, as they were as confused as him. One of his staffers ran in and grabbed the remote off the senator's desk and put on the news. The vice president of the United States stood behind the podium. Stevenson was stunned.

"After much deliberation," said Vice President James Wicks, "and with few objections, the legislature of the United States has certified the election for President and Vice President of the United States. With three hundred ninety-seven electoral votes received, Governor Thomas Baker of the great state of Montana has been certified as the president-elect, and with three hundred ninety-seven electoral votes received, former United States Senator Elizabeth Hanford of the great state of California is certified as the vice president–elect." The vice president hesitated for a moment. "I want to address the disgusting show we have all been watching unfold at the Capitol this morning. The crowd that had been fired up and called to arms by Senator Oliver Stevenson has shown the world America at its worst. The peaceful transfer of power is one of the things that makes our democracy the shining light throughout the world, and this morning that incredible principle came under attack by a group of thugs. The disgusting behavior we all witnessed will not be forgotten, and I hope that the newly elected president, when he is sworn in on January twentieth, will make sure that all those responsible, including Senator Stevenson, are held responsible. I know I speak for the entire executive branch and the legislative branch when I offer my condolences to those brave officers and National Guards and their families, who did not lay down their weapons to prevent the peaceful transfer of power, but who instead fought back to protect this august body. I am saddened to report that there have been many serious injuries and several deaths among the defenders of our democracy.

I would also like to thank President Roman Diggs for having the entire legislative body moved in secret to a hangar at Joint Base Andrews, so we could conduct the business of this country without having to fear for our lives. I thank the legislature of this great nation for doing their constitutional duty and certifying the election results. God bless you all, and may God bless these United States."

Stevenson stood in stunned silence, staring at the TV screen. The vice president had been replaced by the network news anchors, who were now working to get a grasp of the story that had unfolded without their knowledge.

Stevenson's chief of staff ushered everyone out of the office and closed the door. Stevenson sat behind his desk, fuming.

"They can't do this. I am the majority leader of the United States Senate. They can't certify the election without me being there. How can they do that? I'll sue."

"Senator," said his chief of staff. "They certified the election without you being there because you chose to stand on the steps of the Capitol and incite a riot that cost people's lives. I wouldn't be surprised if the FBI was on their way right now to arrest you."

"This is an outrage!" yelled Stevenson. "How dare you speak to me like that, after all I've done for you, you ungrateful shit?"

The chief of staff dropped an envelope on the desk. "You won't have to worry about firing me for insubordination. That's my letter of resignation. I'm out of here."

With that, he turned, walked to the door, opened it and stepped through. Stevenson looked at the letter in his hand and stared at the open door. The office was quiet, and he stood and walked to the door. His office suite was empty. Phones on every desk were ringing, but there was no one in the office to answer them. He closed the office door and walked back to his desk and sat. He pulled the burner phone out of his pocket and dialed the preprogrammed number. The phone rang but remained unanswered. He put the phone down on the desk and placed his head in his hands.

Robert E. Lee Richardson looked at the burner phone ringing on his desk and sat back and sipped his bourbon. He was pissed. The militia groups were prepared for this morning. Everything would have gone off without a hitch if it hadn't been for the spontaneous speech by Stevenson. The result would have been the same, carnage and destruction at the Capitol building, but he would have been able to control the narrative and keep Stevenson out of it. But that asshole and his ego couldn't resist the chance to grandstand. This was going to change everything. He pulled another phone out of his desk drawer and speed-dialed a number.

"What the fuck happened?" asked Calvin Mace. "This is a fucking nightmare. You were supposed to keep him away and let the militias do their thing."

"That's why I'm calling," said Robert. "We need to have a meeting tonight at my house."

Robert disconnected the call and dialed Warren

Turlock and Harold Wahls. He got the same response from them as he did from Calvin. No one was happy about Stevenson's involvement. More important, they were all pissed because President Diggs had defeated their plans. Robert was not looking forward to having this meeting, but he knew it was long overdue. Their candidate had just stepped in a big pile of shit, and if he wasn't arrested by the FBI today, he would be in the coming days, and they all knew that he would not stand up under questioning. They had a real problem, and now they needed a way out.

Chapter Thirty-Three

Mike Branik watched the assault on the Capitol on the TV in his motel room. He wasn't surprised. There had been rumblings for weeks on conservative media that this would happen. Most people blew it off as a bunch of people protesting the election. Violence was to be expected. That all seemed to change when Senator Stevenson gave his address to the protesters gathered on the lawn in front of the Capitol. Funny how not one of the news channels mentioned anything about the rioters being armed. You could almost get the impression that someone had given them advance notice to bring weapons.

Mike picked up his phone and dialed a number. The phone was answered immediately.

"Sir, I know you're busy," said Mike. "I wanted to tell you what a brilliant move it was to relocate Congress. Might have saved a lot of lives today."

"Thanks, Mike," said President Diggs. "But I'm assuming that's not the sole reason for your call."

"No, sir. I'm concerned that the conspirators have been embarrassed and will not wait to move on Baker and Hanford. I need to secure the pieces on the chessboard. Can you discreetly contact the president-elect and let him know I will come by his ranch today? We know he's in Montana, and I would like to meet without his Secret Service detail being present."

"Do you have a plan, Mike?" asked the president.

"Yes, sir. But I'm going to keep you in the dark."

"I'll make the call, Mike. What about the VP-elect?"

"Two of my guys are on her California home. She arrived early this morning after deciding not to meet Baker in Montana. A message to her to expect Bill and Stosh would be helpful."

"Will I be able to reach you?"

"No, sir. Once we make our move, we are going dark. Ronnie has identified the men we got pictures of in North Carolina, and they are all on their way here. Sir, this is going to get dirty, and I'd rather you weren't anywhere near this. If you need something, go through Mary. You know the procedure."

"Okay, Mike. Do what you have to do. I'll give you what cover I can. Semper fi."

Mike disconnected the call and called Jeff to be ready in ten minutes. He put his phone in his pocket, grabbed his weapons and his coat and headed for the SUV.

The snow was falling lightly, and for the first time in a couple of weeks, there was no wind to stir it up. Mike looked across the valley. It was a pristine picture of white. He hoped it was a good sign.

Jeff stepped out of his motel room and slipped into the SUV. Mike turned up the heat.

"Did you talk to Roman?" asked Jeff.

"Yeah. He's making the calls. We should be set by the time we get to the ranch."

"I wish we had a better handle on who the bad guys are on his detail. I hate going up against our own people."

Mike looked at him as he pulled onto the road. "You watched what happened at the Capitol. I don't know how many members of the guard units helped the rioters, but it was a significant amount. Once they helped the rioters, they were no longer our people. They crossed the line. We have to assume everyone is bad until we know different."

Mike followed the interstate until he got to the intersection with U.S. Highway 191 and turned south, heading towards Yellowstone and the Gallatin National Forest. The snow had gotten heavier as they left the valley and headed into the mountains, but they made good time and arrived at the ranch as the snow slowed to small flakes.

Mike drove to the gate and stopped at the guardhouse. He rolled down his window and held up his and Jeff's Homeland Security ID cards. The uniformed Secret Service officer took the IDs and stepped into the trailer that acted as the guardhouse. Mike could see him talking on the phone, and they waited. The officer stepped from the guardhouse as the gate slid sideways. He handed back the ID cards.

"Follow the road till you get to the ranch house. You'll be met by an escort. Have a nice day."

Mike thanked the guard, rolled up his window and drove past the gate. After a half a mile, he pulled to a stop in front of the ranch house. He looked at the building and wondered if they had crossed into a different timeline. The house was dark rustic logs, blackened with age. The roof was red metal, and there was smoke coming out of the fireplace at one end of the house. He wouldn't have been surprised if a cowboy wearing a six-shooter had stepped out to meet them. Instead, a young woman carrying an assault-style rifle waited at the front door and approached their SUV. Mike and Jeff opened their doors, slid out and approached the woman. She asked to see their IDs, which they handed her, and after looking at them, she turned and asked them to follow her into the house. Inside, the house was warm and comfortable. The fire in the huge fireplace burned brightly and gave the room a yellow tint. The ranch house was larger than it appeared from the outside and was filled with large well-used leather furniture and handcrafted tables. The lamps and ceiling fixtures were all hand-forged wrought iron, and the entire space felt like you could sit down and fall asleep, and no one would care.

"You can leave your coats here," said the Secret Service agent, who waited for them to remove their coats and then stepped to a huge kitchen table that looked like it had been crafted from one gigantic tree.

"Please place your weapons in the lockbox and take the key with you." She waited, and when they were ready, she ran a wand over them to scan for anything else that needed to be checked. "Please follow me."

She led them through the great room and down a long hall with several rooms branching off to the sides. One room looked like a lounge for the presidential detail, and several agents were sitting around drinking coffee and watching the continuing news coverage of the assault on the Capitol.

She approached a door at the end of the hall and knocked. The door was opened by a second agent dressed in jeans and a flannel shirt. They stepped through and came face-to-face with the former Montana governor and president-elect Thomas Baker. Baker was a good-looking man with a full head of white hair and a rugged complexion. He was six feet tall. Mike noticed when they shook that his hands were calloused from hard work. Mike wondered how much of the furniture in the cabin had been handmade by the president elect.

Two Secret Service agents stood at the door, which had been closed.

Mike took a seat while Jeff stood.

“Sir, it’s an honor to meet you, and congratulations on your win,” said Mike.

“Gentlemen, forgive my rudeness. Can I get you something to drink or eat?” said Baker.

“Coffee, if you have it and it’s not too much trouble,” said Mike. “Black for both of us.”

Baker picked up the phone, pushed a button and ordered three black coffees, telling whomever he spoke with to bring an assortment of Danishes. He placed the handset back in the cradle.

“So, what can I do for Homeland Security?” asked Baker, looking from Mike to Jeff.

Mike looked over his shoulder at the two Secret Service agents by the door. “Sir, this is for your ears only."

The president-elect looked at Mike and then at the two agents. "Gentlemen, please give us the room."

The agents opened the door and stepped out, closing it behind them.

Baker got a serious look on his face. "Okay, guys. What's going on? When Roman called this morning, he was tight-lipped about your visit."

"Sir, we have it on good authority that an attempt will be made on your life and the life of the VP-elect."

Baker laughed. "I get death threats every day. What's different about your information?"

"There's a major conspiracy that will make sure neither you nor the VP-elect will be inaugurated on January twentieth. Right now, several of my team are tracking about a dozen skilled militia members from around the country as they make their way to Montana and California. These guys have serious money backing them."

Baker sat back in his chair. "Does this have anything to do with the speech Stevenson gave this morning before the Capitol riot?"

"Yes, sir. Stevenson will be voted into the office of the presidency by Congress on the afternoon of the inauguration. If both you and the VP-elect disappear and can't be inaugurated, then Congress gets to pick the next president. According to my sources, this is untested and will probably lead to the Supreme Court, who will side with Stevenson."

"So, we're not meant to just disappear until after the

inauguration. These folks mean to kill us?"

"From what I've been told," said Mike. "If you show up after the inauguration, you will be installed as the president and vice president. So yes, you have to be eliminated."

Baker ran his hands through his hair. "These people are serious?"

"Yes, sir," said Mike. "But that's not the biggest problem. We know that several members of your security detail and members of the FBI are part of this plot. We just don't know who they are at this point."

"Well, after watching those cowards in the National Guard this morning give up their weapons and join the rioters, I can't say that I disagree with that assessment. That's why all the secrecy?"

"Yes, sir. My team and the president are the only ones who know we are onto this threat, and now you and, in a few minutes, the VP-elect."

Baker looked hard at Mike. "So even if you and your team can neutralize this threat, we could still be murdered by our own security people?"

Mike looked at his hands and then looked up. "Yes, sir. That is a likely scenario."

There was a knock at the door, and a member of the kitchen staff entered with a tray containing three coffees and an assortment of pastries. She placed the tray on the desk, gave a coffee to each person and left. The president-elect sipped his coffee and looked at Mike.

"Roman told me you were a straight shooter. He also told me he would trust you with his life."

Mike sipped his coffee and nodded. "As would I."

"What are we supposed to do?" asked Baker. "Sit here until it happens? How the hell can I trust any of these people?"

The president-elect stood and walked over to a large window looking out at the mountains behind the house. The snow had stopped, and the sun was breaking through the cloud cover, causing the mountains in the distance to glow. It was a beautiful sight.

Baker turned. "I've devoted my life to taking care of the people, first here in Montana, and now I have a chance to make a real difference for all Americans and some crazy group may take that chance away from me."

"They're not crazy," said Jeff. "They're just following a crazy guy who can't accept he lost by millions of votes. These people have all the money in the world. The one thing they don't have is a lot of time. Sometime in the next two weeks, sir, you will die, and this country will be torn apart."

Baker looked at Jeff. "Do you have a plan?"

"Yes, sir. We are going to kidnap you out from under your security detail," said Mike.

Baker looked up from his coffee. "Seriously? You drove through the front gate. There must be a hundred news vans parked out there with a couple of hundred reporters, plus my security detail. How the hell are you going to kidnap me?"

Mike smiled. "Let's not call it a kidnapping. Let's call it a vacation. You will still have contact with your staff because I know you have things to do over the next two weeks. But for everyone's benefit, you are going to take a break, and we're going to help you."

"When is this going to happen?" asked Baker.

"Tonight, sir. You will go to bed as normal, but you will dress warmly and be ready. We're gonna have a bit of a walk and then a bit of a drive to get you where I can keep you safe."

"What about my VP?"

"I've got two of my best people meeting with her this morning, and they will spirit her away tonight as well. You and the VP will be able to communicate, but neither one of you will know where the other one is. I'm not going to go into any more details. The less you know, the better. Go about your regular routine today but be ready to go after dark. We are traveling light. You'll have everything you need at the other end."

"What about the people you said were coming to kill me? What happens to them?" asked Baker.

"With any luck, we will kill them all before they get the chance. That's why I need you someplace safe surrounded by people I trust."

Chapter Thirty-Four

Vice President–elect Elizabeth Hanford had spent a good portion of her adult life serving the people of the United States, first as a congresswoman from Northern California, then as the United States Senator from California for three terms and now as the vice president–elect. At fifty-eight years old, she was entering her fourth decade of service. With her blond hair still vibrant and her skin tan, Hanford attracted a lot of attention wherever she went. She was a handsome woman. Her family, now comprising her and her husband, with her youngest child having left in the fall for college, was less hectic than when there had been six children at home, but her days were filled with the rigors of the new job. She was not pleased to be pulled away from those duties to take a meeting the president asked her to take with two Homeland Security agents.

She walked into her office and stopped and stared at the two men. She was expecting two people in suits, dressed to look like the rest of her security detail. What she found sitting opposite her desk were men who looked like they had come off the battlefield. Hard men who looked like they didn't take anyone's shit.

At their request, she dismissed her Secret Service agents and sat behind her desk. "Gentlemen, what's this all about? I don't have a lot of time for nonsense."

Bill Rogers smiled. "If you call a serious threat on your life nonsense, then I guess we've wasted our time coming here." Stosh stood and turned towards the door. Hanford was taken aback. She wasn't used to being spoken to like that, and it unsettled her.

"Wait," she said. "The president said on his call this morning that I had to meet with you, and I have to say, you're not what I expected. I apologize if I came across a little surly."

Stosh turned and sat down. "Ma'am. We may not look like the Homeland Security agents you're used to talking to, and for a damn good reason. Our job, by order of the president, is to keep you alive. There is a team of highly trained operatives making their way here and to Montana. Their job is to make sure that neither you nor Baker is available on Inauguration Day, at which time Oliver Stevenson will be elected president by a vote of Congress. We are to make sure that doesn't happen. Now, we may not look the part, but I can assure you that when it comes to keeping you alive to make that date, you want us and not some stuffed shirt from Homeland."

Stosh sat quietly. That was more words than he usually spoke, but he had read her attitude, and he felt that the best way to reach her was to be direct and in her face.

Hanford sat back in her chair. "The threat is that serious?" she asked. Her face was a little paler than when she first sat down.

"Yes, ma'am," said Bill. "These operatives are well funded and extremely well trained. The biggest problem is we don't know who on your security detail can be trusted, which is why the president has asked us to intervene. As of right now, everyone outside our small group is considered a hostile, and we will take whatever measures are needed to make sure you stay safe until January twentieth."

"What about my staff? Can I trust them? Some of them have been with me for years."

"Sorry, ma'am," said Bill. "But as of right now, besides your husband, the only people you can trust are sitting in this room. I realize that's asking a lot, but if you are concerned, call the president back. He'll tell you the same thing I just did. You get death threats all the time, we get that, but this is way above anything you've ever received before. If you watched the riot at the Capitol this morning, then you'll understand. Watching members of the National Guard surrender their weapons to the crowd is the most disgusting thing we've ever seen in our lives, and we've seen some disgusting things, but that's what we are dealing with."

"Okay, Agent . . ."

"Bill and Stosh are fine, ma'am."

"Okay, Bill. How are you going to keep me alive?"

"We are going to kidnap you, ma'am, right out from under your security detail. You are to tell no one what is happening other than your husband. Once we have you settled, you will have full contact with your staff and with the president-elect, but neither of you will know the other's location. Once we are out of here, you will tell key members of your staff that you have decided to take a much-needed vacation for a few days, and they will not be able to contact you. You will not discuss any of this with your security detail. Let them know that you will initiate all contact. Tonight, when you and your husband retire for the evening, you will dress in casual clothes and sturdy shoes. We will walk for a ways, and then we are going for a boat ride, but once we reach our destination, you will be safe."

"What about the people coming after me?" she asked.

"You let us worry about them. If they get past us, we have a team ready to cover the rest of your family to make sure they remain safe and can't be used as leverage."

"That's not what I'm asking. How do you intend to handle them?"

"Ma'am, we are the best at what we do, but we don't always follow conventional processes. What we do is get dirty to keep you alive. That's all you need to know."

Hanford looked serious. "Why are you doing this?"

"Because the president asked us to," said Stosh.

"All right, Bill. We will be ready tonight, and we will place ourselves in your hands."

Bill and Stosh stood and shook her hand, turned and left the office. Hanford sat in her chair and tried to get her hands to stop shaking. She had been threatened before, but after speaking with Bill and Stosh, she had a new understanding of fear.

Chapter Thirty-Five

Robert E. Lee Richardson was not happy. Calvin Mace sat opposite him at the dining room table and sipped his drink. Robert did not want to repeat himself, so he waited for Turlock and Wahls to arrive. Calvin had seen him like this before, and he knew better than to engage him in even casual conversation, so he sat and picked at the cheese plate Mrs. Richardson had set out on the table before disappearing into the kitchen.

Wahls and Turlock arrived together and could tell immediately what the mood in the room was. They stepped over to the bar, poured a couple of bourbons and sat at the table.

Robert looked around. "This has turned into a real clusterfuck. First, that fucking president spirited away the entire Congress so we could not stop the certification. How the fuck do you even do that? Then that stupid sum bitch Stevenson gets on national TV and incites an insurrection, and since the entire Congress was gone, our people looked like fools."

Wahls sipped from his glass and picked up a piece of cheese. "I told you from the beginning Stevenson was the wrong choice, but you didn't want to hear it."

"Harold," said Turlock. "Now is not the time for 'I told you so' and finger-pointing. What are we going to do?"

Wahls looked across the table. "It most certainly is the time for finger-pointing. Stevenson has been a thorn in the party's side since he ran for president the first time, and each time, he lost by more votes this time than the last. His base and the threat that anyone who opposes him will get primaried keeps him in power. I, for one, am finished with him. He can't primary me, and his stunt yesterday was the last straw."

Robert looked at each man. "Cal, you've been quiet. What's on your mind?"

Calvin Mace set down his glass. "We've lost all credibility. I've been bombarded with calls from militia leaders around the country wanting an explanation for how the president could pull a fast one and move Congress to a secure location. They are also furious that their members put out thousands of dollars to get to Washington at our behest and it was all for naught. The militias look weak, and they are not happy in the slightest. I explained to each person I spoke with that we can still have a plan in place to take over the government, but they are not interested in hearing it. I think we have a hard decision to make. I think it's time we pulled the plug on this entire operation and let the inauguration happen."

"What about Stevenson?" asked Turlock.

"I have it on good authority," said Calvin, "that the FBI will be arresting him in the next day or two, and I might add that they are going to be arresting a lot of militia members as well. This operation was fucked from the start, and I am sorry we had anything to do with Stevenson and his nutty plan."

"Okay," said Robert. "What do we do? Jimmy's teams are still viable, so we can still stop the inauguration, but who do we put into the presidency if not Stevenson?"

Calvin leaned forward. "Bob, you're not hearing us. This thing is over. We've lost all credibility with the militia groups, and we've lost all credibility with the members of Congress. No one is going to support killing the president- and vice president–elect. We need to recall Jimmy and his people before this goes any further."

Robert looked at his hands. "I can't do that. Jimmy has gone dark, as have his people. I can't stop this even if I wanted to."

"What about that guy Branik?" asked Turlock. "Can we get the information on Jimmy's team to him and see if he can stop them?"

"You're asking me to turn on our own people," said Robert.

"We have to do something," said Calvin. "Once the FBI arrests Stevenson, he's going to talk like a parrot, and he will indict us all in this plot. We need to do whatever it takes, and then we need to get the hell out of here."

"We can still salvage this, and with the right candidate, we can still take over the presidency," said Robert.

"How?" asked Wahls.

"We let Jimmy's team continue, and I'll talk to the Speaker of the House and offer a couple of names to replace Stevenson."

"And what about Stevenson?" asked Calvin. "He

won't accept this, just like he doesn't accept the fact that he lost. What are we going to do about him?"

Robert looked serious. "It's time we got out from under his thumb, permanently."

The others looked at him and sat back to think about what he said. Calvin leaned forward. "Do you have someone who can make that happen?"

Robert smiled. "I do, as a matter of fact. One call and Oliver Stevenson will disappear, and if he disappears, the FBI will never know about us. This person will not be cheap but is damn reliable."

They sat for a minute, saying nothing, mulling the idea around in their heads. None of them wanted to leave the country, even though they all had escape plans in place, and this could be their way of solving their problem and not having to leave.

Turlock was the first to speak. "Okay, Robert. Call your contact and set it up."

Robert nodded. "So, to be clear. We are going to provide a different candidate to take over the White House once Jimmy and his team succeed, and we are going to make sure Stevenson can never speak about this to anyone."

They nodded, Robert held up his glass and they all clinked. They set their glasses on the table, grabbed their coats and headed for the door, saying good night to Mrs. Richardson as they left. Robert closed the door and headed for his office.

Calvin stopped the others before they reached their

cars. He pulled up the collar on his coat to block the wind. "You know this is a mistake, right?"

Wahls and Turlock looked at him. "Then why did you go along with the change of plans?" asked Turlock.

"Because Bob is as crazy as Stevenson. We knew from the get-go that this plan had little chance of success even with our people entrenched in the Secret Service. We just agreed to have Bob call an assassin to take out Stevenson. How deep are we going to get into this?"

Wahls smiled. "Cal, you're missing the point. This was never about Stevenson. It was always about taking over the government, and Stevenson was just a means to an end. The original plan may have just gotten shot to shit, but if Bob can succeed at taking out Stevenson, we are one step closer to our reality. Whoever we put into the White House will still work for us. We need to see this through."

Calvin nodded, shook hands and headed for his SUV. He slid in, put the car in drive and headed down the long driveway to the highway. He had a lot of work to do, but once the deed was done, he would grab the wife and head to his private jet in St. Augustine, Florida, and take a quick trip to Belize.

Chapter Thirty-Six

Mike and Jeff moved silently through the woods about a mile from the ranch house. They had decided to come in from the north side of the property and enter along an old forest service fire road. Ronnie and Arnie would stay with the vehicle and act as backup if the need arose.

The trek was long and arduous. The snow had continued most of the evening, and there was now six inches of new snow on top of the old crusty snow that had fallen for the past couple of days. The pine and spruce trees were coated with snow, and visibility was tough. The wind had picked up, and the blowing snow created ground blizzards. They were behind schedule by the time the ranch house came into view.

Mike moved off to the left while Jeff stayed on their original path. They positioned themselves to get a view of the house and the outbuildings and watched. Mike counted three roving guards. Their schedule was more erratic than he would have expected, and he figured the weather was affecting their schedule. It was not a good night to be on guard duty. Mike looked at his watch. He knew that there was a good-sized contingent of Secret Service agents in the house and that more would be arriving.

When they were at the house earlier, they'd made note that there were six agents: four walking the perimeter and the two at the entrance gate. Mike doubled that number to be safe and knew this would not be easy.

Mike clicked his mic one time. "I'm gonna head for the back of the house. Keep an eye out for strays."

Jeff clicked his mic one time. Mike slid from his hiding space and raced towards the back door. There was no moon, and with the clouds and the swirling snow, he looked like a shadow moving in the night. He reached the back wall of the house and crawled behind a snow pile. He knew from the crude map the president-elect had drawn that the patio he was standing next to was off the master bedroom. He waited for a few minutes. Feeling the coast was clear, he moved onto the patio and walked into a cold agent who was guarding the back door.

The agent startled, and Mike wrapped his gloved hand around his mouth and wrapped his arm around his chest. He dragged him to the ground and held him until his eyes closed and his breathing became regular. He pulled him to the door and tapped on the glass. Baker, dressed for the weather, opened the door, and Mike pulled the unconscious agent into the bedroom and laid him in front of the fireplace.

Baker looked at him. Mike smiled. "Couldn't leave him outside to freeze."

Mike used flex-cuffs to bind his hands behind his back and tied the scarf he was wearing around his mouth. He opened the closet doors and slid him into the huge walk-in closet.

He stepped out, closed the door and looked at Baker. "Ready?"

The president-elect snugged into his coat and hat. Mike stopped him.

“Phone,” he said.

Baker handed him his cell phone, which was turned off. Mike placed the phone on the desk on the opposite side of the room. “What about your tracker?”

The president-elect removed a lanyard from his neck and handed the tracker to Mike, who set it next to the phone.

“Have you had any surgeries, medical or dental procedures since you won the election?”

“No,” said Baker. “No one inserted any hidden secret devices.”

Mike nodded and clicked his mic. “Are we clear?”

One click came over the mic. He put his gloves on, opened the door and led Baker onto the patio. He stopped and listened for any approaching noise but didn’t hear a thing. He grabbed Baker by the arm and led him to the side of the patio and then to the tree line. They ducked into the trees, and Mike led the way to Jeff and the trail out. They made better time getting back to the vehicles now that they had a trail to follow, and Mike was glad to see the snow filling in their tracks as they headed deeper into the woods.

They approached the SUVs, and Mike asked Baker to slide into the back seat. Jeff got in the front driver’s side and started the SUV. Mike stepped next to Ronnie and Arnie.

“You know what you need to do. We’ll get back here as soon as we can. In the meantime, let’s introduce ourselves to the militia guys. You understand the rules of engagement?"

Ronnie laughed. "No worries, Mike. We'll get on these guys as fast as we can and cut down the size of the force. The snow is supposed to get worse over the next twenty-four hours. I don't think they'll try anything, but we'll be ready. Good luck."

Mike nodded and jumped into the passenger seat. The inside of the Jeep Wagoneer was warm, and he slid off his coat and hat. Jeff put the SUV in drive, and they headed for the main highway and the trip north. Forty miles north of Bozeman, they turned onto a farm road and followed it to an old cabin and a large barn. Mike checked his watch. Even with the delays due to the weather, they were ten minutes early. Mike slid out, ran to the barn and swung open the door. Jeff pulled into the barn and parked the SUV.

Jeff and Baker climbed out and joined Mike by the door. Jeff had opened the rear hatch and walked past Mike. About fifty yards into the farmyard, Jeff clicked a button on the unit he held in his hand and set it on the ground. The beacon was a specialty item, and even if found, it would take whoever found it months to figure out what it did. But within ten minutes they could hear a low rumble, and then a dark chopper with no markings or lights dropped from the sky and landed next to the beacon. Mike closed the barn door.

Jeff, Baker and Mike ran and climbed into the chopper. There was no conversation, and as soon as the door was closed, the chopper took off. They sat back in their seats and rested. The flight took a little over two hours, and when they landed, the field they landed on was pitch-black. The pilots had been flying with night vision goggles the entire flight, and there had been no lights lit either in or on the chopper for the entire flight. The door opened, and they jumped out and ran to a waiting Humvee and slid in. The drive took another twenty minutes, and the president-elect looked surprised when they passed through a checkpoint that seemed to appear out of nowhere. They drove another mile or two, and then the Humvee pulled under a porte cochere and stopped. Mike, Baker and Jeff left the SUV and made their way into a large house.

Baker slipped out of his coat and handed it to a young woman who appeared through a side door. She was tall, well-built and wore a sidearm on her left side. She took his coat.

"Mike. How in the hell are ya?" came a booming voice from behind them.

Mike turned; standing in the doorway was a bear of a man. He had long gray hair and a beard that reached the third button down on his chest. Mike and the giant embraced, and then Jeff and the giant did the same. Mike turned and faced Baker.

"President-elect Baker, meet Sergeant Major Larry McGreavy, Canadian Special Forces. Larry, meet the next President of the United States."

Larry walked over, and his hand swallowed the president-elect's hand. "Truly an honor, sir. Welcome to your home away from home for the next couple of weeks."

Baker shook Larry's hand and looked at Mike.

"We needed to get you someplace safe that was

outside the influence of the United States government. Larry and his team are the best in the world at protecting high-value targets. We are roughly twenty miles over the border, in a secure base that is not listed on any map. This is one of several bases used by the Canadian government to protect people from around the world who need protecting. Here you are surrounded by the best of the Canadian Special Forces, and they will protect you at all costs. Anything you need, just ask. Larry will see that you have access to secure communications so you can get in contact with your transition team, and he knows how to contact me if the need arises. For the duration, you are in the best hands you could be in. One more thing. If something happens and my team cannot complete our mission, there is a procedure in place that will get you safely back to the United States in time to be inaugurated."

The young woman returned and stood next to Larry.

"Mr. President," said Larry. "This is Yvonne. She will take care of you here in the house. The rules are simple. Never step outside the house. No one other than a handful of people knows who you are, and we want to keep it that way. Yvonne will arrange all your communications needs, and if you have any special dietary needs, she can help with that as well. Everyone in this house is here to ensure your protection, and I am very proud that over the last fifteen years since I have been here, we have never lost a protectee. Now, I know you've had a long day. Yvonne will show you to your room and in the morning she will take you to the communications office so you can contact your chief of staff."

Baker approached Mike and Jeff and shook hands. "I'm not sure how you arranged all this, but thanks."

"It's our pleasure, sir," said Mike. The president-elect turned and followed Yvonne. Mike turned to Larry.

"I owe you, brother," he said.

Larry laughed heartily "As many times as you saved my ass, it will be a long time before you owe me anything. The Humvee is waiting to take you back to the chopper. Good luck."

They shook hands, and Mike and Jeff pulled on their coats and hats and left the warmth of the house.

Chapter Thirty-Seven

Elizabeth Hanford and her husband, James, sat on the patio behind their house and looked out over the Pacific Ocean. It was a calm, clear night, and the stars shone like a billion diamonds laid out on a black cloth. They sat in two Adirondack chairs and whispered between themselves. The wine was perfect, and the small tray of cheese and sausages made the evening sail by.

Elizabeth looked at her watch. She nodded to James, stood and walked towards the corner of the house where one of the three Secret Service agents covering the backyard was stationed. He straightened up as she approached.

"Yes, ma'am," said the agent.

"Robert, James and I would like to spend a little time in the hot tub. I know this isn't protocol, but neither of us has a swimsuit, and we'd like to get in the hot tub now."

She giggled like a schoolgirl, and the agent's face turned red.

"Would you be a dear," she said, "and turn off the backyard lights and move your team a little farther down the house so we can have a little privacy?"

"I don't know, ma'am," said Robert. "We're supposed to have a visual on you at all times."

She giggled and faked falling to one side but recovered. "Please, Robert. It would mean so much to me, and I would hate to wake your boss and ask him. By then the mood would be gone. I promise we'll go to bed as soon as we're done, and we won't bother you guys any more this evening." She batted her eyes at him.

The agent looked uncertain, but he went along and pushed his lapel mic. "Team, this is four. Rainbow is going to be using the hot tub, and she is requesting privacy. I'm going to kill the back lights and each of you move to a position away from the backyard."

His team acknowledged, and Elizabeth thanked him and headed back for the patio. The backyard lights went off, and within a minute he could hear splashing in the hot tub, and he smiled and moved a ways down the side of the house. The blower in the hot tub drowned out all the sounds, and he relaxed.

Stosh had been lying against the sand berm behind the house, hidden by the dune grass. Bill was down the beach keeping watch. A few minutes after the lights went off, he climbed the berm, scouted the area with his night vision goggles and raced to the hot tub.

Elizabeth and James were sitting with their feet dangling in the water, splashing and making noise. They started when Stosh suddenly appeared. Hanford couldn't believe that someone Stosh's size could move like a ghost. She stared at the rifle slung over his shoulder.

"Nothing to worry about, ma'am. Just a precaution."

James Hanford, the vice president–elect's husband,

stood and looked at Stosh, who walked over and held out his hand.

"Stosh, sir. Nice to meet you." He turned and faced Hanford. "Ma'am, sir, we'll need your phones and also the Secret Service tracker." Hanford pointed to the patio table, and Stosh looked over and nodded. "I have to ask. Since the election, have either of you had any medical or dental procedures?" They shook their heads. He picked up their phones and the tracker and disappeared into the bedroom. He returned without them.

"Okay, folks. Please grab your go bags and follow me." The bags were hidden in the pool toy box, and they walked over and grabbed them.

Stosh looked at James. "Sir, you're up."

"Honey, another glass of wine for my lovely bride," he said louder than a whisper, enough that the agents would hear him.

They followed Stosh down the patio steps, raced across the lawn, slid down the berm and waited.

Stosh tapped his throat mic. "We good?"

"Go," replied Bill.

They traveled a mile along the beach when Bill stopped and walked behind a lifeguard station. He pulled out a Zodiac inflatable raft with a small gas motor attached to the back and dragged it to the edge of the surf. The Hanfords slid into the Zodiac, and Stosh and Bill pushed it into the surf, jumped in and, using two paddles they pulled from under the seats, paddled through the surf. Once clear of the breakers,

Bill started the motor, and they stowed the paddles. Bill headed a few hundred yards offshore and then turned the Zodiac south.

Thirty minutes after they entered the water, Bill looked at his phone and, following directions on an app, turned the raft out to sea and headed into the darkness. With no moon, the water was as dark as being in a cave. Twenty minutes later, a red dot appeared in front of them, and Bill headed towards it.

The dot turned out to be a laser finder attached to a massive yacht that was running completely dark. Bill turned the Zodiac towards the bow, and a large hatch opened on the boat's side. He directed the raft through the hatch, which closed behind them. A few overhead lights came on, and the space revealed itself as a toy hangar, filled with all kinds of watercraft, including some that looked like small submarines. Bill angled towards a ladder in the side of the chamber, and two deckhands tied the raft to the side wall. The Hanfords, grabbed their go bags and climbed the short ladder to the deck above. Bill and Stosh followed. A young man asked them to follow him, and they left the toy deck and entered a long, brightly lit hallway. The young man stopped outside a door and knocked.

"Enter," came a voice from inside. The young man pushed open the door and stepped aside. He closed the door once they passed him.

"Stosh, old boy. Good to see you. It's been too long." The accent was British.

The man stepped around the table and gave Stosh a big hug. He did the same to Bill. He then turned to his guests.

"Madam Vice President, I'm Captain Hugh Graham, His Majesty's Royal Navy. Welcome to the *Endeavour.*" He shook their hands and stepped back.

"Captain," said Hanford. "The pleasure is mine. My husband, James." They shook hands.

The captain invited them to have a seat at a large mahogany table. He looked at Stosh and Bill.

"Ma'am, Captain Graham and his crew have most graciously accepted the role of host for you and your husband for the next two weeks. The *Endeavour* may look like a luxury yacht, but she is one of the most elaborate spy ships in the British fleet. Among her crew are some of the most prolific electronic surveillance folks in the world, and her crew is augmented by two teams of SBS special operators whose job it will be to protect you and your husband. If you are not aware, the SBS teams are the equivalent of our Navy Seals, and these two teams are trained in security and protection."

The captain took over the briefing. "For the next two weeks, you will be our guests, and the food and accommodations are as luxurious as you would expect. For your protection, I ask that you remain in the cabin area, which includes a swimming pool, a common area with all manner of entertainment and a gymnasium for your use. You will have limited contact with the crew. All communications will be arranged by your steward, Peter. Over the next day or so, we will familiarize you with the ship and escape procedures, if needed. Your room has been made up, and our communications center will be available in the morning so you can contact your team and let them know you are safe. Your meals will be served at your convenience. If you have any questions, you can come straight to me or ask your steward, who is also a trained protection officer."

They all stood, and Hanford shook the captain's hand. Peter entered and led them to their room.

The captain turned to Stosh. "How bad is it? Mike wasn't clear when we spoke."

Stosh stepped over to the counter, opened a bottle of water and took a long sip. "It's bad, Hugh. We know that a team of trained operators is coming after them. The problem is, we know that members of their security detail have been compromised, but we don't know which ones. That's why we needed to go outside for help."

"Well, don't you worry, mate. We'll treat them like the king. You or Mike let me know when you want them delivered, and we'll make sure they're on time."

Bill and Stosh headed for the toy deck and the waiting Zodiac. They needed to be ready to greet whoever came to the VP-elect's house and make sure they didn't leave. They climbed into the Zodiac and headed for the coast.

Chapter Thirty-Eight

Ronnie and Arnie hadn't wasted any time after making sure Mike, Jeff and President-elect Baker got off safely. They'd headed back to Bozeman and started tracking the guys they'd identified from the pictures taken at Jimmy Bronson's compound. They'd found two of them in a small motel about six miles west of Bozeman. Ronnie and Arnie had been parked in a restaurant parking lot across the highway from the motel for several hours, waiting for the guys to show themselves. Just after midnight, wearing dark camo shirts and pants, the two left their motel rooms, climbed into a red Ford pickup truck and pulled out of the motel parking lot.

Arnie put his truck in gear and followed as they headed west for a few more miles and then took the exit that would take them south towards the Baker ranch. While Arnie drove, he kept an eye on the road conditions because of the ground blizzard from the earlier snow; he didn't want to drive off the road. Ronnie loaded several weapons and added extra magazines to their ballistic vests. She also checked to make sure their night vision goggles were working and put new batteries in several flashlights.

Arnie caught the bright brake lights and knew they had arrived at a small dirt road south of the ranch, a couple of hundred yards from the entry checkpoint that was guarded by uniformed Secret Service officers. The truck had turned off its headlights and crept down the dirt road until they got to a spot where they could hide the truck. They knew the Secret Service would not be flying drones in weather like this, so they felt confident no one would find their truck.

Arnie parked his truck at the end of the dirt road in a small copse of pine trees, and they slid out, put on their ballistic vests and grabbed their weapons. They headed down the road to where the truck was parked. They watched as the two men grabbed several assault-style rifles, several handguns, night vision goggles and helmets. These guys came prepared.

Arnie moved into the woods off the side of the road and paralleled the path of the two guys as they made their way to the barbed wire fence that surrounded the property.

Ronnie moved towards the truck, watching as the two guys entered the woods, and after they were out of sight, she pulled out her KA-BAR knife and flattened all four tires. If these guys tried to make a run for it, they were shit out of luck. She moved off to the west and tracked the guys on the opposite side from Arnie.

They both slowed when the two men crossed the barbed wire and moved towards the back of the house. Arnie had no idea if these guys were meeting another team or if they were the advance team until they reached the tree line at the back of the house and dug in behind an old dead tree. They opened their packs and pulled out two cameras with long lenses and several spotting scopes, and they set up a surveillance nest.

One man sat with his back to the tree and opened an MRE. The other sat and looked through one of the spotting scopes. He reached over and pulled a satellite phone out of a backpack and dialed a number. After several clicks and whirring noises, the phone connected.

"Are you set?" asked the voice on the phone.

"Yeah, got a good view of the side and back of the house. No movement yet, but it's early."

"Okay," said the voice. "Stay on task and report in every two hours. We will update you on one of those calls."

The call disconnected, and the guy put the phone back into the backpack. He continued to watch the house through the scope.

The first guy finished his MRE and moved to his knees. "Gonna go take a leak. Be right back."

"Fuck, man," said the second guy. "We just got here. You must have a kidney the size of a golf ball."

The first guy picked up his rifle and, staying low, walked back into the woods. Ronnie was waiting behind a large tree. As the guy relieved himself, Ronnie came up behind him and shoved her knife into the side of his throat and raked it across his neck. She grabbed him around the chest and lowered him softly to the ground. Blood poured from his neck, his eyes closed and he stopped breathing. She wiped the knife off on his jacket and placed it into the sheath attached to her thigh. She pulled him deeper into the trees and relieved him of his weapons and communications gear.

While Ronnie was dispatching guy number one, Arnie had moved within five feet of guy number two, who was focused on the uniformed Secret Service officer who stood on the patio looking out over the field behind the house. The officer rubbed his gloved hands together, stepped off the patio and moved around the house and out of sight.

He checked his watch. “It’s almost zero hour. Where the fuck did he go to piss, fucking China?” he whispered to himself.

He was about to key the throat mic when he heard the snow crunch behind him. He turned his head slightly.

“Bout fuckin’ time. Where the hell have you been? Something’s going on. I need to move to a better spot.”

Not receiving a response, he turned his head, and Arnie shoved his knife into the guy’s left eye and covered his mouth with his hand. The guy struggled for a minute and then lay quiet. Arnie had to duck down as two Secret Service agents walked across the patio on patrol then disappeared around either side of the house.

He stripped the body of weapons and communications gear, grabbed the backpack and slid deeper into the woods. He found Ronnie about fifty meters back in the woods, and they headed towards the back of the property and Arnie’s truck. Two down, but they had no idea how many were left. It was going to be a long night, and it was just starting.

Chapter Thirty-Nine

Jimmy Bronson and one of his lieutenants sat in a coffee shop on Main Street in Bozeman, Montana. He sipped his coffee, constantly looking at the encrypted satellite phone. The coffee shop was quiet. The smell of fresh coffee and pastries filled the air, but Jimmy didn't care about any of that. He was concerned.

"They've missed their check-in. What the fuck is going on?" asked Jimmy.

"You don't think they were caught, do you?"

Jimmy looked up from his coffee cup and sneered. "How the fuck would I know that? I'm sitting here with you. Stupid comments I don't need right now."

The lieutenant got red in the face, picked up his coffee mug and drank. He set the cup down and looked at Jimmy. "You want me to take a couple of guys and head out there? See what's going on?"

"No," said Jimmy. "We'll stick to the plan. Make sure everyone is ready to go at three A.M. I want to hit the ranch house at four on the dot. If we make any changes now, our guys inside won't have the info, and that could fuck everything up."

They finished their coffee, stood and left the coffee shop. They never noticed the gray pickup truck with Alabama plates sitting across the street. Jeff Halsey watched them leave the restaurant, and he set the small laser microphone on the seat next to him. He picked up the encrypted phone from the passenger seat and dialed a number. After a minute of clicks and whirring noises,

Mike answered.

"What ya got?"

"They plan to meet up at three A.M. and hit the ranch house at four. They are worried because they lost contact with their two guys in the woods, but it sounded like they have no way to contact anyone inside the ranch house to change plans, so they're moving forward."

"Stupid tactical move," said Mike. "But good for us."

"You want me to keep following them, see if we can hit them earlier?"

"No, head back to the motel and we'll meet Arnie and Ronnie at three A.M. and get ready for the assault."

"On my way." Jeff disconnected the call, started the truck and pulled onto the street. Twenty minutes later, he pulled into the parking lot of the small motel he was staying at, parked, grabbed his gear and entered his room.

The room showed signs of age, but it was clean, which was all he cared about. The wood walls gave the room a cabin-like feel, and the coffee maker sitting on the credenza was getting a workout. The motel had a small attached restaurant, so he headed over to grab dinner before he knocked off.

He pulled open the door, took a step and retreated into the room. Walking out of one of the rooms on the other side of the parking lot was Jimmy Bronson's lieutenant. The same guy he saw at the coffee shop. He closed the door and headed for the restaurant. Jeff closed his door and stepped over to the window, hiding behind the curtain. He watched as the guy entered the restaurant and grabbed a seat by the window. He could see the waitress approach his table with a menu and a pot of coffee, which she poured into a cup. She wrote his order on a pad and walked away.

Jeff sat on the edge of the bed. He doubted they knew who he was, which was good. He decided on a course of action and stood. He grabbed his duffel bag off the floor and rummaged around until he found the small .380-caliber pistol at the bottom of the bag; he pulled the silencer from the side compartment and screwed it to the barrel. He slipped the pistol into his waistband and pulled on his leather vest. He checked the mirror. The pistol was well hidden. He opened the door and headed for the restaurant.

A light snow was falling as he walked, and with no wind, it was pleasant. There was little traffic noise, which was why Jeff had chosen this motel. It sat a little ways back in the woods and was surrounded by huge pine trees.

Jeff pulled open the door to the restaurant and the first thing that hit him was the smell of bacon cooking. That smell made him realize how hungry he was, but it also made him remember he hadn't had a lot of sleep since he and Mike made the trip to Canada and back. He stepped inside.

The waitress, a young gal with blue hair who was snapping a piece of gum, told him to grab a seat anywhere. Anywhere was not a lot of options. There were three stools at the counter and four tables, each with four chairs. The tables had red laminated tops with chrome edging, and the chairs were red vinyl. The walls were painted a pleasant cream color and were covered with framed pictures of various sizes showing hunters with lots of different dead animals. He grabbed the table next to the lieutenant, pulled out the chair and sat. The waitress—Glory was the name on the little plastic tag that hung over one of her breasts—filled his coffee cup and handed him a menu. He ordered a cheeseburger platter and asked her to put a bunch of extra bacon on it.

"You get a lot of hunters in here?" he asked Glory as she poured his coffee.

She looked at the pictures on the walls. "Yeah, some," she said, then she turned and walked away.

The lieutenant laughed. "I tried to get her to talk to me too. No dice." He shoveled a forkful of mashed potatoes into his mouth. "You passin' through?"

Jeff looked at him and smiled. "Yeah, stopped for the night. Left Alabama yesterday mornin'. Couldn't keep my eyes open any longer. You?"

"Up here with some friends doin' a little hunting. Make sure we get a couple of elk before the gov'ment takes our guns away."

"Yeah, know what you mean," said Jeff. He noted the patches on the lieutenant's jacket and pointed to them. "You serve?" he asked.

"Missouri National Guard. Never got the chance to kill any rag heads before that chump president ended the war. How about you?"

Glory set the plate on the table and refilled Jeff's coffee mug. Jeff took a big bite of his burger and washed it down with some coffee. He wiped his mouth.

"Yeah, couple of tours in Afghanistan. Ranger battalion. Got out a couple of years back."

The lieutenant was all smiles. "Bet you saw some great shit over there."

"Don't know about great," said Jeff. "Saw some shit, that's for sure."

They both finished eating at about the same time, and the lieutenant stood and stepped over to Jeff's table. He held out his hand. "Name's Dooly, like the pickup truck. It's actually Randolph, but I never did like that name." Jeff shook his hand. "Jeff. Nice to meet you, Dooly. You have a good night."

"Oh, I plan to," said Dooly with a big smile. "I plan to."

Dooly left the restaurant, and Jeff waited a few seconds, paid his bill and then followed. Dooly had just put his key in the door when Jeff called out.

"Hey, Dooly. Hold up a sec."

Dooly stopped and smiled as Jeff walked up. Jeff fired one bullet into his chest, and as he slid down the door, he put another round into his skull. He looked around, unlocked the door with the key that was hanging out of the lock and dragged Dooly into the room. He laid him on the floor and tossed the room. He found what he was looking for in the front pocket of a backpack sitting on the bed. It was a picture of an American flag pendant on a silver chain. Around the pendant, someone had drawn a circle with a line through it in red Sharpie. Under the circle, someone had written *Our guys* in the same red Sharpie. Jeff pulled out the sat phone, activated the camera function, took a picture and sent it to Mike, Ronnie and Arnie.

He found a duffel in the closet with a couple of handguns and a broken-down rifle, grabbed the comm gear and Dooly's phone, threw it all into the duffel and stepped over to the door. He opened the door a crack and scanned the parking lot. Nothing seemed amiss, so he pulled open the door, stepped through, locked the door behind him and threw the key up onto the roof. He put the duffel into the back seat of the cab and slipped into his room.

Jeff grabbed his gear, made sure there was nothing left in the room and, using a bath towel, wiped down the room. He walked out, threw his bags on the back seat and slid into his truck.

Chapter Forty

Jimmy Bronson stood next to his truck in the rest area parking lot off Interstate 90 and looked at his watch. He was getting more pissed by the minute. The snow was coming down heavier, and the wind had picked up. There was already four inches of snow on the pavement, and it didn't look like it was going to stop anytime soon. He snugged his coat up around his collar and looked at his watch again.

"Where the fuck is Dooly?"

"I'm sure he'll be here soon," said the guy standing next to him. "You know Dooly. He's easily distracted."

Jimmy looked at the older guy standing next to him. He was concerned. So far, counting Dooly and the two guys he had on surveillance whom he hadn't had any contact with in more than four hours, he had lost five guys, and the op hadn't even started yet. As it was, he was going to have to use the six local guys he had recruited. He wished he had more time to vet those guys. They all seemed to have the same views of the government as him, but that wasn't saying much.

He looked at his watch and waved all his guys over. Since there were no other cars in the rest area parking lot, he wasn't concerned about being seen. His team gathered around him. He decided not to mention that Dooly hadn't shown up.

"All right, guys. This is it. We know there are sixteen Secret Service agents on the property. Six in uniform on the gate and the perimeter and ten inside the house. You've all seen the picture we passed around of the flag pendant. We have three agents in the house and one guy at the gate who are part of our team. They will be wearing those pendants. Make sure you don't shoot them. You all have your assignments. Stick to the plan and we'll all go home tomorrow, and the president-elect will be dead. If all goes well, we will have done our part to save our democracy from the radical lefties. Last words. Anyone in the house who is not one of our people is to be considered the enemy. No one is to remain alive when we are done. We've trained long and hard for this op. Let's make our friends proud. Saddle up."

The team headed for the vehicles, and Jimmy slid into his SUV and pulled out of the lot. He could barely see through the whiteout conditions, but he had driven the same roads several times over the last couple of days, and he felt he knew where he was going. After ten miles, he exited the interstate and turned onto the highway that would lead them to the Baker ranch. He could feel the adrenaline kick in, and he moved his head into combat mode. His people were the best the militias had to offer, and he was proud of how hard they had worked to prepare for this op.

As he approached the road leading to the gate, he drove past and watched as the various vehicles behind him peeled off and headed for their entry spots. He pulled onto a small forest service road that paralleled the Baker ranch, drove in about a quarter mile and stopped. The three vehicles behind him pulled in, and six members of his team piled out and grabbed their gear. They all wore camo clothes, black ballistic vests and black watch caps. Several of them had painted their faces with black camo paint. They checked their weapons, climbed over the barbed wire fence and disappeared into the trees.

Jimmy checked his watch and pushed the button on his throat radio. “All teams, go!”

Chapter Forty-One

Thomas Baker was an early riser, so every morning at 4 A.M. the maid would bring him his first coffee of the day and the morning newspapers. This morning, she encountered a locked door. She wasn't sure what to do. Ever since she had worked for Baker, the bedroom door had never been locked. She walked to the kitchen, where one of the interior agents was pouring himself a cup of coffee. She explained the situation, and the agent set his cup on the table and followed her to the bedroom. He tried the lock.

"The door's locked," she said with a strong Hispanic accent. "Mr. Thomas, he never locks the door."

The first agent banged on the door. "Sir, is everything all right? Sir, please open the door. Mr. President, open the door or we will have to break it down."

Agent Thompkins, the lead agent on the security detail, came down the hall, stepped up to the door, pushed the other agent away and inserted a key into the lock. He pulled his pistol and pushed open the door. He and the other agent rushed into the bedroom, fanned out and checked the sitting area and the bathroom.

"He's not here," said the agent as they pushed open the patio door and stepped onto the patio.

They heard a groan coming from the closet and took positions on both sides of the door. Thompkins nodded to the agent and pulled open the door. They walked into the walk-in closet with guns drawn and flipped on the lights. Lying on the floor and just coming around was one of the outside agents. Thompkins kneeled next to him and shook him. The agent on the ground sat up.

"Someone jumped me on the patio. How long have I been out?" he asked.

Thompkins stood, stepped out of the closet and looked around. "The bed hasn't been slept in," he said. "Check the closet and see if his coat is here." The other agent standing next to the bed looked down.

"Sir, his phone and tracker are here." He pointed to the nightstand. He walked into the closet and stepped out. "His heavy winter coat is missing."

"What the fuck?" said Thompkins. He turned as Mallory St. Claire, the president-elect's chief of staff, rushed into the room.

"What the hell is going on?" she asked. She looked around the room and stared at the tracker and phone on the nightstand.

"Where the hell is he?" she asked.

Outside, they heard gunfire coming from the front of the house. Agent Thompkins turned and saw the other agent in the room raise his pistol and aim it at him. Instinct and training took over, and as he raised his pistol, he fired from the hip. He hit the agent in the thigh as the agent fired, and the bullet struck Thompkins in the chest. His ballistic vest stopped the bullet, but at that range it slammed him into the wall. He caught himself before he fell to the ground, located the other agent through tear-filled eyes and fired a second round. This one caught the agent in the head as he was raising his pistol. The agent flopped back onto the ground.

More gunfire rocked the house, and Thompkins looked at Mallory. "I don't know what the hell is going on, but wake all the house staff and get them into the panic room."

Mallory stood frozen in place, looking at the dead agent. Thompkins grabbed her arms and shook her. "Mallory, snap out of it. You need to get everyone to safety, NOW!" he yelled.

Mallory shook her head, looked into his eyes and nodded. She ran out the door and headed for the staff wing. Thompkins took a deep, painful breath and clicked his collar mic.

"This is Thompkins. Give me status."

His second-in-command responded, "We're under attack. The shots are coming from our guys. What the hell is going on?"

Thompkins could hear gunfire in the background.

"Stand firm if you can," said Thompkins.

He walked over to the side of the bed and hit the panic alarm. A piercing siren went off throughout the entire house. He pulled out his phone and hit the emergency button.

"Nine-one-one," said the operator. "What is your emergency?"

"This is the Baker ranch. The president-elect is under attack."

He dropped the phone as another agent ran into the room and fired into his leg. He dropped next to the bed and raised his pistol, but he was staring down the barrel of an assault rifle.

"Where the fuck is he?" yelled the agent, the gun held steady on his face.

Thompkins remained quiet. The agent shoved the gun into his face. "Where the fuck is Baker?"

A man wearing camo stepped up behind the agent, pushed him out of the way and grabbed Thompkins by the collar. He dragged him to his feet while another camo-clad person pulled over a ladder-back chair. They plopped Thompkins into the chair and tied his hands behind his back, then they tied a rope around his chest to secure him to the chair.

Thompkins was losing consciousness from the loss of blood, and his head lolled against his chest. The guy in camo slapped him across the face, and his head slammed to one side.

"Where is Baker?" he asked.

Thompkins looked up, blood dripping from his lip. "Fuck you," he said.

The guy punched him in the face, and his head snapped back.

"Where the fuck is Baker?" he yelled.

"Fuck you."

The second guy in camo punched him, and this time teeth and blood sprayed the room.

Another agent stepped through the door. "The alarm

just went off in the panic room in the staff wing. Baker must be in there."

Jimmy Bronson looked up. "Show me," he said as he ran out the door, following the other agent.

Chapter Forty-Two

Mike and Jeff had taken up a position in the woods not far from where Ronnie and Arnie had taken out the surveillance team. They had a great view of the side and back of the ranch house. They hunkered down under a couple of pine trees with branches that hung almost to the ground and waited.

Ronnie snuck into the barn and climbed into the hayloft. She found a spot where several boards on the hayloft door had been cracked or were missing, lay down and slid the rifle barrel through the opening. From her nest, she could cover the side of the house and most of the front. She charged her rifle and waited.

Arnie was covering the entry gate. There were two uniformed Secret Service officers working the gate, and he spotted two more inside the trailer that they were using as an office. He had a good view and spotted the first two attackers moving up the edge of the road, just inside the tree line. The communications gear he had taken from Dooly proved invaluable. He heard Jimmy Bronson give the order to proceed. He waited.

The two guys approaching the gate moved as one, and before Arnie realized, both officers were down. He heard a silenced weapon go off in the trailer and saw a flash. The lights around the property went out, and the property was engulfed in pitch black.

Arnie looked through his night vision scope and

sighted in on the gatehouse. He could hear a gunfight in the distance that sounded like it was coming from inside the ranch house. He held steady. The two guys checked the guards who were down and finished them with head shots. Arnie targeted the first bad guy, took a deep breath and blew his head off. The second guy went down before he knew the other guy was dead. He switched his aim to the trailer door. A uniformed officer pushed open the door and waved his rifle around. Arnie caught the reflection of the American flag pendant on the officer's chest, took a breath, held it and pulled the trigger. The officer's head exploded all over the wall of the trailer, and he slid down in a lump.

Arnie jumped up, pulled his pistol from his holster and bolted for the gatehouse. He made sure all three bad guys were dead and checked the two officers. Both were dead. The gunfire from the ranch house intensified, and he holstered his pistol and ran towards the house.

Mike and Jeff were surprised when all the perimeter and house lights went out. They grabbed their night vision goggles and spotted six figures crossing the field, heading for the house. They shifted positions, sighted in and opened fire. Three of the attackers went down, and the other three dove for cover and returned fire. None of the return fire came close to where Mike and Jeff were because they had already moved towards the house.

The three attackers rose and moved towards the house. One of them branched off towards the front of the house, and as he rounded the corner, he was thrown backwards by a round to his ballistic vest. He'd started to rise when the second round found his nose. He stopped moving.

Ronnie spotted two more guys coming through the woods to her left, and she repositioned and opened fire. Both attackers fell, and she spotted Arnie racing across the field. He approached the two guys who were down in the field and finished them off with head shots. He waved to Ronnie and headed for the front door.

The other two attackers had made it to the house and smashed open the front door. The gunfight was still going on inside, but there was a lot less noise than before, and they entered the fray.

The patio door to the bedroom blew in, and two men rushed in. Mike fired as he crossed the threshold, and the head of the agent wearing the flag pendant around his neck exploded, spraying blood and brain matter into the face of the guy wearing camo, who raised his hands to wipe his face. Jeff Halsey's shot found its mark, and the camo guy went down with a bullet to his throat. He crashed onto the dresser and sunk to the floor. They had their Homeland Security badges clearly visible hanging around their necks as they moved through the house.

Jeff pulled his med kit off his belt, found a tourniquet and wrapped it around Thompkins's leg. He tore his pants, opened a compression bandage and slapped it on the bullet hole. He tapped him on the shoulder and followed Mike.

Mike stepped towards the hall as bullets slammed into the doorjamb. He crouched next to the jamb and, staying low, returned fire, and a camo-clad guy fell into the hall, bleeding from several wounds. Mike stood and moved cautiously along the hall. Jeff was behind him, facing in the other direction to cover his back.

Several rounds peppered the hall, and Jeff grabbed his left arm and hit the ground. Mike grabbed Jeff and pulled him into the nearest room. Jeff was already pulling a compression bandage out of his med kit on his belt when Mike tore open his sleeve and looked at the wound. The bullet had gone through and through, and there wasn't a lot of bleeding. Mike took the bandage from him and wrapped it around the wound. Jeff nodded and picked up his rifle.

Mike moved into the hallway, staying low, and moved towards the front door. He heard two voices, and he stopped.

"What the fuck do you mean, he's not here? Where the fuck is he?" yelled Jimmy Bronson.

"He wasn't in his room. I don't know where he is. He's probably in the panic room with the staff. We tried to get in, but they won't open the door."

Jimmy was pissed. "Without Baker, this was all for fucking nothing."

Mike stood next to the doorjamb, sighted his pistol and shot the Secret Service agent in the head. Jimmy Bronson fired from the hip and ran for the front door. Bullets slammed into the doorjamb where Mike had been standing. Jeff fired from the hall, and he saw Jimmy grab his arm as he ran.

Jimmy jumped into the first SUV he saw, started it and tore away from the house. He headed for the driveway and the gatehouse. Mike fired after him, and the rear window exploded, but the SUV didn't slow down. Mike keyed his throat mic.

"Ronnie, you got him?"

Ronnie was too busy watching the SUV through her scope to respond. She knew that there was a small window when the SUV would turn parallel to her position, but it would be only for a few seconds before it made the final turn towards the gate. Ronnie picked her spot and waited.

Jimmy Bronson saw the turn towards the gate ahead and knew he would soon be in the clear. He couldn't believe this was all a waste of time and the damn president-elect wasn't even on the property. If most of his team weren't already dead, he would have liked to kill someone. His arm ached, and his sleeve was covered in blood, but he knew he needed to get clear of the house. He saw the road straighten out, and then he saw the turn.

Ronnie took a breath, let out half, held the rest and pulled the trigger. The SUV left the road at full speed and slammed into a tree just past the final turn. She could hear the engine revving as the SUV tried to push through the tree.

Jimmy knew he was home free. He would head to where he had parked his SUV and then race back to

North Carolina to regroup and see what Plan B was. The driver's side window exploded, and he felt a searing pain as the bullet passed through his head and blew out the passenger window.

Chapter Forty-Three

Bill and Stosh had made their way back to shore a little after midnight. They stashed the Zodiac in a small marina a mile from the house and headed for the truck. Twenty minutes later, they were staked out at a small motel in the next town. Ronnie had given them information on three of the guys they'd photographed, and through various methods they had learned that these guys were registered under fake names at this small mom-and-pop motel.

Stosh sat back and closed his eyes. He was trying to remember when they had slept last. He knew it had been a while. After making sure the VP-elect was settled in, they had grabbed the Zodiac and headed back to the marina where they had stashed Bill's truck. Lucky for them, the weather had held, and the sea was running about three feet, so the ride back was quick and mostly dry.

Back at the truck, they changed into dry street clothes, loaded the rest of their weapons and headed for the motel. The area they drove through was dry, and the crops they passed looked like they needed a good bath, but there was no rain in sight for the near future and there hadn't been any in several months. Wildfires were everywhere, and as they drove, they were on the lookout for spot fires. In several places, the smoke was dense as they continued their drive. Once at the motel, the air quality improved dramatically, and they could breathe. Bill let Stosh sleep while he kept watch through the camera and spotting scope. The motel parking lot had two cars parked in front of rooms. The rest of the lot was empty.

Twice over two hours, one of the men would leave the room and fill up the ice bucket with more ice from the machine at the end of the building near the office.

The motel was quaint, with adobe walls and a metal roof. The doors were painted in vibrant colors, and Bill had watched the manager or owner sweep the sidewalk around the office and then prune out dead leaves and flower buds from the plants in the planters on either side of the door before locking up for the night.

Stosh woke up and took over the watch as Bill slipped out and walked down the highway to a small Mexican restaurant. He brought back several burrito platters and an assortment of soft and hard tacos. They ate in silence while they watched the motel.

Just before 1:30 A.M., two young women—and Bill used the term "young" because they looked to be as old as his high school daughter—left one of the rooms the three men were registered in. They hurried down the street and slid into a newer-model Volkswagen Beetle and drove away.

They had a sense that it was showtime. They checked their weapons and made their way across the street to the motel. Bill took up a position behind the dumpster on the opposite side of the parking lot, and Stosh found a spot at the end of the building with good protection. They didn't have to wait long.

Almost simultaneously, the three doors opened, and the men strode out. They were dressed in camo and had used camo paint on their faces to minimize light reflection. They each carried a large, heavy duffel bag, which they placed in the back of a large black SUV that sat in front of the rooms.

Bill and Stosh looked around to make sure no one was watching, but it looked like the entire small community shut down after midnight. Even the highway was empty of vehicles, and the lights in the office had been out for over an hour.

They moved as silent as death from the hiding spots and approached the vehicle from two sides. Before the men even knew what hit them, they both opened up with silenced rifles and cut them down. Their ballistic vests did little to stop the bullets as each round found its mark. Bill moved towards the guy who had fallen into the back hatch, blood pouring from a wound in his neck and his thigh. He spun him around and slipped his pistol under his chin.

"How many more on your assault team?" he asked, pushing the gun harder under his chin.

"Fuck you," said the guy with a deep Southern accent.

"Fuck me, huh," said Bill. "Friend, you are going to die tonight, but you have the choice of how you die. I have no problem throwing you in the back of my truck, taking you out into the desert and helping you die a slow, painful death, or you can die like your buddies here, like a man, instead of a screaming little girl. Your choice."

Bill noticed a strong smell of urine. The guy shook, and Bill looked at his watch.

“We need to get a move on. I’m surprised no one has called the cops already.”

They picked up the dead bodies, shoved them into the back of the SUV and closed the door. The third guy they threw into the bed of Bill’s pickup truck; Stosh climbed in with him, and Bill pulled out of the parking lot. The drive out into the desert didn’t take too long, and when they arrived, Stosh opened the tailgate and threw the third guy out. He landed hard. He screamed with pain and grabbed his leg. His pant leg was covered in blood, as were his neck and shoulder.

Stosh walked over and put his foot on the bullet hole in his thigh. The guy screamed. He pushed his foot harder into the wound, and the guy’s body shook. He lifted his foot off the guy’s thigh and kneeled next to him.

“How many more of you guys are in the assault group?” he asked.

“Fuck you.”

Stosh smiled, pulled out his silenced pistol and fired a round into the guy’s other thigh. He screamed and grabbed his leg. Stosh leaned closer.

“One more time. How many guys are on the assault team?”

The guy opened his mouth, and Stosh hit him in the nose with the butt of the pistol. Blood exploded from his nose and covered his black T-shirt.

The scream was now garbled by the blood flowing out of his nose and into his mouth. Stosh held his pistol against the side of the guy's head.

"Next is your ear," said Stosh, his voice level and calm. "After that, we're gonna get more personal, if you get my drift."

"Six," said the guy. His voice was a whisper.

Stosh smiled. "Very good. And when is the assault to take place?"

The guy shook. "Three A.M. today."

"Last question," said Stosh. "How many members of the Secret Service detail are compromised, and how were you supposed to recognize them during the assault?"

The guy was quiet for a minute and then gained a bit of composure. "Four of the team. They will each have an American flag tie clasp. That's it. I swear."

Stosh turned the pistol that was next to the guy's ear and pulled the trigger. The body jerked and fell sideways. Stosh stood and looked at his watch.

"We have about an hour. We'd better get a move on."

Chapter Forty-Four

They jumped into the truck and headed back to the VP-elect's house. Traffic was light for California, and they made it back with twenty minutes to spare. They parked at a public beach parking area, slid out and pulled out their gear. They had their ballistic vests on, so they grabbed more full magazines for their weapons and ran down the beach. They covered the half mile to the beach behind the VP's house in five minutes and slid up onto the dune grass-covered berm. They checked their ammo and waited.

The house, which earlier had been bathed in light from the outside, went dark. Not a good sign, and a violation of protocol. They moved off the berm and ran to opposite ends of the building. Flashes could be seen through some windows, and gunfire erupted from inside the house.

Bill slid open the sliding glass door to the patio and slipped inside. He could hear muffled voices. He spotted Stosh as he came into the family room from the kitchen. He held a finger to his ear, and Stosh stopped and listened. He nodded and pointed towards the bedrooms. Gunfire was sporadic both inside and outside the house. They moved forward.

Lying on the floor in the hall was the body of a Secret Service agent. He had been shot in the back and the head. They found a second body lying in one of the smaller bedrooms. They stopped and listened.

"Where the fuck is she?" asked a deep Southern

voice. There was a loud smack and a moan.

"There must be a secure room somewhere in the house," said another voice, this one with a nondescript accent.

"Wait," said a voice. "Don't hit him again. We've been assigned to Hanford since the beginning of the campaign, and we've never seen a safe room in the house. They must have her stashed someplace else."

"How the fuck would they have known we were coming?" asked the first voice. "Did you guys get an alert?"

"No," said a voice. "But what about your other three guys? Where the fuck are they?"

"Who the fuck knows?" said the guy with the deep accent. "They were supposed to be here half an hour ago and never showed."

There was a loud slap and a groan. "We're getting nowhere. Let's put a bullet in him. Bet he talks then."

Bill and Stosh hated to go into any situation blind, but they felt they had no choice. They heard a silenced round go off, and whoever the victim was moaned.

"Enough fucking around," said another voice. "Drag the broad over here. Maybe he cares more about her than he cares about himself."

They could hear a scuffle and then a thud. There was a tearing sound and a woman's voice screaming obscenities.

"Tell us where Hanford is or I'll put a bullet in her pretty little face."

"Don't you fucking dare tell them!" screamed the woman. There was a loud thud, and something hit the floor. The woman moaned.

"I swear to God," said a ragged voice. "We don't know where she is. Last we saw her, she was heading for bed with her husband."

"So, what?" said Deep Accent. "She just up and fucking disappeared. What, like fucking aliens came down and grabbed her?" There was a moment of silence.

"Put a bullet in her," said Deep Accent.

Bill and Stosh hit the partially open doors at the same time and fired as they entered, spraying the room with bullets. Several rounds came from the bad guys but didn't find their mark and hit the wall and the doorframe. Stosh shot the guy standing over the Secret Service agent lying on the floor, and the back of his head exploded. One of the guys in camo died with the follow-up shot. Bill took out two guys wearing suits as they grabbed for their weapons. The guy in camo kneeling next to the woman on the ground died as Bill and Stosh emptied their magazine into him. He fell next to the woman.

A guy in a suit and a camo-clad attacker entered the room from a sitting area off the main bedroom and died before they could get off a shot.

Bill and Stosh cleared the rest of the bedroom area, and then Stosh cleared the rest of the house. Bill untied the agent on the floor. He held up his Homeland Security badge.

"Homeland Security. Who are you?" he asked while the guy rubbed his hands together to get some feeling back.

The guy rubbed the bruise on his face. "Todd Grissom," he said. "I'm the VP-elect's lead agent. Where the fuck did you guys come from?"

"Later," said Bill. "Is there anyone else in the house?"

"Yeah. Should be five more agents, plus a cook and a housekeeper."

Stosh stepped into the room and kneeled next to the woman on the floor. She was coming to, and he pulled out a knife and cut her restraints. He moved over and checked the four guys wearing suits. He looked at Bill.

"Each guy has a flag tie clasp. I found three more agents in a media room down the hall. They're all dead."

Bill nodded.

"What's the flag tie clasp mean?" asked the agent, who was guzzling a bottle of water Bill had picked up from the nightstand.

"We were told that that's how the bad guys would know which of your agents were part of the attack. The bad guys had to have some way to recognize each other."

The agent looked at Bill. "I've worked with some of those guys for years. I can't believe they're dirty. How did we not know?"

Stosh stepped over and helped up the female agent

and sat her on the edge of the bed.

"This plan goes to the highest levels of the government and has been in the works for months. You guys were collateral damage."

"But how did you guys know about the attack, and where is Mrs. Hanford? We didn't know she wasn't here until these guys dragged us in here and demanded to know where the safe room was."

"The three guys they were missing," said Bill. "One of them is out in the desert. The other two are dead in the back of an SUV at a small motel outside town. As far as Mrs. Hanford, you don't have to worry about her. She and her husband are safe."

"You guys have her?" asked the female agent.

"We took her and her husband earlier tonight."

The male agent looked closer at Bill. "You guys were here earlier today and had a meeting with her. I remember."

"Right," said Stosh.

"We need to get to her," said the male agent.

"The only place you're going is to the hospital, both of you," said Bill. "As far as the VP-elect is concerned, she is no longer your responsibility. We have no idea if there are backup plans in case this first attack failed. The VP's location is need-to-know, and you don't need to know. If you are not happy with that, call President Diggs. He'll tell you the same thing."

Stosh pulled out his phone and dialed 911. He requested police, paramedics and the coroner and hung up before giving the operator any information about himself. Bill looked at the two agents.

"If you care about the VP and her safety, you'll keep your mouth shut when the locals get here, and you won't mention a word about us. As far as the bad guys are concerned, the VP is missing. We need to keep it that way until we can close out this threat. We'll hit the gate button on our way out. Rest up."

Before the two agents could say anything, Stosh and Bill walked through the patio door in the sitting area of the bedroom and disappeared into the night. Stosh ran to the kitchen door, stepped in, hit the emergency gate button on the wall and disappeared onto the beach. They could hear sirens coming from several directions.

Back at the truck, they stripped off their gear, slid in and pulled onto the highway. Stosh pulled an encrypted phone from his backpack and dialed Mike.

***

Bob Fields, the VP's chief of staff, reached for the ringing phone. He checked to make sure his wife was still sleeping, but she was opening her eyes and looking at him. The sun was coming through the curtains. He looked at his watch, looked at the restricted number on the phone and clicked the talk button.

"Bob Fields. Who the hell is this?"

"Bob, it's Liz. I need you to be fully awake."

"Sorry, ma'am, the number said restricted. Why aren't you calling me on your phone?"

"Bob, I need you to be quiet for a minute and listen. There was an attack on our house tonight. Members of a militia group and some of the Secret Service agents assigned to protect us were involved. There are a lot of dead people, from what I've been told."

Bob was sitting on the edge of the bed. His wife leaned across the bed to listen.

"Are you all right, ma'am?" he asked.

"James and I are fine. We were not at the house at the time of the attack."

Bob shook the cobwebs out of his head. "Where are you, ma'am?"

"I can't tell you just yet. We don't know if there was a contingency plan if the attack failed. As far as the agents on the ground are concerned, my husband and I are missing."

"Who's protecting you, ma'am, and did you say some of our agents were involved?"

"Yes, Bob. This conspiracy runs deep through the government."

"But ma'am . . ."

Elizabeth Hanford cut him off. "Bob, I need you to trust me on this. We will conduct ourselves as if I am there at the house. Coordinate everything with Mallory, and let's act like nothing is going on, okay?"

Bob Fields had been with the vice president–elect for more than twenty years and had served as her chief of staff for more than a decade. He could hear something in her voice; he wasn't sure what it was, but he knew it was serious.

"Will do, ma'am," said Bob. "Ma'am, I have to ask. Did something happen that caused you to hide and not inform your security detail?"

"Bob, let's just say that after what happened during the election certification on January sixth, we were told of a serious threat. Our evacuation was directed from the highest office, because if the threat succeeded, it would cause a constitutional crisis."

"Understood, ma'am."

"Good," said Hanford. "You'll need to work out of my downtown office until the police finish processing the house. Call everyone who needs to be on the staff call this morning and have them meet there. I'll call in. Just tell them I'm working remote for a couple of days."

"Ma'am, what about Mr. Baker? Is he aware of the attack?"

"There was an attack on his ranch this morning as well. Tom had been evacuated before the attack and is also safe."

"Shit," said Bob. "I'll take care of everything."

Bob disconnected the call, looked at his wife and headed towards the bathroom. He needed to get moving. He had a lot to do today, and his mind was racing.

Chapter Forty-Five

Mike could hear sirens approaching the house. Lots of them. They had cleared the house and found two Secret Service agents who were wounded but not critical. Everyone else in the house was dead or dying. They applied pressure dressings where they could. They stepped through the door and waited on the front porch, weapons holstered and badges in full view.

The first local sheriff's department SUV pulled to a stop next to the SUV that was smashed up against the tree. The deputy looked inside, reached in and turned off the ignition. Silence filled the woods.

The sky was brightening, and the snow had stopped as the first vehicles approached the house. It was a mix of sheriff's office SUVs and Montana Highway Patrol SUVs, followed by several ambulances. Two black SUVs followed the vehicles into the yard. Officers and deputies approached the front with guns drawn, and Mike and his team put their hands up, holding their badges in their hands.

"Homeland Security," Mike yelled. "Our weapons are holstered."

Gallatin County Sheriff Caleb Winslow looked behind him to make sure his people had the folks on the porch covered and walked towards the porch. Mike stood, keeping his hands in plain sight.

"Sheriff," he said. "Mike Branik, Homeland

Security."

The sheriff was younger than Mike, but his eyes showed a life that hadn't always gone his way. He was tall and trim, with a bright smile and a sturdy handshake. They shook hands. He studied Mike and the others for a minute. "You were in my office a few days ago picking up some prisoners. Why is Homeland Security here, and what in the hell happened?" He noticed the blood on Jeff's arm.

"I need paramedics up here and in the master bedroom. We cleared the house," said Mike over his shoulder, as he walked into the house.

Four paramedics raced towards the house. Two approached Jeff, who stepped aside and sat on one of the wooden benches that lined the porch. The other two ran deeper into the house.

***

Mike and Ronnie had cleared the house. All the Secret Service agents except Thompkins were dead, as well as all the attackers in the house and on the lawn. The attackers who were injured were dispatched quickly. They spent ten minutes trying to convince Mallory to hit the release button and open the panic room. It took a call from President Diggs to convince her that Mike was on their side. She released the lock, and Ronnie led the staff out the nearest door to the yard and then to the back of the house.

Mallory looked at the carnage, and her body shook. She walked down the hall and stopped at the master bedroom and looked inside. Paramedics had Thompkins on a stretcher and had IV fluids dripping into his arm to stabilize him before they transported him to the hospital. Mike, standing next to her, sent a text to a secure number.

"Where is the president?" she asked as tears rolled down her face. Her phone chimed, and she pulled it from her pocket. She looked at the unknown number.

"Answer it," said Mike. "Put it on speaker. Quiet, everyone."

Mallory hit the green button. "Hello," she said, a quiver in her voice.

"Hi, Mal. It's me."

Her face broke into a huge smile, but before she could say anything Thompkins leaned over.

"Sir, where are you? Are you okay?" he asked.

"I'm fine, Paul," said Baker.

"Sir, where are you? I'll send a team to come get you."

"Unnecessary, Paul. I'm safe. Now, let me speak to Mal."

Mallory held up the phone. "I'm here, sir. The ranch was attacked. We thought you were dead. What's going on?"

"Mal, I need you and the transition team to stay focused on our plan. Let's make sure that we get all the remaining cabinet nominees into the Senate so they can start the hearings. Have communications put out some press releases about the transition and keep social media active. Now, this is important, and this is for your team as well, Paul. As far as the world is concerned, I am working behind closed doors and will be until it's time to head to Washington for the inauguration. It's business as usual. No leaks to the press."

"When will you be back here, sir?" asked Thompkins.

"I will keep you both posted, but for right now, keep a lid on my whereabouts. Understood?"

"Sir," said Thompkins. "I need to let my superiors know what's going on. What do I tell them? You can't just up and disappear and keep us in the dark."

"I'm sorry, Paul," said Baker. "But that's what I did. Tell your superiors whatever you want, but you did nothing wrong here."

An FBI agent stepped into the room and whispered into Thompkins's ear. Mallory looked at him.

"Sir. I've just been informed that the vice president–elect has also gone dark. Is she with you, sir?"

"No, Paul. I do not know where Elizabeth is, but I know that wherever she is, she is safe," said Baker.

"How can you know that, sir? This is a serious breach of protocol. Now, I'm sorry, sir, but we are responsible for your safety, and I need to know what the hell is going on." Thompkins's voice could not mask the aggravation he was feeling.

Baker's voice grew stern. "Paul, you are responsible for my safety, and as such I am telling you to do your jobs as if nothing has changed, because if you don't, my life, Elizabeth's life and our democracy will be in serious jeopardy. I'm asking you to trust me and not ask any more questions. I'm asking you to keep this as quiet as possible. I will explain it all to you once the inauguration is over."

Thompkins looked around the room. Mike nodded to the paramedics, and they wheeled the gurney from the room. As they passed Mal and Mike, Thompkins leaned to the side.

"Okay, sir. I hope you know what you're doing," said Thompkins.

"Thanks, Paul. Now, I need to speak to Mallory. Please give her the room."

There was silence on the phone while everyone left the room. Mallory walked into the office and sat at the desk. Mike stood by her side.

"Okay, sir. They are all gone. What's going on?"

"Look, Mal. Like I told Paul, I'm safe. That's all you need to know. I will tell you this in strictest confidence. The threat against Elizabeth and me, as you are now aware, was real, and I was serious about democracy hanging in the balance. For now I need you to keep the ship afloat. We will talk every day. Anything I tell you moving forward is on a need-to-know basis. There are people around me that can't be trusted."

"People on our staff, sir?" asked Mallory.

"Not necessarily, Mal," said Baker. "I don't have enough information yet to know who I can trust, so I am trusting you. Keep the team focused, and I will call you tonight."

"Yes, sir. You can count on me."

"I know I can, Mal. I'll keep in touch."

The phone went dead, and Mallory sat there looking at the blank screen. She mulled the conversation around in her head. Thomas Baker was one of the toughest people she had ever met, but she could hear in his voice that he was spooked. He told her not to worry, but that was one order she would not follow. She looked at her watch. She had two hours until the Zoom call with the transition team. She needed to get ready.

***

Mike walked up as the paramedics were ready to lift Thompkins into the ambulance. He looked confused. He grabbed Mike's arm.

"What the fuck was all this about?" Thompkins asked. He thought for a minute. "The only thing I can think of is that some kind of verifiable threat was made against Baker and Hanford and that caused them to go into hiding. But who helped Baker and Hanford get away? They were taken right out from under our eyes. Who the hell does that?" He looked up at Mike, who leaned next to his ear.

"Here is what I will tell you," said Mike. "The threat to Baker and Hanford was real, as you can see around you. They are safe and under my protection. You need to focus on getting well."

Thompkins looked at him.

"You got him out of here? The meeting earlier. That's when you planned his escape. Why didn't you tell us? It's our job . . ."

"Some of your agents were compromised. The agents in the house were killed by members of your team."

Thompkins's face showed the shock of the revelation. Mike nodded, and the paramedics loaded Thompkins into the ambulance and closed the doors. Mike walked over and joined the sheriff.

"What the hell happened here? It looks like a war zone," asked the sheriff.

A man and a woman in dark suits and wearing trench coats walked over to Mike and the sheriff. The man looked at Mike. "Where is President Baker?"

"Unknown. We were a little late getting to the party, and most of the festivities were over before we arrived." He faced the sheriff. "Everyone we found, good guys and bad, are dead. We cleared the house, but you need to send in more paramedics to confirm the deaths. The house and campaign staff that were on-site have been taken out to the back patio. They were all in the panic room. You'll need to let them get their coats."

The sheriff turned and ordered five deputies to clear the house again so he could send in the paramedics.

The man in the trench coat stared at Mike. "You got ID?" he asked.

Mike smiled at him. "Who are you?"

"That doesn't matter. I need to know who you are."

“I believe it does, because my boss is going to want to talk to you, and he likes to know who he’s talking to.”

“Who’s your boss?” asked the man in the trench coat.

Mike held up his cell phone and handed it to the man.

“This is FBI Agent Frank Turner. To whom am I speaking?”

Turner stood up straight, and his smirk disappeared. He listened for a few minutes. “Yes, sir. No, sir. I’ll take care of it, sir.” He handed the phone back to Mike, who stepped away from the group. The FBI agent stepped over to the sheriff and the woman he was traveling with, and they were joined by two more agents.

“Mike,” said President Diggs. “You guys okay?”

“Yes, sir. Jeff took a round to his upper arm. But other than that, we’re fine. You got a lot of dead Secret Service agents though. Not sure who you need to call, and how you’re gonna spin it, but right now there’s four FBI agents talking with the sheriff.”

“Mike, are Baker and Hanford okay?”

“Yes, sir. We got them to safety before the shit hit the fan. Bill and Stosh are going through the same thing right now in California. You might want to call out there and give them a hand. I’m also going to need a MATS flight out of Bozeman as soon as you can arrange it.”

“Unfinished business?” asked the president.

"Yes, sir."

"Okay, Mike. Finish it. There is still a lot of danger facing Baker and Hanford over the next couple of days. How do you plan to get them to the inauguration unhurt?"

"Don't you worry, sir. We're working on contingency plans just in case."

"Okay, Mike. Get to Bozeman as soon as you can. I'll make sure there's a plane waiting for you."

Mike disconnected the call and joined the sheriff and the FBI agents. The sheriff had sent more deputies and state troopers in to secure the house, and he had called for two helicopters from Bozeman for medical evacuations.

Sheriff Winslow turned towards Mike. "Don't suppose I could get your weapons to run ballistics tests?"

Mike smiled. "No, sir. Much as I'd like to help, that's not going to happen."

"So, you have the President of the United States on speed dial. Interesting," said the sheriff. He took Mike by the arm and walked away from the group.

"Don't suppose you'd like to fill me in on what happened here and where the president-elect is?"

"I'll give you this much," said Mike as they walked around the side of the house. "The guys in camo are a highly trained group of militia members sent here to kill the president-elect. The Secret Service agents and the officers at the gate who were wearing flag pendants around their necks were working with them. I think you'll find that most of the damage inside was caused by agent-on-agent violence. As far as the president-elect is concerned, for right now, all you need to know is that he is missing. Between you and me, he's safe."

The sheriff looked at him and nodded. Mike walked back to the FBI agents.

"We need to head to Bozeman. If you need anything from us, you won't get it, but you can try. Call your deputy director and he will help you out."

"But we have some questions for you," said the agent.

"We'd like to help, but our jobs are not done yet."

"I got a call," said Agent Turner. "It seems there was an assault on the vice president–elect's house in California last night. She is also missing. Anything you'd like to share?"

"Not at this time," said Mike, and he turned and joined Ronnie, Jeff and Arnie and they headed off into the woods to where they'd parked their vehicles.

Chapter Forty-Six

Robert E. Lee Richardson paced in front of his desk. He checked his watch. He should have heard from Jimmy Bronson by now. He picked up the remote and turned on the national news. The news anchors were looking at pictures of a large police and government presence outside the entrance to President-elect Baker's ranch house. They were also flipping to another camera outside a posh residence in California that belonged to the vice president–elect. The camera feeds showed flashing lights and a long line of police and medical vehicles lining the entrance to each location. So far, neither the president nor the vice president–elect had issued a statement, and the internet conspiracy mill was churning out all kinds of ludicrous theories. None based on any factual information.

Robert picked up his phone and dialed a number. The phone was answered.

"Get the plane ready to fly," said Richardson.

He disconnected and dialed three more numbers. As each phone was answered, he said the same thing: "Time to leave." He disconnected each call, sent a text and turned off the TV. He put his laptop into his satchel, opened the office door and walked towards the kitchen. His wife was brewing fresh iced tea, and he walked up behind her and placed his hands on her waist.

"Honey," he said. "I need you to pack a small bag. We need to take a trip, and we need to leave now."

She turned and looked at him. "But Robert, I invited the kids for dinner. When will we be back?" Her eyes showed disappointment.

"We're going to be gone for quite a while. We'll call the kids from Brazil, and they can come visit us for a couple of weeks once we're settled in the house."

She wiped the tears from her eyes. "Okay, Robert. I'll go pack." She turned off the stove, untied her apron, hung it on the back of the door and left the room. Robert went to his closet in his office and pulled out a go bag. He loaded the go bag and his satchel into his SUV and then walked back into the house. His wife was standing at the bottom of the stairs with an overnight bag, and he took the bag and carried it to the car.

He stepped back into the house and noticed his wife looking at the pictures that lined the hallway walls. "Will we ever come back to this house?" she asked.

"Someday, dear, but not for a while."

"Does this have anything to do with whatever you and the boys were doing with that Senator Stevenson? I never liked him," she said.

Robert gave her a hug. "You don't need to worry about that." Robert grabbed their coats off the wall rack by the door and helped his wife into hers. He was putting his on when his phone rang. He looked at the number and told his wife he would be just a minute, and he walked back to his office and answered.

"It's time. I need you to proceed. The money will be in your account tonight." He disconnected the call and walked back into the hall. He took his wife by the arm and led her to the SUV. She climbed in and he did the same, and they headed for the airport.

Warren Turlock wasn't concerned about the call from Robert. He knew Robert would make a run for it once the shit hit the fan, and he assumed, after watching two hours of internet coverage, that the shit had indeed hit the fan. The internet was buzzing with stories of early morning gunfights in California and Montana and with speculation that the president- and vice president–elect had been either kidnapped or murdered. He hooked the boat trailer to the back of his old pickup truck and hauled his boat to the lake outside of town for a little relaxation.

By midafternoon, a press conference was called, and the media descended on the White House. President Roman Diggs stepped up to the microphone. He was dressed casually in gray slacks and a light blue button-down shirt. He wore a navy-blue suit jacket that was unbuttoned as he stood behind the podium.

"My fellow Americans. In the early morning hours today, the homes of the president-elect and vice president–elect were attacked. Authorities in Montana and California are on the scene, and I have sent the attorney general and FBI Director Shavor to oversee the investigations into these heinous and treasonous acts. Preliminary information is that the perpetrators of these acts were home-grown extremists and not foreign terrorists, as some in the media have reported. At this time, we do not have information pertaining to what militia groups might be involved. The terrorists who took part in these cowardly attacks have been killed, as have several members of the Secret Service and the house staffs of Thomas Baker and Elizabeth Hanford.

"At this time, the whereabouts of the president- and vice president–elect are unknown. There is no indication that they have been kidnapped or killed, and the authorities are working diligently to find them. We will keep the American people informed and pass along all information as it becomes available."

The president paused for a moment, then looked into the camera.

"These attacks, though cowardly and heinous, were designed to play on our emotions. This country has never been so divided in its ideology, and this type of event is what happens when those ideologies collide. These were attacks on the two democratic principles that make us a great nation: free and fair elections and the peaceful transfer of power. Good men and women died today because people no longer accept those principles. The men and women who died were doing their duty, and as Americans, we should all be horrified and ashamed by these acts. This is not who we are. We pray for the safe return of Thomas Baker and Elizabeth Hanford, and we pray for these United States."

The president turned and walked away from the podium and down the hall before disappearing into his office. The press was clamoring for more information, but the White House press secretary had nothing new to add. They raced off to file their stories.

Two hours later, the major news groups received a video statement from President-elect Baker. The president-elect appeared on camera, and the message was short and simple.

"Elizabeth Hanford and I are fine, and we are safe. We are horrified by these attacks, and our hearts go out to the families of the men and women who died today defending our democracy. Because of the continued threats we have received, we will remain out of sight until the inauguration. God bless the citizens of our great nation, and God bless the United States."

Conspiracy theorists called the video fake news and reported that both Baker and Hanford were dead or seriously injured. The militias and hate groups disavowed any knowledge of the attacks and condemned further violence, and constitutional scholars covered the airwaves and the internet, discussing what would happen if both the president-elect and the VP-elect weren't able to be inaugurated. No one agreed on what would happen, but they all agreed that it would be a constitutional crisis.

Chapter Forty-Seven

The MATS flight landed at a small Air National Guard base just outside of Nashville and taxied to a small hangar. Mike and Ronnie grabbed their gear, walked down the steps as they were lowered and put their bags in the back of the black government SUV that was waiting for them in front of the hangar. They slid into the SUV, and Mike headed for the gate. He passed through the checkpoint while Ronnie programmed their first destination into the SUV's navigation system. Mike jumped on the interstate and headed deep into the Tennessee countryside.

Twenty-five minutes after leaving the base, Mike pulled the SUV into the long driveway leading to a nondescript farmhouse that sat in the middle of several acres of beautiful farmland and forest. They parked, walked to the back of the SUV, opened the hatch and removed their ballistic vests, which they put on. They checked their pistols, stepped up onto the porch and knocked on the front door. No one answered.

Mike was tired and done with niceties. He reared back and planted his boot next to the doorknob, and the door exploded inward, taking bits of the doorjamb with it.

"Federal agents," he yelled, and they pulled their pistols and stepped into the house. Ronnie took the stairs in front of them two at a time, and Mike stepped into the kitchen. He looked around, then cleared the rest of the first floor. Ronnie cleared the second floor and stepped into the kitchen. "No one's here," she said.

Mike pointed towards the stovetop. “Someone was making sweet tea. Looks like they left in a hurry.”

Ronnie followed him to the office at the back of the house, and they rifled through the drawers and files. Robert E. Lee Richardson had been very careful, but there was a small trail of breadcrumbs. Mrs. Richardson left a note on the refrigerator for her daughter, apologizing about having to cancel dinner and saying she would call once they got to the house in Brazil.

“No extradition,” said Ronnie.

“Yeah,” said Mike. “Let’s see if anyone else is still in town.” He checked the list on his phone. The FBI had identified each of the people whom Bill and Stosh had taken pictures of and recorded with the laser microphone. He picked the first name on the list.

Harold Wahls was a nervous little man, and after watching the television coverage from Montana and California for the better part of the day, he decided to take a vacation and visit his daughter in Florida. It would take a couple of hours, and if he left now, he’d get there just after dark. Harold hated driving at night anymore. His eyesight wasn’t that good in the daytime, but night driving made his eyes hurt. He was putting the small suitcase in the back of his car when a black SUV pulled into his driveway, blocking his way. He watched as two people wearing vests and pistols on their hips slid out of the SUV and approached him. He looked at the badges hanging around their necks, and he panicked and ran towards the front door, which was open. Ronnie tackled him as he got to the door and dragged him to his feet. He rubbed his shoulder where he had slammed into the credenza that sat in the hall next to the stairs.

"What's the meaning of this? I'll be contacting your bosses," said Wahls, but his heart wasn't in it, and Ronnie laughed and led him into the kitchen and pushed him onto a chair at the table.

"Going someplace, Harold?" said Mike as he stepped into the kitchen.

"If you must know, I'm going to visit my daughter in Florida, and I'm late, so if you'll excuse me." He stood, and Ronnie pushed him back into the chair.

"We know what you did, Harold. You and your militia buddies. You know what the penalty for treason is, Harold? Death."

Harold's hands shook, and he tried to deny any involvement, but his voice let him down.

Mike looked him in the eyes. "Jimmy Bronson and his militia fighters are dead, and we have you on tape with Robert E. Lee Richardson and others plotting to overthrow the election and install Stevenson as the president. Where is Richardson?"

Tears rolled down his cheeks. "I didn't want to be a part of it. They forced me."

"And how did they force you, Harold?" asked Ronnie.

He sniffled and wiped his face on his sleeve. "I can help you. I can give you the others."

Mike laughed. "Harold, we already know who the

others are. All you can do is tell us where Richardson went."

"He has a house somewhere in Brazil. I don't know where. He probably headed there."

"See, that wasn't so hard, was it, Harold?" said Mike.

He stood and pulled his pistol out of his holster and pulled a silencer out of his back pocket. Harold's face froze.

"You can't do this. You're law enforcement."

Mike smiled. "Oh, how wrong you are, Harold. We are definitely not law enforcement."

Mike raised the pistol and shot Harold in the head, and he fell to the floor, a puddle of blood forming under his head. They walked from the kitchen and checked the rest of the house.

In the office they found a laptop, and in a desk drawer they discovered an old leather journal. Ronnie opened it up and read what Harold had written. She looked at Mike.

"Harold had an insurance policy. He names names and is detailed in his description of each meeting and conversation. There is a long list of people who were involved in this scheme, who have not hit our radar yet. What do you want to do with it?"

"Take it and we'll give it to our friends at the FBI. There're still a couple of people over there I trust."

Ronnie took the journals and the laptop. They turned off the lights in the kitchen and locked the front door as they left. They slid into the SUV and headed for the next name on their list.

Chapter Forty-Eight

Warren Turlock pulled into his driveway and backed the boat into its spot next to his garage. He grabbed his favorite pole and his fishing box and walked to his front door. He unlocked the door, set the pole behind the door and the fishing box on the table inside the door and turned on the lights. The house was quiet, and he stepped into the kitchen and lit the burner under his old coffee percolator.

He washed his hands, opened the refrigerator and pulled out half a chicken and a small tub of potato salad. He set them on the counter. He turned and stepped into the dark family room. He picked up the television remote and clicked on the news. He stood for a second and watched as the coverage continued from the day's attacks. He laughed, shook his head and turned and found that he was looking straight into the barrel of a pistol that, this close to his face, looked huge. He stepped backwards and felt the cold steel of another pistol pushing against his head.

"Hello, Warren. You don't know us, but we're here to ask you a couple of questions."

Warren stared at the badge hanging around the neck of the person in front of him and realized it was a woman. He sneered. "Do you know who I am? I'll have your jobs."

Ronnie hit him in the forehead with the butt of her pistol, and he fell backwards. Mike caught him and sat him in his lounge chair.

"You can't do that," said Warren as he rubbed his head and looked at the spot of blood on his hand.

Mike stood next to him. "Warren, you are in big trouble. You see, we have video and audio of you conspiring with several others to overthrow the last election. We know you guys planned to have the new president and vice president murdered so they couldn't be inaugurated. You've been on a lot of conservative talk shows explaining how them not being available would result in Stevenson being made president. Going against the will of the people."

Warren laughed. "The people are sheep. They will do whatever we tell them, and you have nothing on me. It's not against the law to express my opinions. It's one of our most important rights. You can't touch me. I know people, and I'll be out of jail before you can finish the paperwork."

Mike looked at Ronnie. "One question, Warren. Do you know where in Brazil Richardson has his house? Could save us a lot of time tracking him down."

"You think I'd tell you even if I knew? The guy is a billionaire. He can go wherever he wants and do whatever he wants, and there isn't shit you can do to stop him. If we're done here, then arrest me and let's get a move on. I don't want to miss my favorite shows."

"We're not here to arrest you, Warren. We've found you guilty of treason against the United States. We're here to execute you."

Warren Turlock looked at Mike and then at Ronnie. He tried to say something, but Ronnie shot him just above his upper lip. Warren Turlock fell back into his recliner, and Mike pulled the lever to make it lie flat. They went through the house and found another laptop and some other documents they thought might be helpful. They turned off the coffeepot and put the chicken and the potato salad in the refrigerator. They turned out the lights and locked the front door as they were leaving. They had one more stop to make in Tennessee, so they headed for their SUV that was parked around the corner.

Calvin Mace could not reach either Richardson, Turlock or Wahls, and he grew concerned. He knew Jimmy Bronson had failed in his attacks, but he had no way of knowing if he was sitting in an interrogation room spilling his guts about the people involved, if he was dead or if he was running. He hoped it was the last, but the other two options concerned him.

Calvin had spent most of the day on the phone rounding up people from the militias that he knew he could trust to get them to Washington before the inauguration to create a cordon around the Capitol and stop the swearing in—by force, if necessary. He wasn't having a lot of luck. The news of the failed attacks was spreading across the media like wildfire, and anyone who was the slightest bit involved in that fiasco had gone into hiding.

Cal had feared that this was going to be the result when he first got involved with Oliver Stevenson. He knew the senator was unstable; yet, he fell under his spell. The man was charismatic. Of that, there was no doubt, and Cal understood how so many people had fallen under his spell, but that didn't change the fact that he was nuts. Cal knew he should have bailed early on, but he wanted to be part of the new beginning, changing America into a thing he could be proud of. Now he was working on finding people to stop the peaceful transfer of power and kill the new president and vice president at the inauguration. What the hell kind of insanity was this? He figured he should be on a plane to Belize, where there was no extradition treaty with the United States. He figured that's what the others were already doing.

Cal made a decision. He had a couple more phone calls to make and then he would wake his wife, pack some bags and head to Belize. Once he got away from Tennessee, he could take some time to think about his next moves and decide which country he would head towards permanently.

Cal was sweating, and he needed to clear his head. He felt like the room was closing in on him. He had been at it for hours and realized that his wife had retired several hours before. Cal killed two birds with one stone. Being the good militia general he was, he knew that the best way to do both things was to spend some time outside checking on the people patrolling his house. He grabbed his jacket and phone, walked through the kitchen and stepped out into the night.

The air was crisp, and he felt better as soon as he took a few deep breaths. This farm had been in his family since the Revolutionary War, and he would hate to leave it. Maybe he could find a way to stay. After all, he hadn't pulled any triggers. All he did was organize a coup. Maybe he could use that to his advantage. He stood for a minute and listened. The stillness was broken by the sounds of crickets and cicadas, and fireflies lit up the area around the house, their rhythmic glow a nonstop symphony for the eyes. As a kid, he'd loved catching them in a jar and then sitting in his room, under the covers, basking in the yellow glow of their light until his father came in, took the jar and let them all go in the backyard. Man, how he loved this place. He was going to miss it.

Cal shook off the melancholy and walked around to the front of the house. He had two men standing guard at the entrance gate, so he walked down the driveway to see how they were doing.

Cal knew something was wrong before he got to the gate. It was the silence. He knew that young Carter Groves couldn't keep his mouth shut for more than five minutes, yet as he approached, there was no conversation going on. He also didn't see the telltale red spot of George Ulster's cigarette. George had been a chain-smoker since he and Cal had met in their first year of high school.

Cal pulled the pistol from his holster and walked towards the gate, avoiding anything in the dirt driveway that might make a noise. He approached and found Carter Groves wire-tied to the gate. He looked like Jesus hanging from the cross. His eyes were open, there was a huge gash in his throat and the front of his shirt was soaked with blood.

Cal froze. He might have run a bunch of militias, but he had never served in the military, so he had never experienced the horrors of war. He stared until his stomach could no longer hold the bile, and then he leaned over and vomited all over his shoes. On his knees and with his hands holding him off the ground, he vomited until he had nothing left. Tears filled his eyes. Carter was an awesome kid, and despite the constant chatter, he enjoyed having him around. He looked to his left and saw two boots sticking out from behind an old oak tree. He stood and wiped his mouth on the sleeve of his jacket and, holding his pistol ahead of him, moved towards the tree. As he got closer, he could see old George lying on his back. He would have looked peaceful in his repose, except for the bullet hole in his forehead.

Cal felt like he was flying as he ran up the driveway towards the house. He had two more guards patrolling around the house and two more asleep in the barn. He was running around the house looking for his two men when he stumbled over something in the dark and fell flat on his face. He picked up the pistol he had lost in the fall and looked behind him. The two men were stacked on top of each other like firewood.

Fear rose from Cal's gut, and he raced for the barn. He was scared, but more than that, he felt alone. He pushed open the barn and fell to his knees. The two guys who had been sleeping were hanging from the hayloft, their faces contorted in agony. Their hands were tied behind them, and they weren't wearing shoes. Cal had no idea why that image bothered him, but it did.

He stood and held his pistol out in front of him and waved it from side to side. Panic grabbed hold of him, and he thought about his wife alone in the house. He'd turned to head for the house when a noose dropped from above and tightened around his neck. He was pulled off his feet, and he lost his pistol as it flew out of his hand. He was dragged from one end of the barn to the other, and he could feel the dirt floor tearing at his skin. He wanted to scream, but the noose was too tight, and he had to hold on to it with both hands so he could breathe.

The pressure released, and he tore at the noose to get some air. He sucked in a couple of large breaths and looked up through tear-filled eyes. He wiped the tears away, but the dirt from his sleeve filled his eyes, and he struggled to see. He looked around as two shadows approached. He felt his bladder let go, and he felt the wetness in his pants. He shuddered as the shadows drew closer.

"Calvin Mace," said a male voice. "You and your friends have been involved in some bad stuff."

Cal wasn't certain if that was a question or a statement, so he sat there in his wet pants and didn't say a word.

"We need to know how many groups you have going to Washington to stop the inauguration."

Cal laughed. "You'll find out when Baker and Hanford are lying dead on the Capitol steps. Fuck off."

One of the shadows did something, and the noose tightened and he was pulled off the ground. He hung with his toes touching the dirt floor, and he pulled at the noose and twisted.

"That was kind of an unfriendly answer," said the voice as it circled around him. "Let's try this again."

The noose loosened so he could stand, and he pulled it loose.

"Fuck you. We are patriots and are prepared to spill the blood of tyrants for our cause."

The noose tightened, and Cal's eyes got wide.

"Cal," said the voice. "You need to stop believing the crap you are selling. You are not patriots. You have no idea what the word means. You and your people attempted to overthrow the legal government of the United States, and now you want to interrupt the peaceful transfer of power. That's a criminal act."

The noose loosened, and Cal swallowed hard. "You'll see when the steps of the Capitol are covered with dead bodies."

"Cal. Do you know where Richardson's house is in Brazil? You know that he and your coconspirators have fled the country. They left you holding the bag."

"Fuck you," said Cal, his voice gravelly from the noose. "I'm not telling you shit. I have rights."

The male voice laughed. "Now you have rights. Before tonight you shit all over those rights, and if we were anybody else, we might care about those rights you suddenly hold so dear. Unfortunately, our job is to punish those who participated."

The noose tightened, and Cal was lifted off the ground. He hung in the air, twisting and turning until the life drained out of him, and he hung still. Mike and Ronnie opened the back door to the barn and led the horses out to the pasture. They walked in and closed the back door. Mike took an old kerosene lamp he found hanging off a post, shook it to make sure it had fluid and lit the wick. The yellow glow danced and cast a warm light over the barn and the three victims hanging there. He threw the lamp up into the hayloft and heard the glass break, and the dry hay caught fire. They walked through the barn and shut the door. By the time they disappeared into the trees bordering the farm, the barn was fully engulfed, and the flames lit up the night sky.

Chapter Forty-Nine

Oliver Stevenson sat in his Washington, DC, town house and stared at the television screen. He had been watching for so long that the information was no longer penetrating his brain. He picked up his glass and poured the last of the bourbon down his throat. He couldn't believe how everything had gone so wrong.

"Fucking incompetents," he said out loud, even though the room was empty. "All they had to do was kill one man and one woman. How fucking hard could that be? Yet they failed. I'm supposed to be the president, god damnit. How is that going to work if Baker and Hanford are still alive?"

He stood, walked to the bar and poured himself another drink. He chugged the liquid and refilled the glass. "I won the election fair and square. This is not how things are supposed to work out."

He walked over and picked up his phone. He had left several messages for Richardson, Turlock, Wahls and Mace, and no one had bothered to return his calls. Once he was sworn in as president, he'd make sure the DOJ did a thorough investigation of those guys, and then he'd see them hung for treason. How dare they abandon him in his time of need?

Something on the news caught his eye, and he grabbed the remote off the desk and turned up the volume. He tried to focus his alcohol-addled brain on what the young woman was saying, but he stared at her breasts. He shook his head and focused on her words.

He listened to the report and then flopped into his chair, spilling his drink on his shirt and pants.

She said something about a fire and several dead bodies at the home of Calvin Mace. He looked at the screen.

"Calvin's dead," he slurred. "That can't be. We have work to do."

He picked up his phone, found the number and dialed Cal. The phone went to voice mail. He dialed three more times and got the same result. He threw the phone across the room, and it smashed against the fireplace. He stood and staggered to the bar, picked up the bottle and was pouring a drink when he heard a noise in the hallway outside his study.

He turned, and the bourbon overflowed the glass and poured onto the floor. He knew he was alone. He had sent his staff home early. He stumbled and grabbed hold of the fireplace mantel. He set his glass down on the mantel and picked up the fireplace poker from the rack. He tiptoed to the door and placed his ear against it. He didn't hear anything.

"Fucking mind is going," he said.

He turned and walked to the mantel and then spun around as he heard the old hinges on the door squeak. He held the poker in front of him like a sword.

"Who the fuck are you?" he said to the woman standing in the doorway.

She wasn't tall, maybe five-six, and she had on a long drover coat and a cowboy hat pulled down, covering most of her face. She wore black gloves, and in her left hand was a silenced pistol.

Stevenson stood up as straight as he could and stared at her. “How the fuck did you get in here?” he asked. When she didn’t answer, he said, “Do you know who the fuck I am? One word from me and there’ll be a dozen Secret Service agents swarming this room.”

Stevenson stepped around his chair and pointed the poker at the woman. “I have friends with money. They will pay you twice what you are being paid to not kill me. I’m gonna be the President of the United States.”

The woman looked up from under the hat and smiled. “Your friends are already paying me.”

Stevenson stared in disbelief. He was having trouble comprehending what she said, but he knew it wasn’t good. He reared back with the fireplace poker, and the woman raised the pistol and shot him in the chest. He fell back against the back of his chair and slipped to the floor. He looked up as the woman approached, and she pulled the trigger a second time.

Mike and Ronnie flew from Tennessee as soon as they got the word from the president that Oliver Stevenson had been killed in his townhome. They arrived as the coroner was loading the body into a black body bag that was lying on the floor next to it. They had badged their way through the checkpoint and now stood next to the medical examiner’s investigator.

“One bullet wound in the chest, one in the head. Execution style,” said the investigator, a tall, thin, serious young man with a bald head and goatee. He helped the aide pick up the body and place it in the bag. He looked at Mike.

"I didn't vote for him, but I sure hate to see this happen to anyone," he said.

Mike nodded, and they followed the body down the stairs, through the house and out into the street. They veered off, slid into the SUV that was parked down the street and headed for Joint Base Andrews. They had a flight to catch.

Chapter Fifty

Inauguration Day

President Diggs stood on the platform at the top of the stairs in front of the United States Capitol and waited with all the other dignitaries. He looked out over the crowd and wondered how Mike was going to deliver the president-elect and the vice president–elect to the stage without getting attacked by the crowd.

Ever since the announcement that Oliver Stevenson had been killed in his townhome, the country seemed on edge, and looking over the crowd below, he could see a lot of angry people. The Secret Service had installed bulletproof glass all around the stage, but that would not stop an angry mob if they attacked. The two big-screen televisions on either side of the stage showed the growing mob, and the president was tempted to cancel the inauguration and have the crowd cleared, but he still didn't know who he could trust in the National Guard or the metro police. He checked his watch and looked at the chief justice of the Supreme Court. Everyone was ready. All they needed were the new president and vice president.

At one minute before noon, the two big screens fluttered, and the pictures changed to show a room. There was a wood courtroom bench and an American flag behind the bench. The crowd grew silent. Everyone was focused on the screen. An elderly man with a full head of gray hair wearing a black robe stepped into view. His face filled the screen.

Elizabeth Hanford, dressed in a black pantsuit,

stepped up next to him.

"I am Chief Justice Earl Hastings of the California Supreme Court. Ma'am, please place your hand on the Bible your husband is holding and repeat after me.

"I do solemnly swear, or affirm, that I will support and defend the Constitution of the United States against all enemies, foreign and domestic; that I will bear true faith and allegiance to the same; that I take this obligation freely, without any mental reservation or purpose of evasion; and that I will well and faithfully discharge the duties of the office on which I am about to enter. So help me God."

Elizabeth Hanford repeated the oath, shook the chief justice's hand and turned and kissed her husband.

"Congratulations, Madam Vice President," said the chief justice.

The screens of the two televisions switched to a different room. The room had dark-paneled walls, and there was a small podium off to the side. Behind the podium was an American flag and a Montana flag. Standing in front of the American flag was a man with a bald head and a thin mustache. He wore a black suit, a white shirt and a skinny black tie. Next to him stood President-elect Thomas Baker, wearing a flannel shirt and jeans.

"Good afternoon. I'm County Court Judge Tim Wheeler of Liberty County, Montana. If you have any questions about who I am, you can look me up on the internet."

He turned to Baker. "Sir, please place your hand on

the Bible and repeat after me.

"I, Thomas Baker, do solemnly swear, or affirm, that I will faithfully execute the office of President of the United States, and will to the best of my ability preserve, protect and defend the Constitution of the United States."

Thomas Baker repeated the oath, then shook the judge's hand. "Congratulations, Mr. President."

Former President Diggs watched the crowd from on the stage, and everyone was dumbstruck. Much of the crowd below had walked away when a chorus of cheers and applause erupted from those remaining. The dignitaries on the podium looked around and then applauded as well.

Diggs pulled out his phone and sent a text: "Well done." He put his phone away and walked into the Capitol. His job was done. He had ensured the peaceful transfer of power.

Mike and Ronnie walked up and shook the new president's hand. An hour before, a contingent of Canadian Special Forces soldiers had escorted the president-elect to the border and transferred him to Mike and Ronnie's care. They wished him well, and he thanked them for their hospitality. From the border, they took a chopper to the town of Chester in Liberty County, Montana, where the judge, a former marine gunnery sergeant, was waiting.

Ronnie had worked her voodoo computer magic and had intercepted the screens at the Capitol and the live feeds from the networks. The rest, as they say, was history.

The new president and vice president, with a fully vetted security team, flew to Washington to assume their duties. Mike sent his team home for a well-deserved rest.

Chapter Fifty-One

Eight Weeks Later

Four shadows slipped from the water and moved swiftly across the lawn behind the mansion on Mirante da Peninsula outside of São Paulo, Brazil. The mansion, a steel-and-glass monument to expensive living, was as beautiful on the outside as it was luxurious on the inside. The vast wall of windows looked out over the ocean, and the white marble floors and expensive leather furniture made it look like it could have been taken right from a luxury architecture magazine. The wide expanse of granite patio was perfect for entertaining, and the indoor/outdoor pool was awesome for those inclement weather days.

The house was more than Mrs. Richardson needed and was four times the size of her farmhouse in Tennessee. She never felt comfortable in it, but it was her husband's dream home, and she made the most of it. They had become well known for their lavish parties and expensive gatherings to celebrate local events and to help some of the local politicians with their fundraising needs. In just a short time, many of the major players in Brazilian politics were indebted to Robert E. Lee Richardson and his largess.

Robert still ran his American empire, and his media companies were doing well. The new president had sent the attorney general after him and his media empire, but so far, his lawyers had held them off. Occasionally, when he was feeling down, he would pull out a picture from a hunting trip he had taken several years back. The picture showed Robert, Calvin Mace, Warren Turlock, Harold Wahls, Jimmy Bronson and Oliver Stevenson standing over a large ten-point elk. He would sip his bourbon out by the firepit on the patio, listen to the waves break along the shore and think about his lost friends. All dead now. Following the inauguration, the country had settled down, and the new president got to work shaping the government in his image. Many of the militia groups that had been a big part of their lives had gone underground and were being hunted by the government.

Robert was still pissed every time he thought about how the former president had hoodwinked them, first by moving the certification to a hangar at Joint Base Andrews and then by having the inauguration in some place other than the Capitol. It was a stroke of genius, but it still made him mad. He had spent a lot of money to prevent the peaceful transfer of power, and it had gotten him nothing but exile. But that was okay, for now. He was still in contact with the militias, and he would make a comeback soon.

Robert slid into the outdoor end of the pool and set his bourbon on the deck. It was a beautiful night, and the sky was lit up like a carnival. The sky looked different than it did at home, and he marveled at the number of stars he could see from his patio. The staff had left hours ago, and he noticed that his wife's bedroom light was off. It must be later than he thought it was.

He took a sip from his glass, waved to the two security guards as they made their rounds, leaned his head back on the rubber pillow and closed his eyes. His eyes weren't closed long before he noticed the lights on the perimeter blink out and the yard was covered in darkness. He looked around and noticed that his neighbor's lights were on. He checked his watch. The security guards were ten minutes late making their rounds. That was unusual.

He felt the water ripple around his arms and chest, and he raised his head off the pillow and looked around. All seemed quiet. He'd just taken a sip of his drink when a head suddenly appeared in front of him. The head was covered in black and appeared to be wearing a helmet of some kind. He went to stand up, but his legs were pulled out from under him, and he sunk to the bottom of the dark pool. He pushed off the bottom and grabbed for the side of the pool and the safety of the ladder and was pulled under again. This time, whoever was holding his legs didn't let go, and he gasped for air as his lungs burned.

His head broke the surface, and he took a quick gulp of air before he was pulled under for a third time. He struggled to breathe and fought to escape the grip of his attacker, but it was all for naught. He needed to breathe, and he opened his mouth and pool water flooded in, filling his lungs.

Robert E. Lee Richardson stopped struggling and lay face down in the pool. When he was discovered by the pool boy the next morning, it was too late to save him. The medical examiner for the state of São Paulo, after looking at the glass of bourbon sitting on the edge of the pool, ruled his death a tragic accident. Within forty-eight hours, Mrs. Richardson was on a plane back to the United States. She was going home to the house she loved. The security guards couldn't be found by the police when they came to investigate and hadn't been seen since that night when they made their rounds. Their families gave up looking for them and accepted a gracious gift from Mrs. Richardson as a way of showing respect for their missing men.

Mike, Ronnie, Jeff and Arnie spent four days in Rio de Janeiro, lying on the beach enjoying the weather. They would have liked to have spent a few more days, but Mike received an encrypted message from the new president. It was time to go back to work.

Acknowledgments

A special thank-you to my daughter Christina J. Morgan, my unofficial editor in chief. She devoted a significant amount of time making sure the book was presented as perfectly as possible.

Thanks to my editor, Laura Dragonette, whose efforts helped turn my manuscript into a polished novel. Her help is greatly appreciated. Any mistakes the reader may find are solely the responsibility of the author.

Also, I would like to thank my family for all of their encouragement. I have been telling them stories since they were little, and I always told them that someone should be writing this stuff down. I decided to write it down myself.

A special thanks to my late wife, Jane. She pushed me for years to become a writer, and my biggest regret is that she didn't live long enough to see it happen. I love her with all my heart and miss her every day. I think she would be pleased.

Finally, thanks to the readers. Without you, none of this would be important.

About the Author

2019 Pacific Book Awards Best Mystery Finalist . . . *Crime Delayed*

2020 Pacific Book Awards Best Mystery Winner . . . *Crime Denied*

2020 Chanticleer International Book Awards: 1st Place Blue Ribbon, CLUE Book Awards for Suspense, Thriller Fiction . . . *Crime Denied*

Chuck Morgan attended Seton Hall University and Regis College and spent thirty-five years as a construction project manager. He is an avid outdoorsman, an Eagle Scout and a licensed private pilot. He enjoys camping, hiking, mountain biking and fly-fishing.

He is the author of the Crime series, featuring Colorado Bureau of Investigation Agent Buck Taylor. The series includes *Crime Interrupted, Crime Delayed, Crime Unsolved, Crime Exposed, Crime Denied, Crime Conspiracy, Crime Unknown, Crime Exploded, Crime Spree, Crime Family, Crime Scene, Crime Victims, Crime Unraveled, The Assassin's Heart and Pip's Grand Adventure.*

He is also the author of *Her Name Was Jane*, a memoir about his late wife's nine-year battle with breast cancer. He has three children, four grandchildren and a Siberian Husky. He resides in Lone Tree, Colorado.

Other Books by the Author

Dear Reader, thank you for reading this novel. Please enjoy the other books in this series and follow Colorado Bureau of Investigator Buck Taylor and his team as they investigate new and sometimes unusual crimes in the Colorado mountains. Each novel is a separate story, and they can be read in any order, but you might find it more enjoyable to read them in order.

Happy Reading

Chuck Morgan

"Crime Interrupted: A Buck Taylor Novel by Chuck Morgan is a gripping, edge-of-the-seat novel. *Right from page one, the action kicks off and never stops, gaining pace as each chapter passes." Reviewed by Anne-Marie Reynolds for Readers' Favorite.*

Finalist . . . 2019 Pacific Book Awards Best Mystery

*"**This crime novel reads like a great thriller.** The writing is atmospheric, laced with vivid descriptions that capture the setting in great detail while allowing readers to follow the intensity of the action and the emotional and psychological depth of the story." Reviewed by Divine Zape for Readers' Favorite.*

*"**Professionally written in the style of a best-selling crime novelist, such as Tom Clancy, Crime Unsolved: A Buck Taylor Novel by Chuck Morgan is a spellbinding suspense novel with an environmental flair. Intriguing subplots of fraud, survivalist paranoia and murder** weave their way through the fabric of the plot, creating a dynamic story. This is an action-filled, stimulating tale which contains fascinating details that are relevant in our present climate." Reviewed by Susan Sewell for Readers' Favorite.*

"Chuck Morgan has a unique gift for plot, one that makes Crime Exposed: A Buck Taylor Novel a hard-to-put-down book. *From the start, readers know what happens to Barb, but they become curious as they follow the investigation, wondering if the characters will find out what happened to her. The descriptions are filled with clarity, and they offer readers great images. The prose is elegant, and it captures both the emotional and psychological elements of the novel clearly while offering vivid descriptions of scenes and characters. This is a fast-paced thriller with memorable characters and a criminal investigation that is so real readers will believe it could happen." Reviewed by Romuald Dzemo for Readers' Favorite.*

Winner . . . 2020 Pacific Book Awards Best Mystery

2020 Chanticleer International Book Awards: 1st Place Blue Ribbon, CLUE Book Awards for Suspense, Thriller Fiction

***"It's really progressive to see a female serial killer portrayed with such intelligent writing and depth of character**, and the cat and mouse chase dynamic is thrown off nicely by the switching of genders. What results is a really enjoyable thriller and crime mystery novel, and overall Crime Denied is certain to please fans of both hard-boiled detective tales and action/adventure crime novels."* Reviewed by K.C. Finn for Readers' Favorite.

2021 Chanticleer International Book Awards Finalist, CLUE Book Awards for Suspense, Thriller Fiction . . . *Crime Conspiracy*

"This makes for a truly dynamic story where anything is possible, and a hero you can root for even when it looks like all is lost." Reviewed by K.C. Finn for Readers' Favorite.

"This is a book you can't put down, which will entertain you on many levels, and at times make your skin crawl; the

kind of book that remains in your thoughts long after you finish reading." Reviewed by Steven Robson for Readers' Favorite.

"I read Crime Unknown in one sitting. The plot is intense and the main character agent Buck Taylor is a hero like no other. *This book has everything a thriller needs to be and more. I thought I knew the story at the beginning. Buck will solve a tricky murder case, I thought. But Chuck Morgan adds a twist to this story that expands it and makes it one of the most enjoyable books I've read in this genre. I loved that the lead was such an awesome well-rounded fellow but that he also had a support team who were just as important to the story."* Reviewed by Maureen Dangarembizi for Readers' Favorite.

"Crime Unknown is a thoroughly enjoyable read and I would not hesitate to recommend this book to fans of the crime genre and those looking for a gateway in." Reviewed by K.C. Finn for Readers' Favorite.

2022 Chanticleer International Book Awards Finalist, CLUE Book Awards for Suspense, Thriller Fiction . . . *Crime Exploded*

*"**Action-packed and fast-paced, I was sucked into the story the moment I opened the novel.** The author built the story to perfection. Chuck Morgan gave just the right amount of suspense, mystery, and action to keep readers' attention on Buck and his team. There was never a dull moment in the story. The narrative ran smoothly until the end; it followed the development of the story and the pace set by the characters. I enjoyed the twists and turns. What I loved more than anything else in the plot was how calculating Buck was. He was smart; he didn't let the FBI discourage him and kept his head in the game. The action gave me an adrenaline rush. Absolutely brilliant!"*
Rabia Tanveer for Readers' Favorite.

2022 Chanticleer International Book Awards Finalist, CLUE Book Awards for Suspense, Thriller Fiction . . . *Crime Spree*

"It is one of the best crime novels I have read in a long while, with real characters developed in a way to let you get to know them intimately, understand them, and appreciate their strengths and weaknesses. *The plot is tight, exciting, and tense, with plenty of action, and it will grip you from the start. The bizarre storyline is enthralling, written in descriptive prose that lands you right in the middle of the action. Forget sleep; once you pick this book up, you won't want to put it down until it's finished. Fantastic story, and highly recommended for fans of high-octane crime thrillers."* Reviewed by Anne-Marie Reynolds for Readers' Favorite.

"Crime Family is the tenth book in the Buck Taylor series. Chuck Morgan had me hooked from the first page until the end. *There was never a dull moment with all the action; one chapter flowed into the next. The story was fast-paced and kept me on the edge of my seat. I kept turning the pages to find out what would happen next. I was intrigued, and with all the twists and turns, I could not predict what was looming. The characters were well-developed. Each had a background description, and it was fun getting to know some of them. The story was excellently written with a fitting ending." Reviewed by Alma Boucher for Readers' Favorite.*

"Crime Scene is a must-read for lovers of mystery sleuth and

murder tales with a touch of conspiracy." Reader's Favorite review.

"Crime Scene has a carefully designed intrigue that deepens with every unforeseeable turn of events and a dynamic narrative." Reader's Favorite review.

"This is a great book. Holds your attention and you don't want to put down. I would recommend this book to anyone who loves a good crime novel." Amazon review.

"Spellbinding, gripping, powerful, and relevant are just a few words that come to mind after turning the last page of "Crime Scene: A Buck Taylor Novel, book 11, by Chuck Morgan." Amazon Review.

"A riveting plot and good pacing keep the reader in suspense as Buck Taylor and his team establish evidence beyond a reasonable doubt. *The author sustains interest by skillfully showing the art and intuition involved in crime investigation and the science behind it, as well as the elements that can delay or confound it. There are a lot of quirky characters in the novel and the author gives them mannerisms, voices, and descriptions that make them distinctive and realistic. The details and descriptions of the work and everyday life of the players are both pleasantly appealing and revolting, depending on the scenario. What's most captivating and intriguing about the*

character development is the backstory of the unhinged characters and how the author uses them as part of the perplexing trail of a horrendous crime. Themes of sadism, cruelty, grief, forensics, police procedures, and even a little bit of romance can be found in this installment of the Buck Taylor series. Highly recommended for crime story fans who especially enjoy the information as well as the twists, turns, and the untangling of intricate and cold case crime sprees." Reviewed by Carmen Tenorio for Readers' Favorite.

If you are looking for a mystery murder novel with a touch of crime, Chuck Morgan's Crime Unraveled is just what you should be looking for.

Chuck Morgan took me on a roller coaster ride with Crime Unraveled. The action started on the first page and continued until the last.

Filled with suspense and action, Crime Unraveled, A Buck Taylor Novel: Book 13 by Chuck Morgan delivers a compelling and realistic story with historical and legal elements.

The 13th book in the Buck Taylor series, Crime Unraveled by Chuck Morgan is a fantastic addition to the series. I've read a few books in this series and they never fail to leave me in awe. This is the type of high-

octane, fast-paced thriller I've come to expect from this author.

Delia Cahill is one of the world's elite assassins, but her next assignment has gotten into her head. Will Delia carry out her assignment or risk everything, including her life, to protect her intended victim?

"If you are looking for a thriller with brains, heart, and just the right amount of edge, this one is a must read. 5 stars, no doubt."

"Chuck Morgan's The Assassin's Heart will keep the reader's heart thumping from the first page to the last."

"Overall, I enjoyed the novel very much. If you're craving a fast-paced, action-packed thriller, you will not be disappointed!"

www.ingramcontent.com/pod-product-compliance
Lightning Source LLC
Chambersburg PA
CBHW071351300726
48976CB00006B/1840
* 9 7 8 1 9 6 8 1 7 9 0 6 9 *